# Missing Persons

## *Book III from the Inspector Lambert Trilogy*

## David Barry

*Missing Persons*
First published in 2012
This revised edition
Published in 2022 by
**Acorn Books**
acornbooks.uk
an imprint of
**Andrews UK Limited**
andrewsuk.com

Copyright © 2012, 2022 David Barry

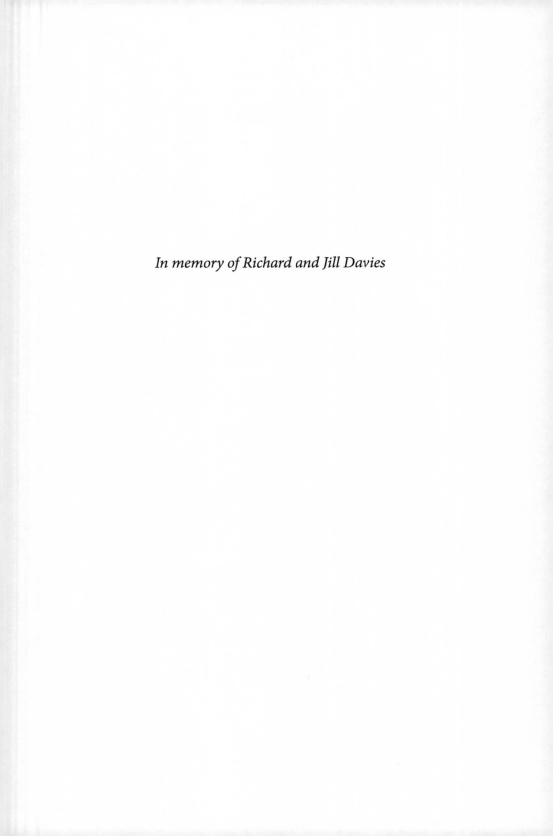

*In memory of Richard and Jill Davies*

# Contents

# Author's Notes

This novel is set in March 2011, when the tragic events of the tsunami ravaged Japan. Also, the Six Nations Rugby match between Wales and Ireland at the Millennium Stadium in Cardiff had a controversial result when Wales won 19-13. There have also been a few changes since 2011. Car paper tax discs, for instance, ended in October 2014, and since then all vehicle tax is now dealt with on the internet or paid for by Standing Order.

I am deeply indebted to South Wales Police for providing me with information and setting me right on details of police procedure. Any deviation from police practice and procedure is either an error on my part or for reasons of dramatic licence.

*Revenge is a kind of wild justice, which the more man's nature runs to, the more ought law to weed it out.*

—Francis Bacon, 1561-1626

# Missing Persons

# One

It was almost 3.30 p.m. and Jimmy Harlan was on his eighth pint on an empty stomach. He had reached that drinker's point of no return, everything a blur, a hazy weaving in and out of reality, and he had no idea that his binge drinking on that fateful Tuesday afternoon was about to lead to his downfall and set in motion a sequence of violent and lethal crimes.

He leaned, almost collapsed, over the pool table and attempted to pot the final ball, lunged forcefully, missing the white, and his cue shot forward and fell to the floor with a clatter. The landlord of the pub, an establishment not renowned for catering to the cream of Swansea society, would have asked Jimmy to tone it down a bit or diplomatically suggest he might have had sufficient, but he was upstairs having a snooze before the evening session and had left his son Daryl in charge; and Daryl, not yet twenty, still plagued by teenage acne, feared Jimmy, whose reputation as a hard man was more than bluster, so he tolerated the stream of foul language spewing out of Jimmy's mouth without a break.

Jimmy's pool partner, his old school chum, Jason Crabbe, was slightly less bad for wear, having had the man-sized breakfast in Wetherspoon's just before twelve. When Jimmy decided it was time to move on, Jason was sober enough to persuade his mate to leave the car at the rear of the pub. But Jimmy was having none of it. He was sober enough to drive. Even made a joke of it, saying he was too pissed to stand up but was steady enough to get behind the wheel.

Fortunately for Jason, he lived nearby and could legitimately refuse a lift, even though Jimmy insisted. But it was difficult arguing with a belligerent drunk like his mate who had always been the leader. During their schooldays Jason obediently accepted his role as sidekick.

And over the years, without realizing it, he began copying his mate. His speech patterns and the things Jimmy said were unconsciously repeated in the company of others. And when Jason got his hair cropped fashionably short, bordering on total baldness, Jason adopted the same cloned bullet-head, so they started to look more like brothers than friends. The only difference was, whereas Jason could eat and drink without putting on an ounce of fat, Jimmy was chunky with a beer belly.

Although Jason faithfully accepted his mate's orders, perhaps he had some sort of sixth sense warning him of the events of that gloomy February day. Perhaps he sensed the tragedy that was about to unfold, giving Jimmy his allotted fifteen minutes of fame. No, not fame. Notoriety. Even though Jason couldn't foresee that his mate's arrogant and cocky face was soon to become one of the most reviled on television, he knew better than to accept a lift from him, even the short distance to his house.

He excused himself by saying he had to go to the Gents to take a dump, leaving Jimmy to reel out to the car park, where he fumbled for his bunch of keys, dropped them several times, but eventually managed to fit the car key into the ignition of his BMW.

***

Now she was in sixth form, Alice Mason actually looked forward to going to school. No more school uniform; now she could dress like a young adult. Outgoing and bright, a popular girl with many friends, Alice was pretty much a star pupil and was destined to do well in further education.

As she stood at the bus stop with her friend Amy, slightly apart from a great knot of younger pupils from the same school, they chatted and giggled about the boys they did or didn't fancy, and then something Amy said prompted a sudden reminder in Alice's mind. It was her brother's birthday tomorrow and she had forgotten his card, which she had left in her locker at school and she needed it to catch the last post.

She embraced her friend briefly and then hurried back to school to get the card, which was an outrageously funny one. It wouldn't take long, although she would probably miss the bus and have to wait fifteen minutes for the next one, which meant missing the frantic, girlie noises that was part of the fun of the homeward journey. As she dashed back through the school gates, she checked her watch. It was just after 3.30 p.m.

At 3.32 p.m. Jimmy pulled out of the pub car park and his hands slipped on the steering wheel. He over-compensated by yanking the wheel the other way and the BMW swerved with a squeal of tyres. A pedestrian stared at the car, glaring judgementally, which Jimmy took as criticism of his driving skills, so he accelerated, going much too fast for his inebriated state, zigzagging along the narrow street like Jason Bourne escaping an assassin.

At 3.36, having collected her brother's birthday card, Alice came out through the school gates and saw her bus, the one with Amy on board, flash by. She couldn't see her friend, the bus was too far away, but she waved in any case, because she thought Amy could probably see her. There was no one at the bus stop now. It was cold, and she turned her coat collar up. Somehow, when she was with her friends, the cold was less noticeable. Now that she was on her own, she shivered, and anticipated getting home to warmth and a welcome purr when she stroked their tabby Moggs.

At 3.38, tearing down the hill towards the bus stop, Jimmy's head swam as he tried to focus on the road. He was on automatic pilot now and the messages his brain was sending to the rest of his body were as blurred as his vision.

As Alice watched out for the next bus, she saw the BMW hurtling down the road towards the bus stop. She had no reason to be alarmed at this stage – plenty of drivers drive too fast. But in a split second came the change, the sudden realization that your life is in danger and out of your control.

Jimmy had driven too far to the right of the road and a heavy lorry was coming up the hill towards him. He swerved massively and the car skidded. Unable to hold the wheel, he wrestled and tugged helplessly as it spun in his hands. Everything was a blur in Jimmy's head as he lost control and the car screeched towards the bus stop. With a massive impact, the car hit Alice head on.

And that was what saved Jimmy from any serious injury. He was braking as the car bumped and rumbled over her body, which slowed it down. That and the privet hedge of the house behind the bus stop. Although he wasn't wearing a seat belt, he only suffered a bruised head from where it hit the windscreen.

On the other side of the road a passer-by recorded the accident on his phone camera. Alice Jessica Mason, aged 16 years and five months, was killed at precisely 3.39 p.m.

After the accident, it was said that Alice would have died instantly. But how can anyone really know that?

# Two

As Lambert swung his Mercedes round a sharp bend in the road on the Gower Peninsula, he caught sight of the house chimneys and roof. A high brick wall surrounded the house and grounds, and he was surprised that a high-flyer like Frank Masina was willing to sacrifice flamboyance for privacy. As he drove through the open, wrought-iron gates and into the sweeping driveway, the house impressed Lambert – but in a sneering way, because he was already prejudiced and had anticipated its ostentation. The house was a smaller version of Tara, and Lambert wondered about the mentality of a local official who might have sanctioned the building of this simulated southern plantation mini-mansion on the Gower Peninsula, with its steps leading up to a wide front door, sandwiched by pillars that looked plastic and unreal. But then he wasn't here to admire or sneer at the architecture.

And that was when he began to have second thoughts about the visit. Why *was* he here? There was no ongoing investigation. The coroner's verdict had been clear about that, which meant he was out on a limb. And it was a risky business going it alone. On the other hand, it could work in his favour. It meant there was no paperwork and no team involvement. He was just conducting a routine enquiry and tying up some loose ends.

An enormous Shogun was parked at the bottom of the steps, and Lambert pulled up alongside. As he approached the house, he felt the chill wind through his unbuttoned brown leather coat, smoothed it around him and rang the front doorbell. He waited as the bell chimed majestically through the house, and expected an overweight black maid to answer the call in true *Gone With the Wind* style. Instead, the door was answered by an attractive blonde white woman, her skin an orange tint of faked tan. She couldn't have been more than mid-twenties, had wide baby-blue eyes and a figure that stopped short of anorexia, suggesting excessive workouts and a micro diet.

She was clearly not the hired help, and Lambert wondered if it was Masina's daughter, but the wedding ring she wore suggested she was far more likely to be the trophy wife.

He gave her his most endearing smile. 'Is Mr Frank Masina at home?'

Her eyes flitted to his Mercedes, assessing his worth. 'And you are?' she said.

He showed her his warrant card. 'Detective Inspector Lambert.'

Her face registered confusion, and she glanced over her shoulder as if she wanted assistance in dealing with the situation. 'What you wanna see Frank about?'

'It's just a routine enquiry. Nothing major. Just tying up some loose ends on a case.' He glanced towards the Shogun. 'I assume Mr Masina is at home?'

She sniffed, shivered and wrapped her arms around herself. Her body language was suddenly defensive, or it could have been because she was wearing tight, pale blue trousers and a skimpy tank top exposing her navel.

'Frank's busy right now. In his study. But if you wanna hang on, I'll see if... if he'll see you. You won't mind if I shut the door.'

She was about to shut the door in his face, thought better of it, and invited him in.

'If you wouldn' mind waitin' in the hall. I'll go an' find Frank.'

He watched as she walked down the hall, overdoing the sway of her hips, knowing his eyes were focused on her backside. She turned a corner out of sight and he took in his surroundings. Expensive striped Regency wallpaper and hunting prints; antique tables and cut-glass vases with fresh flowers; cream thick-pile carpet, wide stairway, and china handles on all the doors. It was opulent glossy magazine decor, but cold and soulless.

From a distance he heard a man's muffled voice, booming and getting louder, and then it stopped, and a little later she returned, a worried look on her face, and he thought he could detect fear in her eyes.

'Frank said he'll see you in his study. But only for a minute.'

She made no move, and he was struck by her vulnerability, like a helpless child needing guidance.

'I've not been here before,' Lambert said, firmly but gently. 'Will you show me where the study is?'

Reacting slowly, she said after a beat, 'This way.'

He followed her down the hall, wondering if her brain might work more effectively with a good steak dinner. The hall led to a state-of-the-art kitchen, but just to the left of the doorway it branched in an L-shape leading to another door. She pushed open the door and led him into a large study.

The study was a gadget emporium, awash with every kind of gizmo known to PC World. And seated behind an enormous desk was a broad-shouldered man of about fifty with hair that should have been grey by his age but was uniformly black, and a face indicating great strength: It was gladiatorial, the face of fighter. His chin was robust, like a cartoon hero, and his brown eyes were so dark they were almost black.

He didn't rise to greet Lambert or offer his hand.

'This is an unexpected visit,' he said. 'I'm not sure...' He stopped and waved a hand in his wife's direction. 'This is my wife Vikki, and she had orders that I was not to be disturbed.'

Lambert was about to apologize and thought better of it. 'Detective Inspector Lambert,' he said. 'I just wanted to ask you a few questions. Routine, nothing more.'

'What about?'

'It's about the recent death—' Lambert began, but was stopped by Masina's raised hand, who then glowered at his wife.

'Vikki, I can handle this. You can leave us alone.'

Another beat before Vikki's brain cells computed the information. Before shutting the door, she reminded her husband they were due out for dinner and he snapped impatiently that this meeting would not take long, waving her away as if she was a swarm of irritating insects.

Lambert stared closely at him, wondering which charm school he'd attended. From delving into Masina's past, Lambert discovered how tough the businessman was as a young man. A professional soldier, he had been recruited into the SAS and fought and trained Afghans against the Russians in the early eighties. When he left the army and returned to Wales, the sudden rise of his business empire was meteoric. He married, had two children, both girls, and divorced more than ten years ago. He had one sibling, a younger brother, who was a cabinet minister in the Welsh Assembly, and, like Cain and Abel, there was little love lost between the two.

As soon as his wife had gone, Masina gave Lambert a confrontational look and demanded, 'Well?'

Without being asked to sit down, Lambert slid into the seat in front of the desk and was pleased to see a somewhat dyspeptic look on the businessman's face.

'I just want to ask you a few questions about Graham Nesbitt.'

Masina frowned. 'Who?'

'Minicab driver, worked for Call Cars.'

'Means bugger all to me.'

6

'Nesbitt was found in his cab, asphyxiated. Carbon monoxide poisoning from a hose connected to the exhaust.'

Masina shrugged and pouted. 'Common form of suicide, I believe. Less painful, I suppose.'

'If you didn't know Nesbitt, what makes you think it was suicide?'

'Just made an assumption. Was it suicide?'

'The coroner seems to think so. That was the verdict. Case closed.'

Masina smiled for the first time since Lambert had set eyes on him. 'Well, there you are then. But I still don't see what this has to do with me.'

Lambert sighed and shook his head, feigning bewilderment. 'What I don't understand is why Nesbitt hardly worked – just a few hours here and there – yet he had a healthy bank balance. We checked with neighbours and he hardly left the house – to do any work, that is, but he still enjoyed a reasonably good lifestyle, clubs, pubs and girlfriends. He had an ex and two kiddies, estranged and living in Stoke-on-Trent. Used to visit them once a week, which also helped to bump up the mileage on his taxi's milometer.'

'I still don't see what this has to do with—'

Lambert cut in. 'It's just that it seems odd that you haven't heard of Mr Nesbitt.'

Smiling thinly, Masina said, 'I don't read local papers. Maybe some of the nationals. So the story of this cab driver's suicide escaped my attention.'

'Strange,' said Lambert, pausing for effect. 'Seeing as he was an employee of yours.'

'Oh?' Masina questioned, thrusting his hero's chin out challengingly. 'How d'you work that out?'

'Indirectly, of course,' Lambert smiled. 'Call Cars is registered as one of your companies at Companies House. You're one of the directors.'

'Along with my many other companies. I've got two hotels, several restaurants, a chain of holiday cottages, a meat processing factory and many other interests. Call Cars was one of my earlier companies, and I barely glance in its direction now. I leave the full-time running of it to the manager. If there's anything you want to know about it, or about this driver who topped himself, perhaps you should have a word with him.'

'We already have, when we were investigating Nesbitt's death.'

'Well, there we are then?'

'How do you explain Nesbitt's income when he clearly wasn't putting in the hours?'

Masina shifted in his chair and Lambert saw his fists close into a ball as he attempted to control his temper.

'I haven't a clue. Ask the manager. I have nothing to do with the everyday running of the minicab firm.' He glanced at his watch. 'And now you've taken up too much of my time.' He rose and gestured at the door. 'I'll see you out. This interview is over.'

As they walked to the front door, Lambert could feel the tension in Masina, like a rubber band stretched taut.

'Thank you for your time, sir,' Lambert said as he walked towards his car.

Masina called after him, 'Just a minute!'

Lambert stopped and turned, staring up at the businessman's face which was by now a mask of suppressed fury.

'What the hell did you come here for? You told me the case of this dead cabby's suicide was closed. So what was all that about?'

Lambert smiled. *Just to rattle your cage.*

'Oh, just tying up the loose ends of a case that leaves that proverbial taste in the mouth. Have a good evening.'

As Lambert got into his car, he heard the front door slam forcefully and indulged in another smile. He whistled cheerfully, albeit a trifle tunelessly, as he drove away from Masina's Deep South abode. He had driven less than four miles round the twisting roads when he felt his mobile vibrating in his pocket. As soon as he found a place to pull in, he stopped to check the message. It was from Detective Chief Superintendent Marden, and it stated in no uncertain words:

'Come in and see me NOW. Marden.'

And just as he was knocking off for the weekend. Damn! And then a thought struck him: Marden wanting to see him on a Friday evening immediately after his visit to Masina's place seemed like too much of a coincidence. And Harry Lambert didn't believe in coincidences. It was almost his catchphrase.

Well, coincidence or not, he would soon find out.

# Three

Like a bird of prey crouched on its perch, Marden glared from behind his desk as Lambert entered his office. Geoff Ambrose, recently promoted to detective chief inspector, was sitting in one of the two chairs in front of and slightly to one side of the desk. Standing, leaning against one of the office walls, a stranger in the camp.

The man was blonde and balding, had small squinty eyes and ferrety features. He wore an expensively cut, pin-striped, blue suit, but the stripes were thick chalk marks, giving him the appearance of a rather lugubrious undertaker trying for a more dashing theatrical effect.

Lambert locked eyes with him briefly, and received no vibrations of any sort, good, bad or indifferent. He nodded at Geoff Ambrose and waited for Marden to gesture for him to sit, which the DCS did with a contemptuous motion, like a hand discarding something grubby.

'Why are you still investigating the death of the minicab driver?' Marden said. 'The case is closed. Verdict was death by suicide.'

Lambert wondered how Marden knew and put it to the test.

'What makes you think I'm interested in continuing the investigation of Graham Nesbitt?'

'Don't play games with me, Harry. You know damn well you've been asking questions about his death.'

'Well, as I live in the Mumbles, I thought visiting a key witness not far from where I live—'

He didn't get a chance to finish. Eyes blazing, Marden swooped. 'What the hell did you have to go and do that for?'

'Tying up the loose ends to the case.'

Even as he said it, Lambert realized it sounded weak, and a glance in Ambrose's direction told him it had been a grave error on his part. He got on

9

well with Geoff Ambrose, who seemed embarrassed by the reprimand and avoided eye-contact with him.

Marden slammed an open palm onto his desk. 'There are no loose ends. There is no case. It's over. Finito. And Frank Masina is not a key witness. He never was.'

Lambert shifted uncomfortably in his chair and his voice wavered when he asked the question he'd been dying to ask. 'So how did you know I'd been to question Masina?'

'Because Frank Masina phoned to complain, wondering why a detective called to interrogate him about a suicide that had absolutely nothing to do with him.'

Lambert shook his head. 'Well, that's where I think you're wrong—'

Marden shouted, almost screamed, the veins standing out on his neck. 'You think you're so fucking clever. But you do not go it alone – ever. That's the way you compromise an ongoing investigation.'

It wasn't like Marden to swear. *Especially not the f-word.* Although they'd had spats in the past, Lambert had never seen Marden so uptight and angry, and he began to worry about his prospects. But he was still far from repentant, especially as he felt aggrieved because they had been holding something from him.

'Ongoing investigation?' he questioned with a frown. 'I don't understand.'

Marden stared at him for a moment, deliberating. Then he gestured toward the stranger. 'This is Superintendent Richard Bewes from the Serious Organised Crime Agency. And he's now in charge of leading the war against drugs in South Wales, working in close cooperation with Geoff. Over to you, Richard.'

As Lambert nodded, acknowledging the brief introduction to Bewes, he tried to gauge the man's mood. But the blank expression was a well-practised stratagem, a deliberate smokescreen for the man's thoughts and feelings.

'What made you visit Masina in the first place? I mean, how come you found a tenuous connection to the minicab driver's death?'

Lambert wasn't certain, but he could have sworn that Bewes already knew the answer to this.

'Because when I checked up on who owned the minicab firm, Masina's name came up as a director.'

'Go on.'

'And when I was investigating Nesbitt's so-called suicide, I discovered that he did very little actual driving, yet he was loaded and enjoyed a flashy lifestyle. There was no suicide note, and anyone we questioned couldn't seem to explain any sudden depression or deterioration in his moods or behaviour. And the post-mortem revealed a small trace of the date rape drug GHB in his blood.'

Bewes's lips tightened into a thin humourless smile. 'Hardly grounds for conducting a fresh investigation, Inspector. And the man went clubbing regularly. He probably used recreational drugs, along with Gamma-Hydroxybutyric Acid.'

Lambert noted the way Bewes reeled off the full name of the drug with studied ease. *It'll take a lot more than that to impress me. Wanker.*

'The chief superintendent is accusing me of compromising an ongoing investigation. And it doesn't take a high IQ to work out this is a drugs investigation to do with Masina. So why wasn't I kept in the loop?' Lambert stared accusingly at his boss. 'If I'd been told what was going on, none of this would have happened.'

Marden's jaw clenched tight as he tried to control his temper. 'You would have been told, but – no – you had to go conducting your own investigation. Disgraceful behaviour. Bloody disgraceful.'

Lambert decided it was time to get the discussion back on track. He looked towards Geoff Ambrose and Bewes. 'You think Masina's a dealer and using his businesses to launder the proceeds?'

Geoff Ambrose, who had kept out of the discussion so far, gave Lambert a cursory smile before answering, demonstrating how unemotional and professional he was, unwilling to get involved in upbraiding his colleague. 'The problem is, Harry, he's clean as a whistle. We've never been able to find anything. We get so close and then it's as if he's got a sixth sense and we draw a blank.'

Lambert looked up at Bewes. 'And I guess this is where SOCA comes in, to assist us village idiots.' He could feel Marden about to explode again and added quickly, 'Joke, sir.'

'Hardly a laughing matter, Inspector. And I'm finding your unprofessional behaviour difficult to tolerate.'

Lambert decided it was time to play his offended and injured card. 'OK, I admit I acted alone in this cock-up, but I really think blaming me for something that happened, which wouldn't have happened had I been kept informed, is – frankly – not on. I was kept in the dark, and now I'm being blamed.' He saw Marden opening his mouth to object and continued hurriedly. 'I thought a simple little enquiry – acting on my initiative – could have helped with Geoff's enquiries. I'm aware of his involvement in drug enforcement, and I thought the little information I'd obtained about Masina's activities might help. I was going to bring you the info first thing Monday morning.'

He stared at Marden. *So stick that up your backside.* Lambert was still smarting over a major case he and his team had investigated about six months ago. As part of his investigation he needed to visit London and had booked a first-class train ticket. Marden went ape, with the result that Lambert had to cough up the difference between standard and first-class travel. Lambert felt justified because he had got a good result. But Marden informed him that the chief constable and deputy chief constable recently attended a conference held by Thames Valley Police at the Sheldonian Theatre in Oxford, about Positive Action on Race in the police service, and they had driven there in the one car. And the smug way the detective chief superintendent held his superior officers as shining examples of frugality had rankled with Lambert.

Marden stared back at him. A long pause, eventually broken by the SOCA investigator.

'I suppose the inspector's unwarranted investigation has given us a further insight into the way Masina thinks. He thinks he's invincible. Anyone else might have ignored the inspector's intrusion and thought no more of it, especially as his investigation turned up little of worth in terms of intelligence.'

Lambert felt a resentful tightening in his stomach as he took this on the chin from the bloke he had already inwardly nicknamed the spook from MI7.

'But Masina,' Bewes went on, 'had the audacity to telephone and complain. Unusual behaviour if you think about it, because it solved nothing. He could have just let it rest.'

'Unless he was sending out messages of innocence,' Lambert said. 'An upright citizen who has been wrongfully accused. Sorry to disagree with you, Richard.'

There was not a flicker in Bewes's expression at Lambert's use of his first name, but Marden jumped in with that petulant voice that always grated on Lambert.

'And now that Masina has been approached and interrogated in his own home, it will give him reason to be far more cautious in future. Because of your interference, Harry, he won't take any stupid chances.'

Lambert was about to mumble an apology, but Marden thrust out his wrist and looked pointedly at his watch.

'I think we're all done here.'

Marden caught the slight smirk on Lambert's face.

'You find something amusing, Inspector?'

He wanted to say: *Yes, you prick, 'I think we're all done here' is straight out of American TV cop series. Life imitating art.* Instead, he said, 'I was just anticipating a good day out tomorrow at the Millennium Stadium.'

Marden's mouth opened, a mixture of shock and surprise. 'You've got tickets for the Wales v Ireland game? I couldn't get any. Left it too late.'

Lambert suddenly felt more cheerful. As he left Marden's office, he said, 'Well, I expect you can catch it on television, sir.'

# Four

Just over two minutes into the match and Brian O'Driscoll scored a try for Ireland. Yells and screams of delight from the Irish supporters and a collective groan from the Welsh fans. Disappointed cries and squeals from a row of girls in front of Lambert and Ellis, their heads enshrouded in mock daffodils. And close by a man yelled, 'And that's in less than three bloody minutes.'

Across the other side of the vast stadium, Irish supporters, faces painted in Irish colours, bounced jubilantly, their flags and scarves weaving and waving exultant patterns, and the massive rows of seats became one co-ordinated mass of celebration.

Tony Ellis turned to Lambert, who was shaking his head with foreboding. Cupping a hand against his cheek to project over the noise of the crowd, especially the Irish supporters, who were going berserk, Ellis shouted, 'Early days yet.'

Lambert looked doubtful. But after the successful conversion, increasing Ireland's score to seven-nil, Wales soon took possession of the ball, and when after eighteen minutes they were awarded a penalty, and James Hook put Wales on the board with three points, the spirits of the Welsh supporters rose. At half time, though, Wales were losing 9–13.

Ellis and Lambert made a break for one of the bars. They had come to Cardiff by rail, so they could unwind, relax and down a few pints. Another pint at half time would be their fourth pint of Brain's SA, and Lambert was feeling light-headed and buoyant, now completely untroubled by his recent clash with Marden. But the beer was having the opposite effect on Ellis, whose movements were beginning to feel sluggish, and his eyelids felt as if they were being pressed down by heavy weights. What he really needed was a quiet night on his own, so that he could sleep. There was little sleep to be had at home. His baby daughter was less than five months old, suffered from colic, and disturbed his and Sharon's sleep regularly every night; there seemed to be no end to their suffering.

As Lambert and Ellis shouldered their way through the throng heading towards the bar, Lambert felt his mobile vibrating. He checked the display screen. It was Swansea Central. He was tempted to ignore it but thought it must be something important if they were calling him just before four on a Saturday. And, however important or urgent it was, they would have to send a car, especially as he had already consumed three pints of Brains' strongest bitter. He decided to take the call, tapped Ellis on the shoulder to halt his progress to the bar and held the mobile screen up.

'Swansea Central calling. I'm going to take it. I won't have another beer.'

'Nor me,' Ellis said as he followed Lambert into one of the corridors leading to the toilets. As Lambert answered the call, Ellis indicated that he was going to the Gents.

When he returned, he saw Lambert ending the call, biting his lip with a chest-heaving sigh.

'What's up?' Ellis asked.

'That was David Davies. Been a major crime and weekend leave is cancelled. The good news is that I've asked DC Jones to drive over in a pool car to pick us up, and that'll take a good forty-five minutes. So, we've got time to watch the rest of the match and see Wales turn this game around.'

Ellis laughed and shook his head, then became serious. 'What's happened to ruin our weekend?'

'Tell you about it after the rugby. Don't want to spoil a good game. I'll just pay a quick visit and join you back in the thick of it.'

Wales's victory in the second half was controversial, as the live television analysis following the match highlighted. Halfway through the second half, the ball was kicked into touch, and it went into the first few rows of the crowd. Lambert and Ellis were only six rows away and saw exactly what had happened.

The ball was quickly taken, and Mike Phillips ran down the field close to the touch line and scored a try. Huge objections from the Irish players who surrounded the ref. The ref asked the assistant ref if it was OK, was told it was, and allowed the try.

But Ellis and Lambert, and many other Welsh supporters, saw the ball had been kicked into the crowd and hadn't been returned, and a ball boy picked up another ball and put it into play. The ball that scored the try was a completely different ball and, not only that, it came back into play further down the pitch, closer to the Irish line. So perhaps there was a niggling doubt over whether the try shouldn't have been given. But it was. And then Wales converted, followed by a drop kick by James Hook, giving a final score of 19–13 to Wales.

When the final whistle blew, the mood of the Welsh supporters was euphoric as they left the stadium. Along with thousands of supporters shuffling out into the road, many singing and shouting exultantly, Lambert and Ellis headed towards Cathedral Road, where Lambert had arranged they would be picked up by DC Debbie Jones. She had made good time, and they spotted her waiting for them no more than a hundred yards on the left as they rounded the corner at the traffic lights.

'Hi, Debbie,' Lambert said as he opened the car door and slid into the back. 'You were quick. Hope you didn't break the speed limit.'

She swung her head round and smiled. 'As if I'd do such a thing.'

Once again he found himself filled with mixed feelings of desire and apprehension. Her jet black shiny hair, unblemished skin with just a hint of light brown from her Asian origins, and intelligent big brown eyes, were a turn on he was beginning to find deeply disturbing. Not because she was at least twenty years his junior, but for reasons of professional standards.

Ellis climbed into the passenger seat and they headed north towards Llandaff and Whitchurch, where they could pick up the M4 motorway at Junction 32. Apart from a muttered greeting acknowledging his colleague, Ellis was strangely silent and moody, and while Jones and Lambert simultaneously wondered what troubled him, he soon provided them with an explanation of his mood.

'I'd better give Sharon a quick call to explain about the weekend,' he said, thumbing his mobile screen.

Embarrassed silence in the car as Ellis argued with his wife. Her voice tinny, shrewish and loud, which they could all hear as Ellis had to hold it away from his ear or risk death by tinnitus. Eventually, nothing resolved, Ellis ended the call.

Another long and embarrassed silence, which DC Jones broke with a falsely cheerful interest in rugby. 'I forgot to ask: how was the game? Any good? Did Wales win?'

'Yes, we won,' Lambert replied. 'But a dubious result. What you might call a pyrrhic victory.'

'Sorry to disagree, Harry,' Ellis said. attempting to lighten mood he was in. 'But if a ball gets kicked into the crowd, and someone hangs on to it as a souvenir, they have to get on with the game and use another ball. It's quite legitimate.'

Lambert leant forward and patted him on the shoulder. 'You're right, Tony. Wales won fair and square.'

\*\*\*

At the entrance to the car pound and breaker's yard at Ogmore Vale, DC Jones opened the window ready to show her warrant card to gain access to the crime scene, but the young constable guarding the entrance raised a hand without looking at them, indicating that the detective's car should wait while he finished dealing with an irate middle-aged man and his wife, the man purple with rage and his wife doing a great deal of finger pointing.

'I want my car NOW!' the man yelled. 'Bloody towed away this morning, it was. We come all the way from Swansea, and now I can't have my own bloody car.'

The lack of concern on the constable's face probably ignited the couple's fury and the woman began screaming obscenities at him. Lambert, Ellis and Jones thought she was going to attack him and would have given favourable odds on her beating him if it came to a fight.

'Oh, for Christ's sake!' Lambert sighed. 'Toot the bastard.'

Jones gave three long blasts on the horn, which suspended the drama. The young constable's demeanour was suddenly that of an official driven to the edge of his patience. He even had a thin-lipped smile as he strutted towards the car, preparing to put this cheeky woman in her place. When she showed him her warrant card he looked as if he'd been slapped.

'Where's the crime scene?' Jones snapped.

'Turn to your right, Miss.'

With barely a glance at the policeman, Jones accelerated and the car shot forward. The irate couple stared at the detectives open-mouthed, as if they were from another planet.

They found the crime scene cars parked in front of a row of towed-away cars. One of them was a white Rover saloon with its boot lid open and leaning into the boot was the senior forensic scientist, Hughie John, dressed in protective clothing, picking delicately at minute traces or fragments of evidence. A police tape had been secured around a very small area and the three detectives gave a duty officer a scrawled signature on his crime scene sheet.

'No need to dress up for this one,' he told them. 'Corpse was towed away from a street in Swansea. Who knows where the murder was committed.'

Lambert thanked him, and he held the tape up for the three of them to duck under. A crime scene vehicle nearby was turning around and seemed to be leaving the scene. There was a small group of bystanders staring with fascination, employees of the car pound Lambert surmised, although there wasn't much of interest to see. Hughie John was the only one working the scene as it was confined to the small area of the Rover's boot.

The forensic officer glanced round as Lambert approached. 'Took your time, didn't you? Divisional surgeon has been and gone, and we're almost finished here.'

The three detectives peered warily into the boot, staring at the body of a man, lying on its side and folded into a foetal position. Lying close to the corpse was an automatic pistol. There was a dark patch of blood on the victim's back, which looked like an exit wound. Because the corpse was folded slightly over they couldn't see an entry wound. And, apart from the body and the gun, the boot was empty, and looked as if it had been recently cleaned. The smell from the corpse was not yet overpowering, but the odour of death and decay was like rotting food and over-ripe cheese.

'How long has this car been here, Hughie?'

'Towed in yesterday, apparently.'

Lambert turned to Ellis and Jones. 'Go and find the patrol officer who was first on the scene and find out who opened the boot and where the car was towed from.'

'Name's Michael Pugh.' Hughie John informed them. 'You'll find him in the site office interviewing some of the staff. Either that or it's an excuse for a cuppa.'

While the two detectives went off to find the uniformed constable, Lambert asked Hughie John if he could speculate about the time of death.

Hughie shrugged. 'Decomposition hasn't long started, otherwise the smell would be a lot worse. Course, I can only hazard a guess at this stage. Thursday or Friday, maybe. There was a frost on Thursday night which could have delayed things. Car had been abandoned in the centre of Swansea on a single yellow line, which, if it had been left on Thursday night, would have gone unnoticed until the next day, when no doubt the Gestapo would've swooped.'

'But if it was a single yellow why would they have called for a tow? Why not just give it a penalty ticket?'

Hughie jerked a thumb to the front of the car. 'There's your answer.'

Frowning, Lambert walked towards the bonnet, glanced at the windscreen, then returned to the rear of the car. 'No tax disc. And judging by the registration of the car, it's... let's see... about 12-years-old. Which means it would have been treated as abandoned. So, someone drives a corpse in a car with no tax disc. Bit risky that.'

Hughie John chuckled. 'You're the detective, you work it out.'

'The person who abandoned the car,' Lambert said, 'removed the tax disc after parking the car, knowing it would be towed away. And hoping it ends up in the crusher.'

'You're not just a pretty face.'

'That the gun that killed the victim?'

'It's a semi-automatic compact Smith & Wesson. No brass casings in the boot. Looks like the ejected cartridge was left at the crime scene, and now nowhere to be found. As to whether that's the gun that killed him, we'll soon find out. But I think he was killed by a single bullet at close range. Right up close, and it looks as if the bullet went upwards through his chest and heart and exited through his shoulder blade.'

'You been through the victim's pockets yet?'

A glint in Hughie's eye as he said, 'Big fat zero. Didn't want to make things easy for you, did they?'

'We need to get an ID on the victim, soon as we can.'

The forensic officer reached up and shut the boot. 'As we are only a stone's throw from the lab, and this isn't strictly a crime scene – that could be anywhere, let's face it – I'm having the Rover towed to the science block at HQ – the sooner the better – and we can go to town on the details. First thing I'll do is get prints off the victim and run them through the AFR system, see if we can get a match. I'll let you know as soon as.'

'What about the post-mortem?'

'Body will be in Cardiff no later than…' Hughie tugged at his sleeve and checked his watch. 'I would say 20.30 hours. That's what time the pathologist is arriving.'

Lambert pulled a face. 'Great. I can't wait.'

'So how was the Six Nations match? Called away at half-time, I don't suppose you know the score, do you?'

'Wales won 19–13. Heard the result on the radio on the way over.'

Hughie looked like a wicked gnome as he chuckled, the jowls on his round face wobbling. 'Yeah, and Angelina Jolie wants to go out with me. Still, I can't blame you for wanting to see the whole game.'

Lambert was about to lie again and protest his innocence, thought better of it, and said, 'I'm going to find Tony and Debbie and get things under way. Catch you later, Hughie.'

'Thanks for the warning,' said Hughie, giving Lambert a wave as he walked towards a police tow-truck.

Lambert hurried to the site office and met Ellis and Jones as they were coming out. 'That was quick.'

Sergeant Ellis held up his notebook. 'Got all the info from Constable Pugh. Good bloke. He was very thorough. The car may have looked as if it had been abandoned since it wasn't displaying a tax disc, but according to DVLA it has a registered owner and is taxed until the end of June.'

'The traffic warden called the recovery firm at 11.09 a.m. yesterday,' DC Jones added, 'and the car was towed away just after 11.30. Got here around noon.'

'How come someone opened the boot?'

'Well these guys have keys and can easily gain access...' Jones began, but Lambert interrupted her abruptly.

'I know that. I mean what made them open the boot? And why did they do that today and not yesterday?'

Jones looked flustered for a moment, then continued hurriedly. 'The bloke who opened it was curious. And a bit suspicious. But he couldn't really explain why. Except for the fact they found out from DVLA that it was taxed and had a registered owner, and he wondered why it looked as if it had been deliberately abandoned minus the tax disc.'

Lambert half smiled. 'Bloke should have been a copper. He'll have touched the outside of the boot. Has he been fingerprinted for elimination?'

Jones nodded. 'He has.'

Ellis tore a page out of his notebook. 'I've got the owner's address here. The car is registered to a Mr John Mitchell and his home address is in Port Talbot.'

As Lambert took the page from Ellis, he said, 'Right, here's what we do. Debbie, you accompany me to see if this Mitchell is at home. Tony, I'd like you to get Constable Pugh to drive you over to Cockett Police Station as soon as you can to organize the incident room. See if you can get hold of Kevin Wallace to report on duty. And try to liaise with the chief super and tell him we're going to need an office manager. See if you can get Roger Hazel – he's a good bloke. Once Debbie and I have finished with this Mitchell who owns the car – depending on what happens, of course – she can drop me off at my place to pick up my car, so I can head back to Cardiff for the post-mortem. But I'll call in briefly at Cockett on my way. Our priority, for the moment, is to ID the victim.'

Ellis raised his eyebrows questioningly. 'You don't think this Mitchell, the owner of the car, had anything to do with it, do you, Harry?'

Lambert laughed. 'If only life were that simple. But we know better, don't we?'

# Five

Even though the Port Talbot estate was dull in its uniformity, at least it was neat and tidy, and many of the council houses had add-on porches and conservatories, suggesting that most had been bought by the residents years ago. The house belonging to Mitchell, the owner of the Rover, was no exception, with its pristine paintwork, double-glazed windows, and a well-tended front garden, with early daffodils and snowdrops growing in the flower beds and a lawn that had been recently cut, shorn of its long winter strands.

DC Jones rang the doorbell, which chimed a Big Ben melody prior to striking the hour, and the door opened before it finished chiming. A gangling teenage girl, freckled and red-haired, stared at them expressionlessly without speaking.

'Is your father home?' Jones asked.

The girl turned her head and yelled, 'Dad!'

She reminded Lambert of his daughter Natasha when she was fourteen, and for a moment he felt saddened by the distance that lay between them now that she had chosen to live in London, and he also felt pangs of jealousy as his ex, Helen, lived not that far away from her, and would see much more of her than he could.

A man appeared from the kitchen at the back, probably no more than early forties, with a mop of brown, curly hair and a dark Joseph Stalin moustache bordering on comic opera. He was followed by his wife, a thin-faced woman, head-cocked on one side and peering inquisitively over his shoulder. Brushing against his daughter, the man scratched his head as he confronted them, like a ham actor performing the part of a baffled scientist.

'Can I help you?'

They held up their warrant cards. 'I'm Detective Inspector Lambert and this is Detective Constable Jones. Are you Mr John Mitchell?'

He opened and closed his mouth, but no words were emitted. His wife seemed less surprised or shocked and took control.

'That's right, Mr and Mrs Mitchell, and this is our daughter Tania,' she said, followed by a sudden intake of breath. 'It's not about Kevin, is it? He's gone over to Swansea for the evening.'

Lambert shook his head. 'If Kevin's your son, this has probably nothing to do with him.'

'So what's it all about?'

DC Jones opened her notebook. 'Do you own a white Rover?' She read out the registration number.

Mitchell, recovering from the jolt, said, 'Not any more we don't.'

'It's still registered in your name,' DC Jones said.

'But we sold it last week.'

'Last Saturday, to be precise,' his wife added. 'Perhaps the chap who bought it hasn't sent in the papers yet.'

Perhaps he never intended to, thought Lambert. Safer to buy a car, leaving it in the old owner's name, than risk driving a stolen car with a body in the boot.

'Do you have any paperwork from the sale, proving you sold it, and the name of the person who bought it?' Lambert said.

'Well, I...' Mitchell began nervously, and then looked to his wife for support.

'Has the car been involved in an accident?' she asked.

'Nothing like that. What about details of the sale?'

Mitchell hesitated and glanced briefly at his wife again. 'Well, the thing is, the young chap who bought it said he would deal with the paperwork and send in the registration certificate. I signed the bit at the bottom as the registered keeper and thought no more about it.'

'And did this chap have a name?' Lambert asked, but the sudden racket of a lawn mower two front gardens away drowned out Mitchell's reply.

'Do you think we might come in and get some details?' Jones asked. 'Bit difficult trying to compete with the noise.'

With some reluctance, they were ushered into the front room, a rather cramped living space, with an enormous television screen which dominated everything like a watchful eye.

Lambert sank into an armchair, Mitchell sat next to his wife on a sofa, huddled close to her for comfort, and their daughter perched on the arm. Jones said she preferred to remain standing, poised with pen and notebook.

'I take it you got this young man's name,' Lambert asked Mitchell.

'Of course. I wrote it down when he phoned to say he was interested in seeing the car. Michael Thomas, that was it.'

'So, you advertised the car...'

'In one of the free papers, yes. And this Thomas bloke telephoned. Only...' Mitchell stopped and stared thoughtfully at the carpet as he tried to remember something.

'What?' Lambert prompted.

'I never thought nothing of it at the time. On the phone, this Thomas sounded different to when he turned up. Like maybe it was his father ringing to make enquiries.'

Mitchell's wife looked at him accusingly. 'You never mentioned it.'

Her husband sighed with frustration. 'Of course I didn't. Like I said, I thought nothing of it at the time. I thought it was something to do with the phone, the way people sound different. It's only now that...' He looked towards Lambert pointedly, who completed the sentence for him.

'That it's become a police enquiry. Of course. That's quite natural. Can you describe this young man for me?'

'He had dark hair. And slightly unshaven. You know, black stubble, but it looked as if it was deliberate. He wasn't bad looking.'

'How old would you say?'

'At a rough guess, I'd say around twenty-two or -three.'

The daughter's high-pitched voice cut in. 'I thought he was quite dishy. Bit like that film actor.'

Lambert leaned forward attentively. 'Which one?'

Tania Mitchell chewed her lip thoughtfully. 'I can't remember his name.'

'Which films has he been in?' DC Jones asked.

The girl tilted her head and looked at the ceiling as she tried to recall. 'I wish I could... oh, there was that one with Jamie Foxx in Miami.'

Her father clicked his fingers. '*Miami Vice*. Colin Farrell.'

'Yes, him. He's gorgeous,' Tania Mitchell said, looking pleased.

'So, this young man resembled Colin Farrell.'

Mitchell turned and looked up at his daughter, shaking his head. 'He was nothing like Colin Farrell, Tania.'

'Well, I think he was.'

'Is he the one from *Ballykissangel*?' Mrs Mitchell asked, getting a nod from her husband. 'No, I think Dad's right, Tania. He was nothing like him. This chap had a longer, thinner face.'

Lambert stifled a sigh and said, 'What did he sound like? You said he looked like this Irish actor? Was he Irish or local?'

'I'd say he was from round here,' Mitchell replied. 'But he didn't have a strong accent. As if he was – well, you know – it was toned down a bit.'

'Like he was middle class, perhaps?' Lambert suggested.

'Yes,' Mrs Mitchell butted in. 'I'd say he was a young professional bloke. The way he was dressed. Casual, but kind of smart and expensive.'

Scribbling furiously in her notebook, DC Jones asked, 'What was he wearing?'

'Blue jeans and a dark shirt, with a short beige jacket with a zip in the collar. I know it seems like loads of blokes dress like that but…' She shrugged. 'It's hard to explain.'

'I think what Eileen means,' Mitchell said, coming to the rescue, 'is that he wasn't at all scruffy and looked as if he could buy a car for much more than the two-hundred quid we wanted for the Rover. I didn't want to sell it, but I've just been made redundant.'

'When he telephoned about the car,' Lambert said, 'did he phone you on your landline?'

'No, my mobile. I put my mobile number in the paper, just in case we were out if someone rang.'

Lambert exchanged a brief look with Jones and tried to keep the excitement out of his voice. 'You've probably got the number on the received calls log. Would you mind checking that for us?'

Mitchell struggled to raise himself from the sofa. 'It's out in the kitchen. I'll get it.'

After he was gone, Jones said to Mrs Mitchell, 'Let's hope he hasn't had dozens of calls since then.'

'Doubt it. No one hardly ever calls on his mobile. Waste of money really.'

Except for the monotonous drone of the lawnmower, a silence followed this niggardly criticism of her husband's extravagance. Moments later, Mitchell was back in the room, scrolling on his mobile. 'Here it is,' he said, standing next to DC Jones and showing her the screen. 'Saturday the fifth of March. That's the only call that day.'

Jones scribbled down the number. 'Got it,' she said.

Lambert stood up. 'Thank you for your help.' He handed Mitchell one of his business cards. 'If you should think of anything else, no matter how trivial it might seem, please give me a call. And if we happen to get a photograph of the young man, we'll send someone round to see if you can identify him.'

The Mitchell family followed the detectives to the front door. As they were about to depart, Mrs Mitchell called after them, raising her voice above the sound of the mower.

'If the car wasn't in an accident, what's happened?'

Lambert paused. He decided he could tell them. They would find out soon enough as it would hit tomorrow's news, and there would be maximum coverage of the car and its parked location, appealing for any witnesses who might have seen something unusual.

'The car was abandoned in Swansea without a tax disc and towed away...' Lambert began.

'That was taxed to the end of June,' Mitchell protested, as if he'd been caught out in a misdemeanour.

'We think the perpetrator may have removed the tax disc.'

'What the bloody hell did he do that for?'

'Perpetrator?' Mrs Mitchell questioned. 'What d'you mean, perpetrator?'

'A body was discovered in the boot.'

The family exchanged fearful looks.

'Bloody Nora!' Mitchell exclaimed.

'If you can remember anything else about the young man who bought the car, or the phone call enquiring about it, however unimportant it might seem, I'd be grateful if you could contact me on the number on the card?' Lambert said and gave them a brief wave before getting into the car.

DC Jones smiled sympathetically, knowing how attached people become to their old cars, and wondered if they were shocked by the news of it being involved in a murder. But as she drove away and glanced in the rear-view mirror, she couldn't help giggling.

'What's so funny?' Lambert asked.

'I just caught a glimpse of the wife rushing to the house next door.'

'Yes, they'll dine out on this for weeks.'

# Six

DS Tony Ellis hadn't let his sleepless home life get in the way of his work, and when Lambert and Jones arrived in the incident room they found everything was up and running and he and Wallace were busy going through the CCTV, both at separate monitors and desks. At another desk and computer sat Detective Sergeant Mick Beech, his enormous buttocks hanging over the sides of a swivel chair. He had close cropped fair hair, a smooth and very pink moon-face, and weighed just over twenty stone.

Lambert tried to show some enthusiasm for Beech's presence on the team, but secretly he felt disappointed in Marden's choice of office manager and had hoped Roger Hazel might work with them once more. Presumably Hazel was not available, which was disappointing, and so Lambert had to tolerate Beech, who lacked social graces. Lambert thought of Beech as an anorak, and it wouldn't have surprised him if Beech's hobby was trainspotting. But in the past, Beech had never given him any sign that he was unreliable or incompetent when it came to running an incident room. In fact, Lambert realized, he was probably compensating for his bulk, which tended to restrict him from more active duties, and so he made up for it by working hard and even gave that little bit extra, but in a taciturn and inconspicuous manner.

'Hi, Mick!' Lambert waved across the office, trying to inject some warmth into his voice. 'Good to have you on the team for this investigation.'

Beech nodded unsmilingly, mumbled, 'Thanks,' and turned back to his computer.

'The bloke who phoned up about the car,' Lambert said to DC Jones. 'What's his number?'

She consulted her notebook, gave him the number, and watched as he dialled it on a landline. 'Anything?' she asked.

He shook his head and hung up. 'It's probably at the bottom of a deep well by now.'

Jones crossed to Wallace's desk and stood looking over his shoulder, frowning at the grey CCTV images of late night Swansea.

Ellis swivelled his chair to face Lambert and said, 'I was going to give you a bell but I knew you'd be here pretty sharpish after finding out the car no longer belonged to the registered owner. I mean, no murderer's going to abandon his own car with a body in it. The car was sold recently, right?'

'OK, smart-arse, but we still had to check it out.' He waved the fingers of his right hand at Ellis. 'Never mind showing off, Dr Watson, I know you've got something for me.'

Ellis grinned and rubbed a hand over his receding hairline. 'Hughie got a result from the AFR, and the victim's been identified. The photo and details are on the desk there.'

Lambert grabbed the paper and stared at the police mugshot at the top of the page. 'Ah!' he exclaimed. 'An old familiar face.'

The man was like a million other hard-nut convicts, about forty-years-old, with a large, protruding forehead and sunken eyes, slicked-back black hair, a crooked, broken nose and thin, downward-curving lips. But Lambert would recognize him anywhere.

'Who is it?' Jones asked.

'Don't you mean, was it?' Wallace corrected her.

'His name *was* Robert Sonning,' Lambert emphasized, 'and he was charged with ABH ten years ago, but the charges were dropped due to lack of evidence. Then, less than four years ago, I worked on a case where a suspected drug dealer was beaten senseless with a baseball bat. It was a vicious assault. Bloke almost died. We got enough evidence for a conviction and Sonning was sentenced to six years.'

Ellis, who had read the details, said, 'He was released just a fortnight ago from Cardiff prison.'

Lambert glanced at his watch. 'I've got an appointment in Cardiff, to attend this charmer's post-mortem. So, I'll be brief. The man who telephoned the Mitchells to purchase the car was a Mr Michael Thomas. See how many of those you can find within a thirty-mile radius and get them checked out.'

A groan from DC Wallace.

'Yes, I know it's probably a false name, but we still have to check it out. Get some uniforms to make enquiries.'

Lambert saw Ellis about to speak and raised his hand. 'I know it's Saturday night, Tony, but it's still early, and our shit-faced citizens won't need police assistance until very much later. See what you can do as soon as you have some Michael Thomas's to eliminate. And tell me quickly, have you seen anything on the CCTV of the Rover?'

'The car was parked in a side street where there was no CCTV camera, so we're having to go through loads of other material to see if we can spot it on the way there.'

Lambert clicked his fingers urgently. 'Hang on: this might be more valuable. As Sonning was released from Cardiff prison a fortnight ago, get on to them and see if they've still got any CCTV from outside the prison after he was discharged. If he was met by anyone, that person could be a key witness. Identifying the driver of the abandoned car may prove difficult, so make the CCTV of Sonning's prison release a priority, and any other information you can get about his release. And see if you can find out who his associates, friends and relatives are.' As he hurried to the door, he called back over his shoulder, 'Sheila Grantham's the pathologist, and she likes to come in under ninety minutes, especially on a Saturday night, so hopefully I can make it back to the Dew Drop well before last orders, and we can catch up on the latest details.'

'Just before you go, Harry,' DC Jones said as she walked over to the other desk to look at the victim's mugshot. 'Do you happen to know what Sonning did for a living?'

'He was a teacher.'

Her eyes widened with disbelief. 'At the risk of sounding like that Scottish actor, I don't believe it.'

Deadpan, but with a twinkle in his eye, Lambert said, 'He was a teacher all right. He taught people a lesson for a living. So, he'd have a few enemies. We might be looking at a revenge motive.'

'What about the baseball bat victim?' Ellis said.

'Check him out. Name's Terry Parsons, but after the beating he become a wheelchair user, and last I heard he was claiming disability benefits, which he spends almost every day from opening time in the Singleton Hotel, so its doubtful he'd have the wherewithal. But you never know.'

# Seven

As it was one of the Dew Drop's busiest night, the detectives were squashed into a corner, leaning against a narrow drinks' shelf, attempting to converse above the hubbub of the bar, especially as a noisy crowd of rugby-shirted men nearby were laughing raucously and clearly trying to outdo one another with a string of dirty jokes. But at least Lambert's team felt secure that their private conversation would be disregarded by strangers.

Lambert leaned towards Ellis and raised his voice above the din. 'Tell me about Sonning's release from prison.'

'He was released a fortnight yesterday and someone in a car picked him up and gave him a lift.'

'What sort of vehicle?'

'It wasn't a Rover. The car the body was found in belonged to Mitchell up until last Saturday.'

'I know that, Tony,' Lambert said with irritation. *Don't treat me like an idiot.* 'I just want to know what sort of vehicle it was.'

Ellis's cheeks reddened and Debbie Jones, knowing how tired he was, came to his rescue.

'It was a blue Renault Megane. But the driver didn't get out of the car so we couldn't get a good look at him.'

'If you couldn't see the driver,' Lambert said, 'how d'you know it wasn't a woman?'

'We got an ID from the car's number plate,' Ellis jumped in, trying to smooth over his blunder. 'The car's registered in the name of Steven Hickson and he's a licensee. Runs a pub called the Earl of Richmond.'

'Not a pub I'm familiar with.' Aware of his shortness with Ellis, Lambert patted his arm supportively. 'And did Sonning appear to get in the car willingly with this Hickson bloke?'

'We think so, from what we could see.'

'He looked more like friend than foe,' Wallace interjected, feeling slightly out of the group discussion as he peered over Mick Beech's shoulder, almost hidden by the sergeant's enormous girth.

'We think,' Jones added, 'that he gave this Hickson a friendly wave.'

'Hmm,' Lambert murmured thoughtfully. 'So it doesn't look as if this was someone seeking revenge.'

DS Beech, feeling he ought to contribute something to the discussion, added rather pointlessly, 'It looked as if this Hickson was a mate of his.'

Lambert shot a look at his office manager which was hard to define. Once again it crossed his mind that Beech, although highly efficient, seemed to lack social awareness, and was cocooned in his own world.

'I suppose old friends can fall out,' Jones suggested.

'And can sometimes become mortal enemies,' Lambert agreed. 'What we need to discover is what happened, and where Sonning stayed during the two weeks between his release and his murder. We need to speak to this pub landlord as soon as.'

Ellis glanced at his watch. 'It's eleven fifteen, and the Earl of Richmond's not that far away...'

'Not tonight,' Lambert broke in. 'If this Hickson's got a busy night – and maybe he does a lock-in – first thing tomorrow morning he'll be exhausted. That'll be the best time to question him. And there's been no media coverage of the murder yet, so he won't be expecting us. Besides—' Lambert broke off and frowned deeply while he downed his lager, then asked Ellis, 'I know I asked you to prioritise the Cardiff prison CCTV, and I'm glad I did, but did you manage to see anything of the car being abandoned in the city centre?'

'Yeah, I did,' DC Wallace said with competitive zeal. 'I spotted the Rover just before it turned into the side street and went off camera. It was around 9.30 on Thursday night. I kept watching on the same camera and, apart from a couple holding hands coming round the corner, a lanky, shaven-headed bloke, wearing an Addidas track suit and trainers came round a few minutes later. I'm sure it was him.'

'What was the facial image like, Kevin?'

'Usual problem of geometry giving distortion. I was looking at images from a camera that was mounted very high up. It's a digital recording so we could use facial recognition software. It might do some good. You never know.'

'Good. At least we've got something to go on. It could be the killer or an accomplice.'

'And,' Kevin added with a grin, 'the suspect has a tattoo on his hand, by the base of his thumb, which we enlarged as much as we could. Might be a butterfly but it's not that clear.'

Lambert nodded approval. 'Good. The design of the tattoo's not important because its location will assist us in narrowing down the man we're looking for.'

'And Tony's been saving the most interesting news until last,' DC Jones announced with a smile.

'Yes,' Ellis said, 'news from forensics. The prints on the gun belonged to Sonning and his prints were also on the casings of the unused rounds in the chamber.'

'And were there no other prints on the gun?'

'Just the victim's.'

'Now that is interesting,' Lambert said, 'especially after what I learnt at the post-mortem. It starts to look as if it was victim who set out to kill someone, but there could have been a fight and he was shot in the struggle. The post-mortem disclosed evidence of a fight: a bump on the back of the victim's head, buttons torn off his shirt, a grazing on one of his ankles, suggesting that he was horizontal and the graze came from his assailant's shoe. It was a fight for life at close quarters, and the victim had other bruises – mainly on his thighs – which probably came from the other man's knees as they struggled. And finally, the bruise on the sternum…' Lambert jabbed a finger at his own breastbone. 'Evidence that the gun had been pushed tight against the victim's chest, and the bullet went up through his heart and exited his shoulder blade. The struggle probably took place indoors, in someone's house or office, as cheap carpet fibres were found on the victim's clothing – suggesting they came from carpet tiles or very poor-quality carpeting.'

Wallace attempted to manoeuvre himself around Mick Beech's bulk to demonstrate what he imagined happened during the fight. He mimed holding a gun in his right hand and grasped his wrist with his left hand and said, 'Sonning was right handed, we know that, and in the struggle the killer must have quickly turned the gun like this, and, when it was pressed hard against Sonning's chest, squeezed his hand tight. Sonning was a big bloke, so the other geezer must have been stronger and fitter.'

Lambert nodded in agreement. 'Sonning's in his late forties, and the killer may have been a lot younger.'

DC Jones took a sip of white wine and said, 'Strange how the killer managed to anticipate the danger he was in, suggesting he was either warned in advance or knew Sonning and the reason for his visit.'

Beech snorted. 'I know one thing: the killer – if we catch him – can legitimately plead self-defence.'

'Self-defence or not,' Lambert said, 'I wouldn't mind betting this pub landlord's heavily involved.' He turned to address DC Jones. 'Fancy calling on Mr Hickson at 9 a.m. tomorrow, Debbie? I'll call for you at 8.45 and we'll go in my car. I like to pamper myself now and then. Especially when visiting the elite of Swansea.'

# Eight

The Earl of Richmond was not as scruffy as Lambert had anticipated. It was small and compact, leftover from the days when pubs were thriving and there were small public houses on every street corner. He noticed it was a free house and this was reflected in the care taken over the presentation of the exterior: hanging flower baskets coming into bloom, fresh paintwork and clean net curtains on the bottom of the windows, and the pub sign hanging over the entrance looked new, which was a portrait of the Earl of Richmond crowned as Henry VI, the first Tudor monarch.

'I think they've jumped the gun a bit,' Lambert said to Debbie as he looked up at the pub sign. 'Earl of Richmond didn't wear the crown till after Bosworth.'

Jones laughed. 'I think you're just showing off you know your history.'

'Yeah, pretentious old fart, that's me. But not so much of the old, eh? Right, time to swoop and get a few answers.'

High up by the side of the door was a bell. Lambert pressed it firmly, and kept his finger on it for a while, although they couldn't hear anything from inside the pub. He stood back on the narrow pavement and craned his neck, staring at the upstairs windows, expecting to see a bleary face complaining about being woken too early on a Sunday. Instead, they heard a bolt rattling and the door was opened by a woman with dyed blonde hair, cut in a deliberately carefree style, giving the impression she had been in a wind tunnel and paid good money for it. She was probably in her early forties and, although it was at least three hours away from opening time, her face was heavily made up. She was what Lambert would describe as voluptuous and he thought she fitted the bill as pub landlady perfectly, chosen for the part from central casting. To her side, looking up at the two detectives, and blinking in the low morning sun, stood a young girl of around eight-years-old.

Lambert showed the woman his warrant card. 'Mrs Hickson? I'm Detective Inspector Lambert and this is Detective Constable Jones.'

The landlady's lip curled. 'You're nearly three months too late.'

'Sorry?'

'You here about the burglary?'

'Burglary? Has the pub been burgled then?'

'Christ! Don't you cops talk to each other? Haven't they given you any of the details?'

'We're not here about the burglary. We're here to talk to Mr Hickson. Is he in?'

The landlady's face lost its animation, stilled by what looked like feelings of guilt or fear. 'What d'you wanna see Steve about?'

'Is he in?' Lambert repeated.

'You've just missed him. He's gone out. He'll be back just after opening time.'

Lambert wondered if she was lying and decided to test the water. 'Would you mind if we came in and had a word. We won't keep you very long.'

Jones, seeing the woman hesitate, said with a slight laugh, 'Neighbours love to gossip, Mrs Hickson, so it might be best if we had a word inside.'

Reluctantly, guarded and suspicious, but also curious, the landlady eased to one side, pulling her daughter by the arm, to make room for the detectives to enter. Inside the pub, which was small and cosy, with blue-and-white china plates and jugs on a shelf over the bar, and a large red dragon flag hanging near a television set, with a laminated list of the Six Nations fixtures stuck to the wall beneath the flag.

Waiting for the landlady to shut the door, Lambert glanced down at one of the tables, which was smeared with last night's beer, and chose to remain standing.

'My cleaner comes at half-nine,' the landlady explained.

'Mum!' her daughter whined. 'Can I have a J2O?'

'Kelly, I've told you before—' the landlady protested and then stopped, deciding it was easier to give in. 'You can have a drink if you be a good girl and drink it upstairs.'

The three adults waited silently while the young girl got a bottle of juice, uncapped it, took a drinking straw, and exited through the door behind the bar. The landlady leant back against the bar, her breasts thrust out boldly, and her demeanour giving the impression that she was defending her territory against intruders.

'So, if you haven't come about the burglary, what's this all about?'

Lambert threw a glance at the door behind the bar and said, 'Where is your husband, Mrs Hickson?'

'I told you: he's out. Don't you believe me?'

'Where is he?'

'He'll be back just after opening time.'

'That's over three hours away. We'd sooner speak to him before that.'

'Tell me what you want him for, and I'll tell you where he is.'

Seeing the defiant expression on the landlady's face, her lips clamped tight, Lambert decided to go for a soft approach. 'We just want to question him about an old friend of his.'

'Who?'

'Robert Sonning.'

She pulled a repugnant face. 'Oh, him! Robbie Sonning. Waste of space he is. I told Steve he shouldn't have nothing more to do with him.'

'How long has your husband known him?'

'Years, I think. Since long before I met Steve.'

'And has your husband been in touch with him recently.'

She shook her head vigorously. 'Robbie Sonning's in prison. Which is the best place for him.'

'And did your husband ever visit him in prison?'

'A few times, I think. I didn't want him to. We had a bit of an argument about it, but afterwards I thought what the hell! At least if he's in prison he's out of harm's way.'

Lambert saw the wheels begin turning in her head, and the cogs slotting into place. She gave him a piercing look and he knew what she was about to ask.

'He is still in prison, isn't he?'

'As far as I know,' Lambert lied, holding her gaze.

'So why d'you need to speak to Steve about him?'

'He may have said something to your husband when he was in prison, to do with an old case which has reared its ugly head.'

'Oh.' She seemed to accept this quite readily. 'If you want to speak to Steve you'll find him working on his boat at Burry Port. Boat mad he is. It's a smallish motorboat called *Esmeralda*. You shouldn't have any trouble finding it. Just the other side of Llanelli.'

'Thank you. Oh, before we go, tell us about your burglary. When did it happen?'

'Bastard broke in upstairs on Boxing Day – our busiest day of the year. And come the end of January he came back and did us again, knowing the insurance would have paid up by then and we'd replaced all our stuff. That's when Steve sussed out who he was.'

'You mean you knew who the burglar was?'

'We had a pretty good idea. It was one of our customers. Not a regular. He was drinking here on Boxing Day and we'd never seen him before. He disappeared and we thought he'd just gone home. After we'd been burgled the first time, we didn't put two and two together. But when he came back in January, we knew it was him after we'd been robbed a second time. We found out his name because one of our regulars knew who he was – sort of. Just by his nickname. He was originally from Swansea and everyone called him Virgil, cos he looked like that puppet character from TV. We told the police and they tracked him down to a pub… on the outskirts of Cardiff, they said. But they had no proof and had to let him go. So Steve…'

She stopped speaking and looked down at the floor, as if she suddenly realized she had said too much.

'So Steve did what?' Jones prompted.

She shrugged and pouted. 'Nothing. He just said if he ever saw him round here again – but of course, we never did. Anyway, if you've come to speak to Steve about that Sonning toe-rag, why d'you want to know about the burglary?'

It was Jones's turn to lie. 'We like to collect intelligence about criminals for future reference. So thanks for that. I only hope we'll be able to apprehend him soon.'

The landlady smiled mirthlessly. 'Yeah. Right.'

***

In the car on the way to Burry Port, Jones asked her boss why he had been so interested in the burglary, and whether he thought it had anything to do with Sonning and his murder.

'Maybe it's got nothing to do with it. But I was interested in the burglary because she clearly had something to hide. You must have noticed her reaction when we first questioned her and said we wanted to speak to her husband?'

'Eye contact went from ten to zero,' Jones observed. 'And it can't have been anything to do with Sonning because she thinks he's still in prison.'

'It looks as if Hickson keeps his wife in the dark about his activities,' Lambert added. 'She obviously knew nothing about him picking up his mate from prison.'

'Harry, you don't suppose Hickson employed his mate to take revenge on the burglar, do you?'

Lambert spluttered, and his voice leapt almost an octave. 'Murdering someone for a burglary. Come off it, Debbie. That's a bit extreme, isn't it?'

'I know, but there have been some brutal crimes for all kinds of petty reasons. Family feuds, jealousies, money-owed. There are people out there – you read about them in the papers every day – too boozed up to reason like other rational human beings.'

'I appreciate what you're saying, Debbie: the sort of losers you get from Scumbags 'R' Us. But usually those crimes are alcohol-fuelled and spontaneous. If what you're suggesting is correct, it looks as if the attempted murder of a petty criminal was premeditated and took a great deal of planning.'

Jones sighed loudly. 'I know. I'm clutching at straws.'

'And this Hickson has no previous convictions, not even for a driving offence.'

'But his friend Sonning sounds an unpleasant villain.'

'Yes, the missus certainly thought so.'

Debbie chuckled. 'But mothers always think it's their son's friend who is the bad influence. Never the son.'

'You could be right, Debbie. This Hickson bloke might be a right hooligan. He just hasn't been caught.'

'Cleverer than his mate, you think?'

'Soon find out, won't we?'

# Nine

At the end of the Gwendraeth valley, about five miles to the south-west of Llanelli, lay Burry Port, a small town with a great deal of history, and a thriving harbour and marina; once a busy coal-shipping port, now it catered mainly for pleasure craft.

When they reached the harbour car park in front of the lifeboat house, they saw there were only three cars, and one of those was Steven Hickson's Renault. Although there were dozens of empty spaces, Lambert parked right next to the Renault and got out. He and Jones stood for a moment surveying the marina, their eyes straining to catch sight of any boats called the *Esmeralda*.

'I can't even see the name of the boat nearest to us,' Lambert complained, squinting as he attempted to read its name, but gave up, realizing that perhaps soon, now that he was in his fifties, there would be the need for prescription glasses, instead of the off-the-peg ones he occasionally wore for reading.

'Time you saw an optician,' Jones replied mockingly. 'The nearest one's called the *Foxy Lady,* and the one next to it's called…'

'All right! All right! Don't rub it in. Let's see if we can find our way down on to the marina.'

Jones pointed to a gate and a steeply angled walkway. 'That looks like the way down. I suppose we can split up and walk a pontoon each until we find it.'

But when they got to the walkway, they discovered a locked gate forbidding them entry. 'I suppose we need a code or a key to gain access.' Lambert said.

Jones nodded towards a building near the lifeboat house. 'Why don't we try the Harbour Master's office? I know it's early on a Sunday morning, but you never know.'

Lambert knocked loudly on the plain, unpainted door. After a moment, it was thrown open by a young man sporting a beard, as if this was a nautical adornment to match his voluminous navy-blue sweatshirt.

'The door was open,' he said, and beckoned them to follow him into an office. They closed the door behind them and followed him into a small office, bare and functional. The young man went behind a counter, leant towards them with his elbows on the counter-top and flashed them a broad smile.

'My name's Tom Bradley. Now what can I do for you?'

'Well, Mr Bradley, we need to find a boat called the *Esmeralda,* belonging to a Steven Hickson,' Lambert said.

'Please – call me Tom.'

'Well, Tom, we're looking for Steven Hickson. Can you tell us where we might find him?'

The young man's smile faded as he frowned thoughtfully. 'Is he expecting you?'

'No. He doesn't know us, and we don't know him. Yet.'

The frown deepened into confusion. 'But you see, I'm not supposed to… I mean we have rules about…'

Before he reached the end of the sentence, Lambert had shown him his warrant card. 'CID. Detective Inspector Lambert. I would be grateful if you could let us on to the marina, and perhaps point us in the right direction of the *Esmeralda.'*

The young man stood up straight and nervously tapped out a rhythm with his fingers on the counter. 'I know Steve quite well. He's a nice bloke. I hope he's not in any trouble.'

Lambert shook his head. 'It's a routine enquiry. We just need to speak to him, that's all.'

'Right, well, I'll give you the access you need. If you'd like to follow me.'

He took them back to the walkway and pointed towards one of the pontoons in the direction of the town. 'The *Esmeralda'* s fourth berth along from the end of that pontoon.'

'Thanks for your help, Tom. We'll find it with no trouble.'

They shuffled down the walkway clutching the rail for support and felt the gentle motion of the sea beneath their feet as they stepped onto the pontoon. Lambert's heavy tread as he pounded along the planks echoed across the stillness of the harbour as he marched determinedly towards the *Esmeralda.* A yacht owner, winding a rope between his hand and elbow bade them a good morning. Lambert, whose thoughts were on his quarry, merely nodded, but Jones offered the yachtsman a bright 'Hi!'

As soon as they reached the *Esmeralda,* Lambert stopped and stared at the two tiny portholes on the cabin's side, trying to make out if there was anyone inside. He was about to step aboard the small craft when the cabin door flew open and Hickson appeared, slamming the door behind him.

'What's your game?' he growled.

He was grey-haired, with a wiry physique, wore glasses with medium-thick black frames and was probably in his mid-forties. He wore a short-sleeved check shirt beneath a beige padded gilet, and his bare arms looked like it was a deliberate intention to show off the Rolex watch strapped to his left wrist.

'Mr Hickson?' Lambert enquired.

Hickson stared at the detectives insolently. 'Who wants him?'

Lambert showed his warrant card and introduced himself and DC Jones. 'What's this all about?'

'We want to ask you a few questions,' Lambert began, 'about your friend Robert Sonning.'

'What about him?'

'It would help, sir, if you didn't answer questions with questions. We're making enquiries about Robert Sonning. There's a great deal we need to know, so perhaps if we came aboard and…'

Glancing back at the cabin door, Hickson said hurriedly, 'The cabin's a right mess and it's cramped and claustrophobic down there. If you want to talk to me, why don't we do it on dry land? There's a park bench over there, and it's not as if it's cold today.'

Lambert and Jones followed Hickson back along the pontoon, up the walkway and across the car park to a park bench overlooking the harbour. Jones seated herself on the bench and Hickson sat next to her, but Lambert remained standing.

Hickson looked up questioningly at Lambert and said, 'Your call.'

'When did you last see your friend, Robert Sonning?'

Hickson took his time replying, as if he was trying to remember, but Lambert could tell he was trying to guess if the detectives knew about his friend's release from Cardiff prison.

'I last saw Robbie just over a fortnight ago.'

'Was this on the day he was released from prison?'

Hickson nodded thoughtfully. 'Yes, I picked him up and gave him a lift.'

'Where did you take him?'

Another pause while Hickson considered his reply. 'First, I thought he could probably use a decent meal, followed by a drink. So, I took him to Cardiff Bay, and we went and had a traditional all-day breakfast, and then we did a few pubs there.' He laughed nervously. 'Of course, I was driving, so I was careful 'bout how much I drank.'

Like a children's staring match, Lambert remained silent as he looked intently at Hickson, deliberately attempting to unnerve him. The publican broke eye contact with him and fiddled with his Rolex, as if this offered him security as a sort of materialistic charm. Lambert wondered briefly if the Rolex was genuine or made in Hong Kong and bought over the internet.

'Sonning wasn't married,' Jones said. 'Did he have a girlfriend? Someone he was going to stay with when he was released?'

'Not as far as I know.'

'The next question is,' Lambert said, raising his voice, 'where did he stay for the last fortnight?'

'I don't know.'

Lambert forced incredulity into his tone. 'You don't know? But, after your booze-up in Cardiff, you must have taken him somewhere. He must have told you where he was staying, seeing as how you were old mates and that.'

Hickson turned anxiously in the direction of his boat as if he was considering his options. 'I brought him here to the marina, just until he got fixed up.'

'You mean he slept on your boat?'

'It's not ideal but he had nowhere else to go.'

'How long was he on your boat for?'

'Just a couple of nights – the Friday and Saturday. To be honest I was relieved when he'd gone, because my wife doesn't approve of our relationship. She doesn't understand that you stand by your friends, through thick and thin.'

'But I can't say as I blame your wife. By all accounts, your friend was a violent man, with a terrible reputation. And your wife never said anything about you meeting him on his release.'

Hickson looked genuinely surprised. 'You've spoken to Pat?'

Lambert nodded. 'How else would we know where to find you? But you say your friend only stayed on your boat for two nights. Where did he go after that?'

Hickson shrugged hugely and showed the palms of his hands. 'I haven't a clue.'

'You mean he just disappeared?' Jones said.

'He left a note in the cabin, thanking me, and saying he'd made other arrangements and would be in touch.'

Lambert looked down at Hickson like a stern schoolmaster. 'Didn't you think that was an odd thing to do?'

'Not really. Robbie's always been a bit of a loner.'

41

'And this note he left you. Have you still got it?'

'Yes, I think I must have,' Hickson said, and then clicked his fingers to make a show of remembering something. 'Tell a lie. I had a blitz on the cabin. I think I must have thrown it out with the rest of the rubbish.'

'You just told us how untidy the cabin—'

'This was a fortnight ago,' Hickson butted in. 'It's such a cramped space, in no time at all it looks as if a bomb's hit it.'

Lambert didn't for a minute believe Hickson's story about the note. He had yet to give him news of his friend's death but, before he did, he wanted to see if there was any connection between the pub burglary and Sonning's murder.

'Does the name Virgil mean anything to you?'

Hickson's face was expressionless, but Lambert noticed glimmer of fear in his eyes, and in that instance the detective knew the man had a great deal to hide.

With a feeble laugh, Hickson recovered and said, 'Isn't he a character in *Thunderbirds*?'

'I'm talking about the man who burgled your pub. Twice. Your wife told us all about it, and she said one of your regulars recognized the man you suspected, and he went by the nickname of Virgil.'

Hickson took a slow, deep breath to keep calm, wondering what the detectives knew about that scumbag in Cardiff. It was two months ago, and there'd been no comeback at the time. So why was this coming home to roost now?

He'd found out which pub on the outskirts of Cardiff the scumbag used regularly. It was one of those large, brash, impersonal pubs, uncarpeted and dark. He'd sat in one of the diner-type booths, biding his time. The petty villain hadn't spotted him, so he'd watched and waited from a distance until the scumbag had sunk enough beer and needed to pay a visit to relieve himself. No one else had gone to the Gents'. It had been a perfect opportunity. He'd given the scumbag about half a minute to enjoy his relief then followed him. Zipping his fly, the arsehole had looked over his shoulder as he entered, and the shock and surprise on his face had been a joy to behold. That was when he'd felt his adrenaline pumping and his heart pounding. He'd whipped out the flick knife, ready to slash. The scumbag pleaded with him, offering to return his property. No way. Too late, sunshine. He'd slashed and slit a bloody stripe down the scumbag's right cheek, and as the loser slid down the urinal, trying to stem the open wound, blood oozing through his fingers, that's when he'd given him the same treatment along his left cheek. Then he'd walked to the door and turned to savour the scumbag's trauma before leaving. He couldn't resist a parting shot.

'Oh, and a word of advice,' he'd said. 'You're supposed to wash your hands after you've had a piss.'

A good line. And his delivery had been perfect. He couldn't resist a smile as he remembered the scene.

'His nickname was Virgil,' Lambert repeated impatiently, noticing the slight smile on Hickson's face. 'Why would you find that amusing, Mr Hickson?'

Hickson shrugged, his confidence growing. 'Probably because he resembled the puppet character, that's all.'

'After the burglary, did you ever set eyes on the man again?'

'No, why would I? I've no idea where he lives or hangs out.'

Lambert decided to go for the jugular.

'Where were you between the hours of six and nine on Thursday evening?'

'I was at the pub.'

'You sure about that?'

'Of course I'm sure. It's quiz night on Thursdays. Why? What's so important about Thursday night?'

'Because somewhere between the hours of six and nine on Thursday, Robert Sonning was murdered.'

The detectives remained perfectly still, scrutinizing Hickson's reaction like scientists examining a specimen. From a distance came a child's playful scream and a dog barked, otherwise the morning stillness was morbidly apt.

And then, like a pan boiling over, Hickson's tears erupted and he clutched at his forehead. DC Jones exchanged a look with Lambert. Neither of them had expected Hickson to react as if it was a major tragedy in his life.

'I'm sorry,' Jones said. 'We had no idea you were such close friends.'

He sniffed noisily and blubbered, 'We go back donkey's years. Even though Robbie was… well, he was a bit of a rogue, but we was very close.'

'And the last you saw of him,' Lambert said, 'was on the day of his release, two weeks from Friday, when you brought him to your boat, is that right?'

Hickson nodded, mumbled something unintelligible, then wiped his tears and nose with a hand, which he then rubbed on his denims. He tried to recover, shook his head as if he still couldn't believe the devastating news, and asked, 'How did it happen?'

Lambert answered, 'He was shot at point blank range and his body was dumped in the boot of a car, which was then abandoned in the centre of Swansea. It'll probably be on the news, even as we speak.'

DC Jones watched closely as Hickson digested this information and seemed to her to be weighing up how this could have happened to his friend, almost as if there should have been an alternative outcome to the episode.

'Did Sonning buy a car recently?' Lambert asked.

Blurry-eyed, Hickson tried to focus on Lambert. 'If he did, I wouldn't have known about it.'

'Why not?'

'Because the last I saw of Robbie was on the day he was released from prison.'

'And he didn't phone you at any time between then and Thursday?'

'No, I never heard a word from him.'

'And have you any idea who could have done this?'

'I think he could have had a few enemies. The reason he went inside was cos he battered someone with a baseball bat.'

'Who is now an alky confined to a wheelchair.'

'The bloke was a drug dealer, so no one's going to lose any sleep over that.'

'But your friend didn't do it to make our streets safer. Rumour has it that he was paid by another dealer whose patch Terry Parsons had invaded.' Lambert thought it was time to use his tactic of a sudden change of subject. 'What time on Thursday does your quiz start?'

'What?'

'It's a simple question, Mr Hickson? What time does your quiz begin?'

'Half-eight. Christ! You don't think I... Jesus wept! He was a close mate. I know Robbie had his faults, and the sort of work he did was... but we was mates, for Christ's sakes.'

Ignoring his protests, Lambert said, 'So where were you between six o'clock and the start of the quiz?'

'At the pub.'

'Any witnesses who can corroborate this?'

Hickson stared at Lambert with hostility. 'Yeah, there's Pat, my wife. There was also a handful of regular customers, about six or seven. And from around quarter-past-eight there would have been at least forty witnesses who can confirm that I ran the quiz. You can check, if you like.'

'Don't worry: we will.'

'Mr Hickson,' DC Jones began, 'over the years, how much did Sonning confide in you about his irregular and illegal activities?'

'Hardly at all.'

'That's a bit unusual, isn't it? Seeing as you and he were great mates.'

'I knew better than to ask. It was better not to know.'

'Not even the occasional man-to-man confidence over a few beers?'

'I knew he was a professional heavy and, because we were mates, I didn't delve into it. I think he appreciated that because he didn't want to involve me.'

'In other words, you have no idea who could have done this.'

'I've already told you: I ain't got a clue. And I hope you catch the bastard who did it.'

'Do you really?' Lambert said sarcastically. 'But when we catch the perpetrator, his sentence might not be substantial, because it looks like he was Sonning's target and killed your mate in self-defence. Would you happen to know anything about your friend's intended target?'

'Of course not,' Hickson replied, glancing away from Lambert's probing stare. 'Why would I?'

'Because it seems a strange coincidence that you visit him at prison a few weeks before his release, pick him up on his release, and then less than a fortnight later he attempts to murder someone. Most people might assume that Sonning's motive was revenge, but it could have been a conspiracy, and he was paid to hit someone.'

'That's bloody ridiculous. I had nothing to do with it.'

Lambert didn't believe him. He could tell he was lying. But he had no concrete evidence, nothing to hold him on suspicion of conspiring to murder. At least, not for the time being.

'OK,' he said. 'For now, you're just another citizen going about his business while we investigate Sonning's death. But we will no doubt speak again soon, and we have some pictures of the man who abandoned the car, who might or might not be Sonning's killer, so we'd like you to see if it's someone you recognize.'

'Of course,' Hickson said. 'Anything I can do to help catch this man.'

'That'll be all for now.'

Lambert turned abruptly and walked off. DC Jones got up and joined her boss as he strode towards the car. Hickson remained seated, staring across the harbour. Lambert glanced back when they had gone some distance and saw him taking a mobile phone out of his pocket.

'He's on the blower to someone already. I'd love to know who he's calling.'

'Shame we haven't got the equipment with us to monitor the call.'

'Shame indeed. But one thing's for certain, Hickson's involved in whatever was going on between his mate and the killer. And I think I'd like to track down this Virgil bloke and have a word with him.'

'He shouldn't be too difficult to trace. D'you reckon he'll have some previous?'

Lambert chuckled. 'What do you think, Debbie?'

'Yes. Silly question, really.'

# Ten

On Monday morning the tsunami that had devastated Japan and was intensifying by the minute as the country faced nuclear disaster, meant that the story of the corpse discovered in an abandoned car in the centre of Swansea was completely overshadowed by the tragic events on the other side of the globe. The report of the murder hit the third or fourth page in most of the tabloids, but because of the in-depth reportage in the broadsheets of the impending nuclear disaster, it tended to become lost somewhere in the national news in brief. But, more importantly, the BBC local news gave it maximum coverage, which would help with the investigation, and might trigger someone's memory who had been out walking in the city centre early on Thursday evening. And Lambert had been right about the headline, and the story became known as the 'Body in Boot'.

No sooner had Lambert arrived at the Cockett incident room but Marden called and insisted he gave a television appeal for witnesses to come forward, which Lambert agreed with some reluctance, but accepted that it was necessary. The police press office had it all arranged, and photographs of the car, taken at the Ogmore car pound, were shown with the appeal, and Lambert gave a description of the man caught on CCTV, stressing details of the tattoo on the base of his thumb. The item was scheduled for use on the 1.00 p.m., 6.00 p.m. and 10.00 p.m. news and he hoped the tattoo details would pay dividends.

While Lambert was busy dealing with press and TV, DC Jones concentrated on tracking down the man known as Virgil, but it was no easy task, mainly because he had so many aliases. Sometimes known as Geordie Pete, even though he was born and bred in Swansea, he also went by the name of Mark Richards and John Gibbon, and his criminal record gave details of his previous convictions in the latter name, so Jones thought this was probably

47

as correct as they would get. She dismissed the name Peter Hartlepool as false, and assumed it was what gave him the Geordie Pete nickname. It was as Geordie Pete that he got his biggest conviction, for stealing mailbags from station platforms. Because of his aliases, it took her all morning to discover his whereabouts. But she eventually discovered he was currently using the name of John Gibbon and traced him to a flat on the outskirts of Cardiff.

It was almost 12.30 by the time she and Lambert pulled up outside his flat, which was above a boarded-up corner shop in a district that had more than its fair share of dumped takeaway cartons and discarded beer cans. The entrance to the flat was round the back, reached by steep iron stairs. At the bottom of the stairs a wheelie bin was overloaded with rubbish, with supermarket plastic bags containing household refuse piled around it, the bags split open, spilling chicken bones and other revolting food waste. Jones wrinkled her nose as she breathed in a rotten egg smell of drains and smiled when she saw the look of distaste on Lambert's face, which she somehow found comical, almost endearing. They mounted the stairs in double-time, attempting to escape the sickening lavatory smell from the blocked drains below.

Lambert knocked a rusted silver knocker and was just wondering how difficult it was going to be to question this Virgil man if he chose not to answer – and there was little justification to obtain a warrant – when the door was flung open by a woman who looked as if she'd had a rough night and gone three rounds with Mike Tyson. Her face was red and bloated, there was a large purple bruise on the top of a cheekbone, and yesterday's make-up gave her the unattractive semblance of a smeared watercolour image in a distorting mirror. She had a top-heavy figure, large breasts crammed into a grubby maroon sweater, but surprisingly slim legs in tight yellow jeans.

The woman blinked blearily and Lambert spoke slowly and precisely. 'I'm looking for John Gibbon.'

'Police,' Jones said, thrusting her warrant card in the woman's face.

'I don't know anyone... that name.'

She sounded slurred, and Lambert pictured the scene of the night before, her and her partner quarrelling drunkenly, and fighting and swearing like two snarling cats.

'Which name does Virgil go by these days?' Lambert said.

'Who the fuck's Virgil?'

'Come on, sweetheart, don't play games. We know Virgil lives here with you. Where is he?'

She stared at him with a stupefied expression, her mouth hanging open, revealing a mouthful of bad teeth.

'We know,' he said more forcefully, 'Virgil lives here, and goes by the names of Hartlepool, Richards and Gibbon. It's all on record. So, you might save us, and you, a bit of time if you tell us where he is.'

'Out,' she said.

'Out where? Where can we find him?'

'Here, there, everywhere.' She giggled. 'I used to like The Beatles.'

He realized she was still drunk and, guessing the flat was chock full of stolen items, decided to apply some gentle pressure. 'We just want to talk to Virgil. And if we don't talk to him today, it means we come back with a warrant and go through the flat. Who knows what goodies we might find? You'll make it a lot easier on yourself if you tell us where we can find him. Otherwise…' He gestured towards the inside of the flat, making it clear that a police search could turn out to be a major problem for her. 'We can either come back and search the flat or have a quiet word with Virgil and be on our way?'

'What d'you wanna talk to him 'bout?'

Lambert felt he was about to explode but DC Jones suddenly found some inspiration.

'We want to ask him about an incident back in January,' she said.

The woman looked at her, as if noticing her for the first time. 'If you can catch the bastard who did that to him, I'll tell you. He's never been the same since it happened. Made my life a misery, it has. So I'll tell you: he's just round the corner at the club.'

'Club?' Jones queried.

'The Working Men's Club,' the woman said, waving a hand in several directions. 'Just round the corner.'

'OK. Thank you,' Lambert said. 'We'll find it.'

Glad to see the back of them, the woman slammed the door. As the two detectives walked to the front of the building, Lambert gave Jones a quizzical look.

'What was that about an incident in January?'

'Just a shot in the dark. A pure guess.'

'An educated guess. And it worked.'

# Eleven

Having asked for directions, Lambert and Jones found the working men's club less than three hundred yards from the burglar's flat, down a lane behind a large ironmonger's. The club was the usual anywhere place offering cheap alcohol, with fluorescent strip lighting, an enormous television screen and plastic rather than wood furnishings.

As they entered they saw the clientele were predominantly men over retirement age. The television was showing golf, to which nobody appeared to be paying attention. From another room came the gentle clack of billiard balls. Their eyes scanning the customers, trying to take them in at a glance, Lambert and Jones walked towards the bar.

'Anyone here called Virgil?' Lambert announced to the barman.

That was when a man, slightly concealed by a pillar in the middle of the long bar, suddenly lunged for the emergency exit, slammed down the metal release bar, and ran out of the door and into a back alley.

'Stop him!' Lambert yelled.

By the time Lambert had responded physically, DC Jones, whose reactions were younger and quicker than her boss, was already out of the emergency exit in pursuit. She saw the man bolting along the narrow alley, his fast-retreating figure heading for the street at the end. She raced after him, her pace steady and controlled, knowing she stood a better chance of catching him in the street where she was less likely to trip over.

As soon as he turned left at the end of the alley, she lost sight of him and put on a spurt. By the time she reached the street, she heard the squeal of a car and an angry blast on a car horn, and saw him darting across the busy street. She followed, dodged between a bus and a white van, and ran flat out after him into a side street, hardly aware of the cacophony of furious tooting she had caused.

She could see the man weakening, and this gave her greater energy as she shortened the distance between them. He glanced over his shoulder to see if she was still following, and this action lost him some ground. He suddenly stopped and then bolted between two parked cars, crossing the street. She saw how he had lost even more ground now, kept going along the same side of the street, her pace never slacking, waited until there were no parked cars, and charged across the street. As she drew level with him, she saw how shattered he was.

'Hold it!' she shouted. 'Just hold it right there!'

He stopped, his body suddenly rigid, and raised his hands in surrender. 'OK,' he wheezed. 'You got me.'

And that was when she was distracted. *Those scars.* She had seen his mugshot back in the incident room, but she didn't recall seeing these two tramlines, one either side of his face. These scars were recent.

And in that regrettable instant of distraction she paid the price. With all his might, the man summoned up one final surge of energy, putting it into a forceful kick which caught Jones in the shin. She doubled up in agony, tears sprang into her eyes, and hot and cold needles of pain shot up her spine.

And in that moment of agony the man was gone.

Lambert, breathless and flushed, came bounding up seconds later, and put an arm round her stooped shoulders as she rubbed at her ankle.

'I'm all right,' she said. 'Get after him.'

'Don't worry, Debbie,' Lambert said, knowing his bird had flown. 'We'll get a description out to apprehend. He'll be wanted for assaulting a police officer, at least. Hopefully, one of our E Division uniform's will get him. How's the ankle?'

'I'll live. It's just bruised.' She straightened up and took a deep breath to calm herself. 'You know what his wife said about catching the bastard who did that to him in January? Well, I had a close look at our *Thunderbirds* puppet-man and he had a deep scar on each cheek. And his mugshot didn't show him with any scars.'

Lambert nodded thoughtfully. 'As the excitement's over, I think we'll head back to the incident room and delve a little deeper. You OK to walk?'

'I'll be fine.'

'Here, take my arm.'

She gladly slotted her arm through his as they began the walk back to the car. And just for a moment, as he enjoyed the feeling of escorting an attractive young woman, Lambert indulged in licentious thoughts, and wondered if his own rule about avoiding a relationship with a colleague could be ignored.

# Twelve

Kyle's greedy eyes stared at the money stacked on the grubby kitchen table in neat bundles. Sitting opposite, his partner and partner-in-crime, Donny Williams, surrounded by KFC debris, swigged from a bottle of Budweiser.

'Not a bad haul from Spar and Costcutter,' Kyle said and snorted. 'There's money in the grocery business.'

Donny yawned. 'Easy pickings but not exactly a fortune. I know I could make twice – three times as much with an ID scam. And it's less risky than armed robbery of small supermarkets in broad daylight. With daylight robbery...' Donny stopped to chuckle at his own choice of words before continuing. 'You only need one punter to have a go – some model citizen and upright wanker – and I'd have to let him have it.'

Kyle gazed in awe at his partner. 'Fuck me. You'd really shoot someone if they got in the way?'

'If I had to. Look at it this way, Kyle: when it comes down to him or me, I come down on the side of *numero uno*. Present company excepted, of course.'

'Eh?

Kyle's jaw went slack, and a dim expression clouded his normally attractive brown eyes, which irritated Donny.

'I mean,' Donny said, talking as if to a five-year-old, 'there's just you and me, boy. And if anyone got in our way—' He pointed a finger with his thumb cocked like a gun and made an explosive sound in the back of his throat.

Kyle grinned. This is what he liked to hear. With Donny he felt invincible, untouchable. After meeting him that night at a gay club about six months ago, he soon discovered they shared the same criminal tendencies, the same lust for illegal activities, and a crazy hunger for risk-taking. And Donny, being older and more experienced in law-breaking, became a kind of mentor to him, encouraging him to consider a life of extremes, a life where moderation is for boring suckers. Not long after their relationship was sealed with this unwritten agreement to run rampant over conventional society, they committed their first robbery.

Remembering it now with fond memories, Kyle laughed and said, 'I'll never forget that Paki shop we did. Geezer's face – looking at that gun. It was brill, man.'

Donny smiled suggestively. 'The first is always the best. You never forget the first time.'

Kyle stared at his partner, who was almost forty, round faced and balding, and pretty average-looking – you wouldn't look at him twice in the street – but there was something lurking beneath his exterior that was electric, aggressive and fiery – but at the same time, congenial. Like an attractive reptile, poisonous but spellbinding.

'Do you mean…' Kyle began hesitatingly.

Donny snapped with sudden irritation, 'What I said was what I meant. It's easy enough to understand. Even for a half-caste like you.'

Shamefaced, and without realizing what he was doing, Kyle wiped a hand across his boyish face, and spoke in a strangled voice. 'I'm not a half-caste.'

'What are you then?'

'Mixed race.'

Donny laughed cruelly. 'That's just semantics.'

Kyle's brows contracted into a confused frown. He hated his partner using big words, the words he'd learnt trying to better himself in prison.

But Donny was now on a roll, and loved tormenting Kyle, his loveable but vulnerable hooligan. Half-teasing yet intentionally heartless, he added, 'Boils down to the same thing in the end. The son of a black whore and white trash.'

'At least if I was going to kill someone, I'd do it properly.'

This was Kyle's ultimate defence, knowing it was his partner's Achilles' heel. In a moment of weakness, Donny had confided in Kyle, telling him the truth about why he was banged up for eight years at the age of twenty. A pensioner he tried to rob in her home fought back, and when he pushed her forcefully, she fell, cracked her head on a coffee table and died. It was more accident than murder and of this he was ashamed. It was pathetic. Not even a proper murder. Ignominious. Which was another addition to his vocabulary courtesy of HM Prison.

Donny's eyes narrowed as he studied his partner, and Kyle was suddenly afraid. The older man was totally unpredictable and unbalanced, and you never knew what to expect. It was exciting, exhilarating and unnerving, and in a way Kyle found it sexually stimulating.

To pacify Donny, Kyle smiled apologetically, and said, 'Mind you, I know if you had to, you'd kill someone, wouldn't you, Donny?'

'Don't try to manipulate me, boy. If there's any manipulating to be done—'

'I just meant,' Kyle said hurriedly, without giving a thought to what he was going to say.

Knowing this, Donny pounced. 'You meant what?'

'I mean, um, killing someone,' Kyle burbled, 'what's it like? What's it like to do someone in? What's it feel like afterwards?'

'D'you feel any remorse, you mean?'

Kyle nodded uncertainly. 'I think so.'

'Let me ask you something, boy? Do you believe in God?'

'I've never really thought about it, like.'

Irritation crept into Donny's voice again. 'You must have given it some thought at some stage in your pathetic little life. You must have wondered what happens after you kick the bucket.'

'I dunno. I guess nothing happens. You just die.'

Donny laughed delightedly, toasted Kyle with his bottle of Bud and took a sip. Kyle felt relieved. He appeared to have said the right thing for a change.

'You see, boy, if you truly believe there is no God and no after-life, you don't have to look over your shoulder. You don't have to worry about paying the price for your crimes. You can sin with impunity. You can play God and you can be God. You can decide who lives and who dies. And the only thing that stands in your way is the law of the country. So, my mottos is: don't get caught.'

Donny was about to have another swig of beer when there was a loud knock on the front door. They were not expecting anyone and froze, staring into each other's eyes as the danger signals bounced back and forth between them. The tableau was broken by Donny, who went to the kitchen cupboard and fetched the sawn-off shotgun.

# Thirteen

As soon as they got back to the incident room, Lambert gave Mick Beech a quick run down on what had happened in Cardiff, and how the man called Virgil had managed to get away, and then he left Debbie Jones to contact Accident and Emergency in Cardiff while he emailed Marden to give him details of the investigation so far.

Ellis was at a desk, hunched over in concentration, and he gave them a cursory wave, his body language indicating that he was close to a discovery and needed uninterrupted time to finish.

Wallace arrived back mid afternoon, exhausted and deflated. Lambert looked questioningly from his workstation and he puffed out his cheeks and shook his head.

'You can forget the Michael Thomases. They've all been checked out – all fifty-eight of them – and not one of them arouses the slightest suspicion. It looks as if the man who phoned Mitchell about the car used a false name.'

'As we thought,' Lambert said. 'But it had to be done. I hope you didn't spend the entire day on it.'

'A few were checked out on Saturday – not that many. And I had some help from some of the uniforms this afternoon.'

Everyone's attention was diverted by DC Jones ending a phone call loudly. 'Yes, thank you. That was very helpful.' She replaced the receiver and stood up to speak to Lambert, unable to keep the excitement out of her voice. 'Accident and Emergency at Cardiff have a record of a Mark Richards, which was one of this Virgil's aliases, being brought in needing attention for two serious knife slashes, one on each cheek. This was the last week in January. Questioned by a police constable about the incident, he said he was attacked and robbed by a gang of youngsters, and when asked to describe them he said it was dark and they were all wearing hoods.'

'It looks as if our publican likes to take the law into his own hands,' Lambert said as he went to the white board and picked up a marker pen. He pointed at Robert Sonning's mugshot, drew a horizontal line from it and wrote 'Hickson', with the word 'Revenge' next to it, followed by a question mark.

'If Hickson took his revenge for the burglar...' He drew a vertical line down from Hickson and wrote 'Virgil'... 'the question is, what did he need his mate Sonning for?'

'Maybe the two are not connected,' DC Wallace said. 'Maybe he told the truth about Sonning disappearing from his boat and then turning up dead, and it had nothing to do with Hickson.'

'That's a possibility, I suppose,' Lambert reluctantly agreed.

'Except,' Ellis said, grabbing the focus now, 'I checked into Hickson's background. He's got no previous of any sort, but he's the brother of Mrs Sheila Mason, whose daughter was killed by a drunk driver towards the end of February. It was on the national news, because after the hearing when the driver was bailed, he was seen leaving the court, laughing and joking on his mobile phone.'

'Yes, I remember it,' Lambert said. 'For while he was the country's most hated man.'

'Yeah, I'd liked to have kicked the bastard myself,' Wallace said.

DC Jones's eyes widened as she said, 'You don't think Hickson, the girl's uncle, would actually have this drunk driver killed, do you?'

Lambert tapped Virgil's name on the board with the felt tip marker. 'If he slashed the burglar for theft, who knows what he's capable of doing. Especially if he was close to his niece. And if he got his mate Sonning to do it, you know what that means.'

'It means,' Ellis said, 'that this James Harlan, the drunk driver, may have killed him.'

'In self-defence,' Mick Beech reminded them.

But his opinion was ignored, as the other detectives were all focused on Lambert, knowing he was ready to make a move now they had some concrete leads to chase.

Lambert stared at the white board. 'Now a pattern is starting to emerge.' He looked towards DS Ellis. 'Got this Harlan's address?'

Ellis nodded.

'Bring him in for questioning right away. If he's not at home you might have to track him down via his parents or friends and acquaintances. Kevin, shoot over to Mitchell's place at Port Talbot – shouldn't take you long – see if Mitchell can ID the CCTV photograph. I'd still like to know who purchased that car. You can meet up with Tony afterwards and try to get as much on James Harlan as you can. Meanwhile, I'll take Debbie to visit the Mason family and see just how close this wicked uncle is to the unfortunate niece.'

As they all put their coats back on, Lambert asked Beech if he had the details of their actions.

'Already started inputting,' Beech muttered, his back to them, making no effort to make eye contact.

As Lambert tapped the pocket of his leather coat, making sure he had his mobile with him, he said to DC Jones, 'Their daughter was knocked down by this Harlan less than three weeks ago, so they may still be feeling—'

'Don't worry. I'll be tactful, understanding and sympathetic. And it won't be a performance. It'll be genuine, believe me.'

Lambert gave her a grateful smile as he opened the door. He was about to dash out when he stopped and held the door open for her.

'After you, Debbie.'

'Sexist!' she laughed, easing the tension of visiting bereaved parents.

# Fourteen

His breathing shallow and excitement pulsing in his chest, Kyle followed his partner stealthily out of the kitchen, along the hall towards the front door. Donny had the sawn-off aimed at the door, and Kyle wondered if he was going to open it and blast whoever it was in the face. He also wondered if this was it. End of the road. *Out of the prison van and into court with a hood over the head.* Like he'd seen in films and on the news.

Halfway along the hall, Donny stopped and listened, then turned to Kyle, with a finger to his lips. Obviously, he had no intention of answering the door. Kyle was relieved. *Pretend there's no one in. Only use the shooter as a last resort, when they break down the door.*

Suddenly both men jumped as the letter box clattered open and a voice yelled, 'Kyle! You in there? It's me. Dad.'

Kyle let his breath out slowly as the tension in him eased. But Donny seemed even more wound up. 'Fuck!' he muttered through gritted teeth.

Before Donny could stop him, Kyle dashed forward and threw open the door. Virgil didn't wait to be invited in and sidled past his son into the hallway. As soon as he saw Donny with the sawn-off, his eyes flickered alarm. But he recovered quickly, and his assessment of the situation was sharp. He kicked the door shut and grinned at Donny.

'Expecting company, were you?'

Donny was about to answer but Kyle noticed the tramlines on his father's cheeks. 'Fuckin' hell, Dad. Who did that?'

'I'll tell you all about it. Aren't you going to ask me in?'

'You are in,' Donny grumbled. 'I suppose you want a drink.'

'Drink would be good. And I want to ask a favour of you.'

Donny's mouth clenched tight. He didn't like Kyle's father but felt he ought to make an effort. After all, like himself he was feral and walked on the wild side.

'OK,' he said with a great effort at civility. 'Let's go in the kitchen.'

As soon as Virgil spotted the neat stacks of money on the table, he whistled. 'You have been busy. Looks like you got a result.'

'It pays the rent,' Donny said as he put the shotgun away in the cupboard, then got three bottles of Bud out of the fridge and put them on the table. 'For a while, until it runs out.'

Virgil snapped the top off his beer with an opener and toasted them both. 'Cheers!' He took a swig, then glanced round the kitchen and nodded approvingly. 'Yeah, not a bad place you got here.'

With a scornful growl from the back of his throat, Donny said, 'Two-up and two-down. We'll have much better than this before long.'

Virgil frowned, fell silent, and downed his beer. Much as he'd had little to do with his son for a while, especially now he was all of twenty-eight – or was it twenty-seven? (Virgil could never remember) – he hated the notion that he could be 'one of them'. His son and this fat bastard nesting together was a sickening thought. But he needed their help, so he had to try and hold his true feelings in check, because all he focused on now was his diabolical plan. It had become an obsession, almost to the point of a screaming madness.

Donny, who sensed Virgil's disapproval, leant towards him with a touch of menace. 'Something wrong, Virgil?'

Virgil laughed foolishly. 'Course not. Why would there be? I just wondered, that was all.'

'What about?'

'Well, even though this is only two-up, two-down, it's still quite... well, I mean, it's not to be sneezed at. Bigger, better place'd set you back quite a bit.'

Kyle chuckled proudly. 'Donny's got it all worked out, Dad. Know how we got this money? Just fuckin' took it from a couple of supermarkets. Got clean away we did and left no traces.'

'In that case,' Virgil said with a sneaky smile, 'how come you answered the door armed with the shooter? Can't have been that sure of yourself?'

Donny slammed his beer bottle onto the table. 'Listen, we wasn't expecting you or anyone, so we was taking precautions, that's all.' He gestured at the money. 'As Kyle said, we got a result and left no traces. So don't be criticising us.'

Virgil ducked his head subserviently, knowing he needed to keep on Donny's good side, and looked up craftily from beneath hooded eyelids. 'I'm not criticizing, Donny. Far from it. I'm impressed how you both managed to get away with it. I mean, nicking a car these days is not easy. You must let me in to your secret.'

'I don't nick cars,' Donny gloated. 'I hire a car to do a job.'

Virgil's mouth opened, confusion spread across his face.

'Yes, if I say so myself, my skills are improving daily. See...' Donny leaned forward, lowering his voice to a conspiratorial whisper. 'I can hire a car because I steal someone else's identity. I'm not like you, Virgil, using loads of fictional names. Mine are for real. Have a look at that.'

Donny fumbled in his wallet and handed Virgil a driver's licence. Virgil stared at it for a moment, his voice dropping to the same level as Donny's.

'This is your photo but it's in the name of Gary Bain.'

Kyle, irritated by the pointless whispering, brought the conversation back to a normal level. 'Donny's got it all worked out. He spends hours on the computer searching for people's weaknesses. And you'd be surprised what people throw out with the rubbish—'

'Not to mention the recent dead giving me a new ID,' Donny boasted. 'But enough about me. What about you, Virgil? Who marked your face for you? If someone had done that to me, they'd be dead meat.'

'It's what I want to talk to you about,' Virgil said. 'I've had a bit of a result myself.'

From the inside pocket of his denim jacket, Virgil pulled out a Sharwood's medium egg noodles packet. It crackled enticingly as he opened and tilted its contents onto the table. Donny and Kyle's eyes widened as they saw the mound of jewellery sparkling like Christmas decorations.

It was Virgil's turn to boast. 'I don't know if you guys read the *Western Mail* but following a burglary at a posh gaff in Penarth, it was reported that this little bundle of goodies is worth around thirty grand. Thirty bloody grand! How's that for a result?'

Donny's eyes narrowed and he felt dryness in his throat as he felt stirrings of jealousy. This was a much bigger and more important haul than their own small supermarket larceny.

'Cash is better,' he sniffed.

Virgil sniggered. 'Yeah? How much would a fence want? Thirty-per-cent, maybe. So that leaves us with ten grand for me, and ten grand for you two.'

Donny eyed him suspiciously. 'And what would we have to do to earn our share?'

'Well, I need a safe house for a while,' Virgil ran the fingers of a hand down one of his scars. 'And I've got a proposition to put to you.'

# Fifteen

Daniel and Sheila Mason, Alice Mason's grieving parents, lived in the Morriston area of Swansea, in a quiet cul-de-sac of typical Fifties-built suburban houses. The Masons' house was detached, with mock Tudor beams and leaded windows. A short gravel driveway led up to a solid oak front door, and a bright yellow Fiat was parked in front of an adjoining garage.

Lambert parked in the road and he and DC Jones, aware of the sensitivity and tact needed to conduct the interview, approached the house with a feeling of dread. As Jones rang the doorbell, her eyes contacted Lambert's, and he felt himself melting in the warmth of her compassion. It was an inappropriate moment to have lewd images flitting through his head, but her sympathy aroused in him feelings of both lust and deep affection. As if she could read his mind, she broke eye contact and fumbled in her coat for her warrant card.

The door was opened by a man whose face had the ghastly pallor of someone who suffered nightly torments and looked as if his once plump physique was imploding. He had a long face, a dominant hooked nose, and eyes that were sunken and despairing. Despite his ravaged appearance, his dark hair, with grey flecks, was neatly brushed and side-parted, suggesting a need for a certain amount of routine and appearance in spite of the recent tragedy.

He wore navy-blue corduroy trousers, a check shirt and a grey woollen cardigan. Although he couldn't have been much more than sixty-years-old, Lambert got the impression that he was terribly old-fashioned.

'Mr Mason?' Jones enquired, holding out her warrant card.

He nodded, his eyes brimming with sorrow and confusion. *What else is there to say or do? Nothing can bring her back to life.*

'I'm Constable Jones and this is Inspector Lambert. We'd like to have a few words with your wife if it's convenient.'

'I don't know what else...' he began but was unable to complete the sentence.

'We're deeply sorry to hear about your tragic loss,' Jones said. 'But we really do need to speak with Mrs Mason.'

'What about? It's not going to make any difference now, is it?'

Lambert remained calm and kept any trace of impatience out of his voice. 'We'd like to speak to your wife about her brother, Steven Hickson. We appreciate how hard it is at this time, and we'll try not to keep you both for very long, but if we could come in and have a brief word about your brother-in-law, we'd be grateful.'

Mason blinked several times as he digested this information. After a moment, he stood aside and said, 'You'd better come in.'

He led them through to the living room and gestured vaguely to easy chairs and a sofa.

'Make yourselves comfortable. I'll go and find Sheila, my wife. I think she's pottering in the greenhouse. Gardening keeps her from cracking up.'

While he went off to fetch his wife, they both sank into the settee in the chintzy surroundings, a room with a stockbroker feel about it, but from another era, as though the room had been created from a description in a Betjeman poem. There was even a Russell Flint picture hanging on one of the walls. On the mantelpiece above an open fireplace, and on top of a mahogany cabinet, were silver-framed family photographs, and one which caught the detectives' eye was of Alice Mason, smiling and posing with a young man they guessed could have been her older brother, both with their heads tilted cutely and closely together.

'You think that's her brother or boyfriend?' Jones whispered.

'There's a distinct family resemblance there. But we'll soon find out, won't we?'

When Mason returned with his wife, they expected to meet a woman who suited the air of cosy and cloistered gentility epitomized by their living room. Instead, they discovered his wife was much younger than him – probably no more than early-fifties – and wore beige cargo pants and a denim shirt. Her dark, red-tinted hair was swept back tightly into a bun, adding to the strain and severity of a face that in other circumstances might be described as soft and attractive. A small silver cross dangled from a discreet necklace around her neck, which she nervously fingered as she stared at the two detectives.

'You must excuse me,' she said, her voice husky with suppressed emotion. 'I've been gardening, and we weren't expecting you.'

'We're sorry to trouble you at this time,' Jones said.

Sheila Mason sank into one of the armchairs, and Jones noticed how heavy her body seemed, wearied by distress.

'Daniel tells me you'd like to talk to me about my brother. I don't understand what this has to do with Alice and that drunken pig.'

She mentioned her daughter's killer unemotionally, the monotone of her voice revealing how dazed she still was.

'Mrs Mason,' Lambert began uneasily, 'how close was your brother to his niece?'

She took her time considering the question, and fidgeted with the cross, as if this talisman could protect her from further harm. After a long silence, she said, 'Well, he got on well with Alice, and she liked him. Although…' She broke off, frowning deeply.

'Although what, Mrs Mason?' Jones prompted gently.

'I don't know. I suppose he and I were never really close as siblings. But when Mark was born – that's my son – Steven made more of an effort to involve himself in family events. And I suppose the same thing happened when Alice was born. And, when Steven became a father himself, it was as if family became hugely important to him. And I have to hand it to Steven, he made more of an effort than I did. I don't know why. Now that Alice has gone, I feel so guilty. I realize now that Steven wanted to get to know his niece and nephew, but I always made excuses, excluded him from the family.'

Her voice quivered as she fought back tears. Daniel Mason shuffled over to her, placed a hand on her shoulder and squeezed gently.

'Was there a reason for you to exclude him from the family?' Lambert asked.

Silence. Sheila Mason's knuckles were white as she gripped the cross tighter, and she looked down at the floor. Her husband came to the rescue.

'I think what my wife means is, her brother had a bit of a reputation.'

Lambert raised an enquiring eyebrow. 'Oh? What sort of reputation?'

'Well, Sheila has two other brothers, and I suppose Steven was considered the black sheep.'

'In what way?'

'I think he was what you might call a Jack the Lad. Bit of a ducker and diver. Always had some dodgy scheme going. You know: bit of a rough diamond.'

Although Lambert knew the answer he would get from his next question, he asked it anyway.

'Was he ever in trouble with the police?'

'Not as far as we know. So perhaps I'm doing him a disservice. I think he changed for the better once he got the pub and started his own family. That's when he made an effort to get close to ours.'

Sheila Mason raised her head and made eye contact with Lambert. 'I don't understand. Why are you asking all these questions about Steven? What has this got to do with that Alice and that drunk driver?'

It was the question Lambert had been dreading, and he hoped his lie would sound convincing. 'We need as much information as possible for the Crown Prosecution Service. We build up a complete picture for them, show how many victims there are, family members et cetera, in order to get the heaviest possible sentence.'

Her face was expressionless, but he could see her mind working as she assimilated the information. Lambert became aware of the mechanical hum of a refrigerator coming from the kitchen, underscoring the strained silence.

'In that case,' Sheila Mason said, finally letting go of the silver cross, 'you'll want details of my other brothers. Jeremy's the eldest, and he lives in Australia. Sadly, he couldn't make it for the funeral as he's been very ill. Gordon lives in Edinburgh, and he managed to attend. I was the second child and Steven, who'll be forty-four next month, is the youngest.'

Lambert inclined his head towards one of the photographs. 'That photo of your daughter: is that your son Mark with her?'

'Yes, that was taken only last year at his engagement do. His fiancée's dad's a professional wedding photographer.'

'I expect,' Jones said, steering the conversation to a more comfortable topic, 'that'll be useful for when they get married. He'll be able to take the wedding photos. When are they planning on marrying?'

'It was going to be April, but they've postponed it until later in the year. Mark felt it was too soon after Alice's... after the tragic accident.'

'And have they fixed another date yet?'

Sheila Mason shook her head. 'Unfortunately...' She stopped and clutched her cross again. 'I expect they'll sort something out soon. Poor Mark was very close to his sister. He's taken it very badly.'

'As we all have,' her husband added. 'You see these terrible events on the news or read about them in the papers, but you never expect it to happen to you. I still can't believe it's happened, and I can't get to grips with the fact that I'll never see her again.'

Sheila Mason stared at her husband for a moment before she spoke, and then seemed to gather strength as she stressed, 'I know we'll never get over it, but we've still got Mark and his future to consider. And I just hope that he and Julia will start a family. And then perhaps our role as grandparents might go some way to ease the loss.'

'I can see why you'd like your son to set a wedding date,' Jones said. 'Were they originally planning a big wedding?'

'Well, big-ish. It was going to be a church service at St Paul's, the Anglican church just round the corner. They both wanted to get married round here, because it's the church we've attended all our lives. And Mark sang in the choir there. But perhaps that will change now.'

'Any reason for the change of venue?' Lambert said.

'Oh, I don't know. It's just that after the terrible event of that awful day, Mark seemed unable to cope. We sent him to see Reverend Eastman – Tom's a good man – and we thought he might be able to help. After all, the immediate family... we've always been churchgoers. Well, I know Mark had a long chat with Tom, but it seemed to make matters worse. Mark seemed angrier than before he'd been to see him, and I could tell he was bottling it up. I've since had a word with Tom, but he seemed reluctant to speak about it. Only to say that Mark may eventually come around to a more forgiving frame of mind.'

'And where is your son now?'

'After the funeral, he went back to work. He lives and works in Bristol, which is where he met Julia.'

'What does he do for a living?'

'He works for Verve Initiatives. He's a management consultant.'

Lambert paused, realizing the next question was going to be difficult. 'Between the accident and the funeral, did your son go back to work?'

There was a brief pause while she wondered about the relevance of the question. Debbie Jones, out of the corner of her eye, spotted Daniel Mason drop his head, avoiding any contact with anyone in the room. It was as if, she thought, he had suddenly built a protective shell around himself.

'I expect it was only a matter of a week after the accident,' Lambert added, pressing Sheila Mason for an answer.

Struggling as she recalled the worst week of her life, she eventually said, 'Mark didn't go back to work. He stayed here until the funeral.'

'What did he do during that time?'

'At first, he helped us to organize things, and get in touch with friends and relatives. Although most of them knew. They'd seen it on the news when that terrible man came out of court and was laughing and joking on his mobile phone. I find it so hard to forgive. But deep down I know I must. He shouldn't have been drunk, and I can't defend his behaviour. But he didn't deliberately set out to kill anyone that day.'

'You say your son helped you organize things, *at first*,' Lambert emphasized. 'You've already mentioned how upset he was. How did he spend most of the week?'

'He spent a lot of the time with my brother. Steven became very close to us after the tragedy. He became a very supportive, caring uncle to Mark, and spent time with him, trying to help him to come to terms with the shock.'

'So I suppose he was out of the house quite a lot.'

'Yes, I don't know where they went to. I was too upset to ask. All I know is, Steven seemed to help Mark to come to terms with it. There was a time during the week when I thought Mark was going to crack up. But Steven brought him out of it, thank God! So that, a few days after the funeral, Mark returned to work.'

Lambert began to rise slowly. 'Thank you, Mrs Mason, for your help, and we'll do our best with the prosecution of this man.'

'I can't believe these questions you've asked will matter when he goes to court.'

'We hope this man's sentence will serve as a deterrent.'

'Well, as long as some good comes out of it, then Alice won't have...' Unable to continue, Sheila Mason fumbled in her trousers pocket for a handkerchief as tears blurred her sight.

'We're so sorry,' DC Jones said, rising awkwardly from the sofa. 'If you don't mind my mentioning this,' she nodded towards one of the photo frames, 'youngsters these days use social networking sites like Facebook. Do you think it might be a good idea if—'

'I think Mark's already sorted that out. Left a message about Alice, which I think he intends deleting eventually. Oh, dear God!' She dabbed at tears blurring her vision and wiped her nose. 'I'll be alright. I'll get back to my gardening. I just have to keep myself occupied.'

Jones gave Mr Mason a sympathetic look. 'And what about you, sir? Do you have anything to keep you occupied?'

'Daniel has his work,' Mrs Mason answered. 'He's semi-retired and goes to the office two days a week.'

'And what is it you do, sir?' Lambert asked.

'I'm a financial advisor for M and M Financial Services. It's a partnership, and my business partner still works full time. I'm due in tomorrow. I suppose it keeps me going, although I feel numb most of the time.'

'I suppose financial advice is the business to be in when you have a family to bring up. I expect your son appreciates your financial knowledge as he's about to embark on one of the most expensive events of his life, especially in these hard times.'

Lambert remembered his own struggle with finances when he married Helen, and the lack of any financial support from his own family. But he had only been making polite conversation to get himself across the living room to the door to make a clean exit and hadn't expected the strange reaction his words provoked in Daniel Mason.

'I don 't know what's going on,' he shouted. 'I really don't.'

'Darling, what do you mean?' his wife asked. 'What's happened?'

'Nothing's happened. It doesn't matter.' Mason looked at the detectives, his eyes glistening with tears. 'If you will excuse me, I can't take any more of these questions.'

He barged past them and exited.

'I'm sorry,' his wife said, frowning and tugging at the edges of her handkerchief. 'Daniel's taking it very hard. He bottles it up, and then…'

'We quite understand,' Jones interrupted. 'And again, sorry for the intrusion.'

She led them to the front door. Lambert thanked her for giving them her time, but she merely nodded and didn't say another word. Her eyes were distant and they could tell she was now concerned about her husband and wanted to go to him. She closed the front door so softly, it seemed to signify a return to a reverent state of mourning.

As Lambert opened the car door, he called over to Jones on the passenger side, 'When you asked about the social networking site, was that genuine concern or was there an ulterior motive?'

'Bit of both. I knew if they're on Facebook, it would make life easier to get their photos. And I know we're going to need the son's.'

Lambert flashed her a smile. 'Good one, Debbie.' Inside the car, he said, 'So the wicked uncle takes the nephew under his wing.'

Jones nodded. 'Think it's time to bring him in on suspicion of conspiring to murder?'

Lambert looked at his watch. 'It's not yet four-thirty. Before we bring in Hickson, we need to find out if Tony and Kevin have tracked down Harlan. And we need to regroup and get an update back at Cockett.'

'Just to make sure we're all singing from the same hymn sheet.'

Lambert laughed. 'Doing impressions of a superior officer, it'll be a desk job in traffic before you know it.'

Jones widened her eyes with mock innocence. 'I don't know who you mean, sir.'

Lambert suddenly became serious. 'Yeah, and what's the betting the chief super will want me to drive over to HQ later this evening. Just as things are starting to boil.'

'You think we might have this case wrapped up in the next twenty-four hours?'

'I know, Debbie, you're thinking what I'm thinking about this case. Hickson takes the law into his own hands, as we found out about the pub burglary and the knifing of this Virgil. And it's starting to look like he's tried to take revenge on this Harlan bloke but used his mate from prison to do it.'

'And it went horribly wrong,' Jones added.

'That's what it looks like, Debbie. But first, before we head back to the incident room, we need to meet with a clerk of the holy orders.'

Jones gave her boss a questioning look which he answered it with a teasing smile.

# Sixteen

Despite there not being much trade on weekday afternoons, The Earl of Richmond remained stubbornly open all day. Phil, the part-time barman, continued working throughout the afternoon, allowing Pat some time to herself after the lunchtime session, and later she would fetch Kelly from school. Phil would leave at five when Pat took over for the start of the evening session, bringing Kelly into the bar with her. The little girl was always on her best behaviour, knowing it was a privilege to join the customers on that side of the bar, and sit at one of the tables doing her drawing and colouring.

Two men, both regular customers, in their early seventies, always arrived, give or take a few minutes, at 5.15. Pat served them, engaged in the usual small-talk, followed by a serious chat about the Japanese tsunami tragedy, before they settled at their usual corner table to discuss local and world events. Pat was relieved when a new customer walked through the door and perched on a stool at the bar. Pat always went out of her way to nurture new customers, chat to them in a very homely manner, and this act of inclusivity occasionally paid off, and she sometimes managed to create new regulars. She was also an inquisitive person and liked nothing better than to hear all the gossip and, because of her outgoing personality, she was an asset to the business. Which was more than could be said for Steve, some of the customers opined, who had a rather 'sarky' way about him.

Pat served the new customer a pint of lager and, as he raised the glass to his lips, she noticed a small tattoo on the base of his thumb. She tried not to stare, but she couldn't quite make out whether it was a butterfly or a spider in a web.

He downed half the pint in one go and sighed with satisfaction. 'Ah! I needed that.'

'Been working?' she said, hoping to discover a customer with a remarkably different occupation. He wore a navy cotton bomber jacket and denims, so

69

it was difficult to guess his trade. But he clearly had no intention of revealing his business because his eyes darted away from hers towards the television set.

'Nice to go in a pub and see a blank screen for a change. Some pubs you go in it's on all the time.'

She couldn't help but notice how quickly he changed the subject when she asked him about work. Nothing unusual in that, though. Not these days, when there was so much unemployment.

'Well,' she said, with an apologetic shrug, 'if you're still here at six o'clock, the TV goes on for the news.'

He nodded approvingly. 'That's OK. We need to know what's going on in the world.'

'I switch the TV off after the local news, and then, unless there's something special on, like football or rugby, it stays off.'

'There might be an extended version of the news tonight. They sometimes do that with incidents like this Japanese earthquake, especially now it's affecting the nuclear power stations. I mean, it was bad enough all that flooding and destruction, but now... who knows what might happen.'

Pat shivered as she thought about it. 'It's a terrible tragedy. Terrible.'

'We're all at the mercy of the sea. One minute it's all calm and gentle, and then the next it's...' He opened and then closed his hand into a tight ball as if crushing an insect. 'I know, because I've got a small boat, so I've been there.'

Pat's eyes brightened, glad he'd given her an opening to get off the subject of the tragic tsunami. 'You've got a boat?'

'Yeah, small launch moored at Swansea marina. I'm looking for a new mooring, slightly less expensive.'

'My husband's got a boat. And you boat people—' She laughed. 'You're like golfers. It's an obsession.'

'You never said a truer word. So, is your husband's boat moored at the marina?'

'Not in Swansea. He's moored at Burry Port.'

'I don't know it that well. I've heard of it.'

'Just the other side of Llanelli. It's quite famous, that woman pilot, Amelia someone – I can't remember her name now – the first woman to fly across the Atlantic, went from Newfoundland and landed at Burry Port.'

Exaggerating incredulity, he let his jaw drop. 'No! Bloody hell!'

Pat laughed. 'I'm Pat, by the way.'

'And I'm Dave. I must talk to your husband about boats, sometime.'

Pat pulled a face. 'Oh, I can't wait.'

'Doesn't he help you out in the pub?'

'Yes, he usually takes over at eight, while I get Kelly ready for bed. It wouldn't surprise me if he's on the *Esmeralda* as we speak.'

'That's his boat, yes?'

'His pride and joy. I sometimes think he loves *Esmeralda* more than he loves me.'

Flirtatiously, Dave grinned and said, 'Now I'm sure that's not true. If I were your hubby I'd consider myself a lucky man.'

Pat was about to respond to the flattery when he looked at his watch, downed the remains of his beer, and became sharp and businesslike. He gave her a wink as he climbed off his stool.

'Well, time I was away. Nice talking to you. Catch you again soon.'

Before she had time to thank him for his custom, he had slipped out of the door. She frowned, deep in thought. There had been something slick about his departure, something unnerving that she didn't like. And normally, she was the one who managed to get customers to spill their most intimate secrets. This time she had failed abysmally and had found out nothing about him, other than he went by the common name of Dave. Dave who loved boats. It hadn't been much of a disclosure. No gossip there. And, she realized, he had found out much more about her and Steve than she had about him.

She was losing her touch.

# Seventeen

As soon as DS Ellis approached James Harlan's narrow, end-of-terrace house, he suspected there was no one at home. The house had a dark neglected look about it, sombre and cold. The front door, despite being white and synthetic, with a small square of mock stained glass, merely added blandness to the illusion of elegance, and the downstairs PVC double-glazed window had a venetian blind closed tight, blocking any view of the front-room.

Ellis pressed the doorbell, and heard it ringing sharp and clear, followed by a silence that seemed sinister as his imagination ran amok. He could clearly picture the thuggish Harlan from his fifteen minutes of infamy, his bloated bullet-head gabbing on his mobile, oblivious to the Masons' anguish for the life he had so carelessly obliterated.

Ellis put his ear to the cold plastic of the door and listened intently. He thought he could hear noises from deep inside the house, but he knew they were the vacuous sounds a building makes when left to its own devices. Of course, Harlan could have seen him parking the car and was lying low, silently waiting for him to go away. But somehow Ellis doubted that was the case. And, monster though he might seem from his image in the media, Ellis was aware that even monsters have the same human needs as everyone else and needed to pop out to get the groceries. There was something about the house that was slightly unnerving. Or maybe it was his imagination playing tricks. But he couldn't help it. There was something – what was it about the house? – it was only a vague impression, but the house felt not only empty but abandoned.

Ellis glanced at his watch. It was just after five-thirty, so hopefully there might be someone at home next door, the front door of which he reached in only three short steps. He knocked loudly and waited. After a moment, he heard a door opening, followed by a slow, shuffling sound, and he pictured an ancient man in carpet slippers, who probably couldn't remember his own family's name, let alone details about his neighbour. But the man who opened the door was no more than thirty or forty – it was hard to tell. He was enormous, at least twenty-five stone or more. He wore old-fashioned, brown check carpet slippers, ragged at the end of elephantine legs, grey flannel trousers held up by red braces and a prayer, and a collarless granddad shirt. His face perspired gently under a ghastly comb-over of less than a dozen strands of greasy hair.

'Good evening, sir,' Ellis said brightly, holding out his ID. 'I'm sorry to disturb you, but I wonder if you might be able to help us with our enquiries.'

The man tilted his enormous head in the direction of Harlan's house. 'This about the prick next door?'

Ellis nodded and half-smiled. 'I gather you don't like him.'

'Bloody great understatement, that is.'

'What can you tell me about him?'

'Bastard should get life for killing that girl. Course, they won't give him anything like that. Bastard'll probably get five or six years and be out in three-and-a-half. Where's the justice in that?'

'What can you tell me about what he was like prior to, as well as after, that incident? What sort of visitors he had. That sort of thing.'

The man leaned against the door jamb for support, his chest wheezing noisily. 'Look, I don't wanna be rude, but I'm an asthma sufferer. D'you mind if we go and sit down and talk. In the back room?'

'Sure. Please lead the way, Mr…?'

'Johnson. But please call me Dan.'

Ellis shut the front door and followed Dan Johnson slowly along the hall, intrigued by his extreme starboard to port and port to starboard waddle.

\*\*\*

The church was unlocked and Lambert and Jones walked into its cool interior, walking slowly along the nave, their footsteps echoing on the flagstones. Lambert coughed loudly hoping to attract someone's attention, thinking there must surely be a presence, because these days no one would risk leaving even a church unlocked or unattended.

As they reached the pulpit, they were both startled by a door slamming nearby, and a tall, reed-thin man, wearing a tweed sports jacket with a thin strip of white showing underneath the collar of an ordinary shirt, came bounding forward, smiling a well-practised greeting.

'Hello. Can I help you?'

'We're looking for Reverend Tom Eastman.'

'You've found him. How can I help?'

'We're police officers and we wanted a to have a word with you about Mark Mason.'

As Lambert showed his warrant card, the vicar's smile faded and the ingenuous expression disappeared. 'Why are you asking about Mark? I thought the man had been charged for his sister's death, and the trial is soon, I believe.'

Lambert told him the same thing he had told Sheila Mason, that they were obtaining evidence for the CPS.

'I see,' he said, staring at Lambert through narrowed eyes. 'And do you mind me asking why a detective inspector is sent to gather evidence for the CPS when a trial is imminent?'

'It's a new initiative,' Lambert said hurriedly. 'I believe Mark Mason was very close to his sister. After her death, he came to see you, I believe.'

'Yes, he did. But it was with reluctance; I think he did it to satisfy his parents.'

'What did he talk to you about?'

'Not much. I did most of the talking. I tried to get him to come to terms with the fact that even though the man was irresponsibly drunk, he still hadn't intended to kill Alice. But I'm afraid my words fell on stony ground. I could see Mark was simmering with anger and refused to discuss his feelings with me. Other than to say he'd like to see Alice's killer dead. It was about the only thing he said throughout our talk. How he'd like to murder the man. I've never seen a man so possessed by vengeance before.' Shaking his head, the clergyman added with a note of apology in his voice, 'But thankfully that hasn't happened and Mark has left the law to deal with the charge of manslaughter.'

Lambert exchanged a brief look with Jones. Reverend Eastman noticed it and added quickly, 'Yes, I think Mark eventually overcame his thirst for revenge, so perhaps our talk hadn't been a complete waste of time.'

'What gave you that impression, sir?' Jones asked, her voice echoing in the hallowed space of the church.

The vicar frowned and stared at the cross on the altar, seeking guidance Lambert supposed. He guessed the clergyman was searching his conscience for an answer and deliberating on how to answer Jones's question.

'There must have been some indication that Mark Mason had come to terms with it by the end of your talk,' Lambert said, not bothering to hide the impatience in his tone. 'What did he do or say that left you with that impression?'

The clergyman stared at him for a moment before answering. 'He suddenly became calm, as if he had eventually accepted it. And he asked me to pray for him. At first I thought he was considering self harm and it worried me. I implored him to consider his parents and how devastated they would be if they lost two children. But he assured me that he had no intention of taking his own life and just repeated his request for me to pray for him. And that was it. He turned and left, almost as if he had resolved something inside himself.'

Lambert cast his eyes along the nave, searching into the gloomy corners, beyond the pillars and across the rows of pews, as his thoughts began to take shape.

'Mark's a good man,' the clergyman added, sensing the drift of Lambert's thoughts. 'He has attended St Paul's since he was a lad. He wouldn't do anything foolish. I guarantee it.'

'I'm sure you're right, sir. Thank you for your time.'

But Lambert felt far from convinced by the clergyman's assertion of Mark Mason's innocence and intended interrogating the young man as soon as possible.

***

Wallace had his warrant card ready as soon as Mitchell opened the front door. He was momentarily taken aback by the man's moustache and, without thinking, began smoothing and tugging his own. He thought Mitchell's looked ridiculous, and for a moment he considered shaving his.

'Mr Mitchell?' he said. 'You on your own, sir?'

Mitchell nodded and glanced over his shoulder, as if to make sure.

'Yes, my son and daughter's at school. Well, they'll be on their way home by now. They usually dawdle with their friends. Who knows what they get up to.' He jerked a thumb towards the row of semi-detached houses to his left. 'My wife's two doors away, if you need her.'

'I don't think that'll be necessary, sir. You recently sold your old Rover to someone...'

'Yes,' Mitchell leapt in before Wallace could finish. 'I saw it on the BBC earlier on. Imagine seeing your old car on the news like that. Body in the boot, the papers said. I've kept a few copies as a memento.'

Despite the seriousness of his quest, Wallace couldn't keep the smile from his face.

'I expect you also saw the CCTV pictures of the man we think parked the car.'

'Yes, and we saw your detective inspector chap appealing for people who might have seen him.'

'Which is why I called,' Wallace said, showing Mitchell the photograph. 'Was this the man who bought your car?'

'That's not him. That looks like the man who parked the car. The same as the one on the TV.'

'And you're absolutely certain about that?'

Mitchell nodded. 'Of course, I'm sure. Otherwise I'd have come forward after seeing him on TV, wouldn't I? This is not a good photo but I can see it's not the same bloke. For a start, the chap who bought the car didn't have cropped hair. It was more... normal-looking. Like yours and mine. Average length.'

As he suspected, Wallace had felt all along this would be a wasted journey. Still, it had to be done. A process of elimination. Fitting all the pieces together.

Mitchell suddenly burst out laughing, and Wallace waited politely for the morsel of dire wit that would undoubtedly be repeated ad nauseam for the benefit of his family and friends.

'Know what I've been thinking?' Mitchell chortled. 'Why did I have to go to all the trouble of hoovering the boot? If I'd known a body was going to be found in it, I wouldn't have bothered.'

\*\*\*

Mr Johnson's back room had a small kitchen extension built on to it, and a faint smell of fish hung in the air. The room was reasonably clean and tidy, but the Formica table in the centre of the room was strewn with books, fiction and non-fiction on a variety of subjects. Ellis sat at the table opposite Johnson, writing in his notebook and trying to concentrate on what he was saying. A clock ticked loudly above a tiled mantelpiece and every so often Johnson's kitchen chair protested loudly beneath his vast bulk. Although Tony Ellis needed as much information on Harlan as possible, Johnson was like a wound-up toy, spinning out his answers with irrelevant observations. Now he had a captive audience, he would no doubt drone on until doomsday if Ellis let him.

'You say Harlan occasionally parked a lorry in the street,' Ellis said quickly as soon as Johnson paused for breath. 'Presumably, that's what he did for a living.'

Johnson snorted. 'He won't be doing no more driving, that's for sure.'

'So how big was this lorry?'

'Big. Proper long-distance vehicle. He sometimes parked it opposite, until Maria's hubby complained to the council. Yeah, nobody in the street liked Harlan, even before he killed that girl.'

'You don't happen to know who he worked for, do you?'

Johnson's chins wobbled as he shook his head. 'No. But I think he went abroad with his lorry. When he went away, he was usually gone some time. Peaceful it was then. No loud music. Always the boom, boom, boom pounding through the walls. Drove me mad it did. I used to bang on the walls with a hammer.' He stopped speaking to point out the dents in the wall. 'Not that it did the slightest bit of good. Except to make holes in the wall.'

'Getting back to this lorry of his: have you any idea what type of load it may have carried.'

'It was a meat lorry. Refrigerated. I'm trying to remember the name on the side.'

Ellis waited anxiously, pen poised over his notebook. 'Did it mention meat?'

'Of course it did, which is how I knew it was meat and not some other food like ice cream or something. Wait a minute, I should have got it straight off, seeing as how it was good old alliteration, like our own Swansea boy, Dylan Thomas. He was fond of alliteration, you know. Bible black, and all that.'

'And what was the name?' Ellis said with a pained smile.

Johnson had a sudden spasm of wheezing and coughing, and Ellis gripped his pen tighter and tried to keep calm. He tried not to stare at the man's heaving and spluttering mass, was tempted to ask him if he was alright, but changed his mind, in case Johnson went off on another tangent.

Once the cough had subsided, Johnson laughed to cover his embarrassment and made a sweeping banner gesture. 'Prime Pork Pies. That was it. Prime Pork Pies. Should have got that straight away.'

Ellis wrote it down, and then asked, 'Was that it? Just "Prime Pork Pies"? That doesn't sound like the name of the firm.'

'I think there was some smaller writing underneath, listing more of their products. All pork, I think. It was probably pig carcasses he was transporting. To be honest, I can't remember the name of the firm – it was in much smaller lettering. But I don't think there can be many meat processing factories in or around Swansea. You'll soon find their whereabouts. They probably advertise in the Yellow Pages. Christ! All this talk about pork. I could really fancy a bacon butty, I could.'

'Did Harlan have many visitors?'

'If he did, I never saw them. Much. I hardly go in the front room, and even when I do, I'm not one of those net curtain twitchers.'

Ellis found this hard to believe. 'There must have been odd occasions,' he said, 'when you might have seen someone calling.'

'I saw him with a young bird once. Tarty-looking kid. Seemed much too young for him. Can't have been more than seventeen. And some of these young girls, the way they dress... and they wonder why they get attacked. But I'm not one of those blokes who reckons they're asking for it when they wear provocative gear, but if they only stopped to think what the word provocative means, they might think twice...'

'What about men friends?' Ellis interrupted. 'Did he have many male visitors?'

Johnson pursed his lips as he thought about this. 'Yeah, I did see blokes calling now and again. No one I'd be able to describe, though. Bit tricky that. Don't expect me to remember someone I might have glimpsed as I was going out of the house.'

'That's OK, Mr Johnson... Dan... you're doing very well. Have a look at this photo for me. See if you recognize him.'

Ellis took the CCTV photograph from his pocket, unfolded it and pushed it towards Johnson, who stared at it for a long time before speaking.

'What's this got to do with Harlan and killing that girl? This looks like a CCTV photo to do with something that happened in Swansea. And the only thing I can think of that's happened recently is somebody being shot and found in the boot of a car.'

'Did you see this on the news at lunchtime today?'

'No, I usually watch the news at six. It was on yesterday's news. Briefly. It didn't give details, they just said a man had been murdered and they found his body in the boot of a car. Has this murder got something to do with that prick next door?'

'We don't know yet. The two incidents may be unrelated. But we think that's an image of the man who got rid of the car. I'm trying to find out if he knows James Harlan.'

Johnson stared at the photograph again. 'Well, I can't be sure, because this bloke's very like the prick next door. Apart from that, he looks familiar.'

'Take a close look at the tattoo at the base of his thumb. I know it's not clear enough to make out the design, but it's quite an unusual place to have a tattoo.'

Suddenly, Johnson thumped his forehead with the heel of his hand. 'Of course, I remember as I was leaving the house one day – popping out to the off-licence – and this bloke drove up in his car and parked outside Harlan's place. I tried not to stare, because if Harlan caught me looking at him I was afraid he might come over and start something. Especially as he'd heard me thumping on the wall.'

'And you're sure this was the same man?'

'Ninety per cent certain. Out of the corner of my eye I saw the tattoo on his thumb as he was parking the car. There can't be many blokes with a tattoo just there, can there?'

Ellis could tell his witness was looking for a pat on the back, so he smiled and said, 'That's fantastic. A great help, Dan. One last question. Can you remember how long ago this was and what sort of car the man was driving?'

'It was quite some time ago. Maybe last October. And the car was a Volvo.'

'You're sure about that?'

'Course I'm sure. I know a Volvo when I see one. Quite a big one. An estate car. Sort of dirty green colour.'

Ellis closed his notebook, stood up and reached across the table to recover the photograph. 'Thank you, Dan, you've been a great help.'

'So now you've connected the two blokes, does this mean the prick next door might have shot the bloke in the boot?'

'We don't know yet. But thanks to you at least we know they're both involved. Don't get up. I can see myself out.'

Johnson's double chins had sunk on to his chest, and he looked far from happy. Ellis guessed that he probably had few friends and very little opportunity to talk to anyone. He felt sorry for the man. But he had a job to do and was grateful for his witness's information.

He let himself out, and crossed the street, hoping he might find a neighbour who could confirm Johnson's story, just to be on the safe side.

# Eighteen

'And now let's go over to the news where you are,' said the BBC presenter, and the familiar theme tune linked the national news to BBC Wales news.

Pat Hickson, busy serving two male customers, only half-heard the item about the body in the boot, but when the newsreader said the victim had been identified as Robert Sonning, her hand dropped slightly, and a cascade of lager foam filled the pint glass. She turned and stared at the television screen in time to see the prison mugshot of Sonning.

'That's a lively one,' the customer said with a friendly laugh.

But the landlady didn't hear him as the foam surged over the edge of the glass. Her eyes were fixed to the screen as she tried to unscramble her confused thoughts.

Reluctantly averting her eyes from the screen, she tipped most of the foam into the tray beneath the tap, slid the beer spout into the remaining half pint of lager, and poured it carefully. But by now the customer and his friends were also engrossed in the news item, and one of them said jokingly:

'Christ! Swansea's getting like Chicago.'

Pat was handed a twenty pound note by one of the men and, as she walked towards the till, her eyes fixed to the television screen, she stopped and drew breath as she recognized the detective inspector who had visited her on Sunday morning when he was looking for Steve. But when she heard the appeal, the search for the man with the tattoo, which she just about recognized as the customer from less than an hour ago, she froze, her eyes glued to the set.

She knew she ought to ring the police immediately, to let them know she had seen the man, but a siren screamed a warning in her head. Her body suddenly felt unreal, like a blob of helpless jelly. She knew her Steve was implicated in some way. What the hell had he got himself involved in this time? He had always been headstrong, she knew that. Perverse and reckless. Like the time they went on holiday to Normandy, and they'd had a lousy sandwich in a small bar. When Steve complained about it and received a Gallic shrug by way of a reply, he had grabbed the proprietor round the throat and refused to pay the bill.

But this was far more serious. A body in the boot of a car. Shot. Murdered. And a friend of Steve's. And the man who likely had killed him, had visited the bar less than an hour ago. And then another missile exploded in her head as she relived the all too recent encounter with the man. Pretending he was interested in boats, he managed to fool her into giving him details of Steve and his boat.

She opened the till quickly, counted out the change and handed it to the customer. He said something to her, making polite conversation, but she didn't take it in.

'Excuse me,' she said. 'I need to make a phone call.'

She grabbed the wall phone behind the bar and dialled Steve's mobile, waiting for him to answer, her eyes tearful with worry now.

Damn! It was switched to voice mail.

Aware that the customers could hear, she dropped her voice and shielded the mouthpiece with her hand. 'Steve!' she said, her voice tremulous, 'I need you to ring me or come home urgently. I can't tell you how important this is. Ring me now. Pat.'

\*\*\*

Jason sat in his Volvo near the marina, wondering how to proceed in his search for the *Esmeralda*. There were many pontoons and dozens of craft and he didn't know where to begin. The fact that he had the information, the name of the boat, should have been enough for whatever Jimmy had in mind. But when he'd rung his mate to tell him, Jimmy had pleaded with him, said it was important, one last favour, could Jason reconnoitre the marina and let him know the whereabouts of Hickson's boat.

Jason agreed, although he was worried about being seen, especially as he'd heard on the radio that police were looking for a man with a tattoo on the base of his thumb connected with the killing, and Jimmy told him they'd shown the CCTV footage of him on the television news.

What he needed to do was buy himself some driving gloves, and he thought a good idea might be to purchase a pair at a motorway services, which might be reasonably busy during the early evening, and he could have his money ready at the checkout and stick his right hand in his pocket.

He was about to get out of the Volvo to begin his search, when a blue Renault pulled up and parked about fifty yards in front of him. He watched as the man got out, carrying a Sainsbury's shopping bag. Jason, never having seen Steve Hickson – and he didn't think Jimmy had either – had no reason to suppose it was him. But it was a gloomy evening, cold and drizzling slightly, and there was hardly a soul about, with no sign of anyone on any of the yachts or boats, so Jason wondered if the man in the Renault was Hickson.

He watched as the man walked along one of the pontoons. There was something determined about his walk. He looked like a man with a definite purpose, which Jason thought was unusual. He knew boat people were a breed apart, geek-like in their enthusiasm for sailing. And the man he was watching was in a hurry, as if he was carrying out an important errand of some sort.

Jason waited for him to reach almost the end of one of the pontoons, and then he saw him climb aboard the last boat in the mooring and disappear into the cabin below. Jason gave it a few minutes before getting out of the Volvo. As he neared the locked gate leading to the walkway, he wondered how he could get access to the marina. He waited, lit a cigarette and inhaled deeply.

He stared over towards the sandy beach beyond the harbour and saw a fine spray of light sand blowing along the shore like an undulating net curtain. And then his attention was diverted to the marina, where he saw a man climbing off his boat and heading towards the walkway. Jason hurried over and reached the entrance just as the man opened the gate.

He smiled at the man and said, 'That was good timing.'

Not thinking anything of it, the man held the gate open for him. As Jason thanked him, he imagined a raised fist in his head. He had scored. Luck was going his way. He walked stealthily along the pontoon where he had seen the man he thought might be Steve heading, straining his eyes for the name of the craft as the planks creaked beneath him. He reached the halfway mark and the name became clear. The *Esmeralda*. He made a mental note of the name of the boat next in line to it, then turned quickly and headed back to the car.

Now all he needed to do was get the hell out of Burry Port, pull over somewhere quiet, ring Jimmy on his mobile and give him the information. Job done. And perhaps, by this time next week, after Jimmy's trial for drink-driving and manslaughter, he could relax, knowing his mate was off the scene for a few years, and unable to put pressure on him by demanding risky favours.

# Nineteen

Keyed up and speaking breathlessly, almost as if he'd been running, Lambert stood by the white board and addressed his team in the incident room. They all knew it was decision time, and their boss was ready for action. There were also six uniformed constables present, four males and two females, awaiting orders. The two women were the only ones taking notes.

'It shouldn't be too difficult to find the man with the tattoo on his thumb,' Lambert said, his eyes sweeping the room. 'OK, the only response we've had from the public so far is several phone calls telling us they saw the man on Thursday evening in the centre of Swansea. We already know this from the CCTV. It's important that we apprehend this man. Bring him in and we'll get somewhere with this case. What I'd like you six to do is...' He stared at the uniformed constables. 'Two of you start at the pub where James Harlan was drinking on the afternoon he ran over Alice Mason. We think he might have been a friend of this man, although we have no concrete evidence yet. The pub's called the Punch and Judy. Anyone know it?'

One of the uniforms half-raised his hand. 'I've been in there twice when I was off duty. It's a shit-hole.'

'OK, Colin, you and Jane make a start at the pub. You wouldn't happen to remember anyone from there who might have looked like our man?'

The young constable, his chin scarred from teenage acne, shook his head, and looked about him nervously, like a bird watching for predators. 'No. But at the time I wasn't looking for anyone.'

Lambert held up his thumb and pointed at it. 'And you don't ever recall seeing anyone with a tattoo here?'

'No, but then...' The constable shrugged. 'I guess nearly everyone who drinks in the Punch and Judy has a tattoo of some sort.'

'Well, if this man ever used the pub, the landlord might remember the

83

thumb tattoo, or one of the bar staff or some customers might. He could live close to the pub. And it's not a vast distance from James Harlan's home either – about a twenty-minute walk – although it's doubtful these guys would walk anywhere, as that poor family know to their cost. And the rest of you check out the district, see how much of it you can cover – corner shops, takeaways, any other pubs. And find out when you go in a pub who the local postmen are. They might deliver to these two men, and, you never know, one of them might remember delivering to the bloke with the tattoo. You've all got your photograph of him, so off you go and good luck.'

While the uniformed constables muttered their goodbyes and shuffled out, Lambert turned to the white board and pointed at Sonning's mugshot. 'This is my hypothesis, for what it's worth. You can contradict me later, if you like. Our man here is picked up at Cardiff prison by his old friend Steven Hickson and is later found dead. Hickson turns out to be the uncle of the girl who was killed by James Harlan, and it appears that this Hickson takes the law into his own hands, as we think he may have taken his revenge on this Virgil man who burgled his home above the pub. So, it begins to look as if Hickson somehow persuaded Sonning to attempt the murder of Harlan, and it went horribly wrong resulting in Harlan killing Sonning.'

'In self-defence,' DS Beech said.

'As you keep reminding us, Mick,' Lambert said testily.

Ellis, who had been listening, but also making a Google search on his computer, slapped a hand on to the desk, claiming everyone's attention. 'I told you that Harlan, until his drink-driving charge, worked as a long-distance lorry driver, specifically for a firm importing meat for pies and other meat products. Well, the owner happens to be an entrepreneur called Frank Masina.'

'Who has a lot of fingers in a lot of pies,' Wallace joked, but nobody laughed.

Ellis stared closely at Lambert, who was frowning and staring into the distance.

'You think we ought to question this Masina, Harry?'

'What?'

'Masina. Think we ought to go and talk to him?'

Lambert snapped out of his troubled thoughts and said, 'No. We'll leave Masina for the time being, until I've had a word with the DCS.'

'I don't understand…' Ellis began, but Lambert interrupted.

'First of all, we'll bring Hickson in on suspicion of conspiring to murder James Harlan.' Lambert glanced at the clock. 'It's into the evening session at his pub, so he should be there. Kevin, I'd like you to go back once more to Mitchell's place in Port Talbot with a photograph of Mark Mason. Debbie'll run you one off from his Facebook portrait. His wicked uncle took him under his wing after his sister was killed and seemed to be influencing him. And the Mitchells said it was a young bloke who turned up and purchased the car.'

'And, according to Mitchell, it sounded like a different person who phoned up about it,' Jones said. 'Maybe that was Sonning or Hickson.'

'But if this was a hit by the ex-con,' Wallace said, 'wouldn't he have wanted paying to do the job? You don't do someone else's revenge for nothing, do you?'

Lambert clicked his fingers. 'Of course. Mark Mason's a management consultant, probably on a reasonable wage with some savings put by. He's someone else we need to bring in. Debbie, get the number of his Bristol flat, or his mobile number and see if you can track him down. I'll take Tony and we'll bring Hickson in for a thorough interrogation. We'll meet at Swansea Central where we're taking him.'

As Lambert and Ellis were half out of the door, Lambert turned back and said to DC Jones, 'And you might like to check with E Division to see if they're making any progress with this Virgil bloke. Apart from the burglary, we still don't know how involved he is in all this.'

***

Although it was Monday evening and quiet in the Earl of Richmond, Pat Hickson still found it difficult to speak to her husband. Every time she started to talk to him about Sonning and the man with the tattooed thumb, someone needed serving. Eventually, there was a slight lull and she took him to a far corner of the bar.

'Steve,' she hissed. 'Will you tell me what the fuck is going on?'

Hickson glanced round the bar to see if anyone was watching, but no one was paying them any attention.

'What are you on about?'

'You know bloody well what I'm on about? Your so-called friend Robbie Sonning was found murdered, and the man who may have killed him was here less than two hours ago.'

Hickson's eyes grew wide with worry. 'What? Here? Are you sure?'

'Yes, and he was asking after you. Are you going to tell me what's going on or not?'

'Nothing's going on, Pat, I swear.'

She stared into his eyes, which seemed to have sunk into his head. 'Don't give me that bullshit, Steve. I want to know what's going on. This affects Kelly and me. So you'd better tell me.'

'Later, sweetheart. It's too complicated to talk right now.'

His wife's voice began to rise. 'I don't care how fucking complicated it is, Steve. I want answers. Now!'

He glanced quickly round the bar. Customers were staring at them, and when he caught their eye, they looked away with embarrassment, presuming it was the start of a domestic row.

He looked back at his wife and began opening his mouth to speak when DI Lambert and DS Ellis entered, already displaying their warrant cards.

Pat Hickson felt herself crumbling, her world collapsing like towers going down. She knew it was bad news, but how bad she had yet to find out.

'Steven Hickson?' Lambert said. 'We'd like you to accompany us to Central Police Station for questioning in connection with the murder of Robert Sonning.'

The bar was deathly still as the customers watched the disturbance with a mixture of enjoyment and curiosity, like the scene from a drama, waiting for the next occurrence. This was provided by Hickson recovering quickly, taking charge of the situation as if this happened to him regularly, behaving like a captured military officer giving instructions to his men.

'Phone Joe Blanche,' he instructed his wife, and then explained to Lambert, 'He's my solicitor. I presume I'll need one.'

'That's advisable, Mr Hickson.'

'Can't this wait until tomorrow?' Pat Hickson said, her voice hoarse with anxiety. 'Steve runs the bar when I put Kelly to bed.'

'I'm sorry, Mrs Hickson. This can't wait. Your husband needs to accompany us right away.'

Her voice rose to a strangled screech. 'What the fuck am I going to do then?'

Embarrassed by his wife's outburst, Steve Hickson deliberately softened his voice. 'Phone Phil, he might help out in the circumstances.'

Pat Hickson stared at Lambert, her eyes glassy. 'How long are you keeping him for?'

'It depends on how your husband cooperates, Mrs Hickson.'

'That's not what I asked you.'

'The sooner we go, the sooner we can resolve the situation. Shall we go, sir?'

Lambert gently held Steve Hickson's arm, guiding him towards the door, held open by DC Jones. Hickson called back over his shoulder:

'Remember to call Joe Blanche.'

Dazed, Pat Hickson stared at the door as it closed behind them. Then, aware of the silence and of being the pub's focus, she rounded on the customers.

'The show's over, folks.'

# Twenty

Joe Blanche, around fifty-something, with wavy white hair spilling over the collar of his hound's-tooth suit, looked more like a bard than a solicitor. He sat next to his client, and had so far interrupted only once, when Lambert made an observation instead of asking a question. But now, fifteen minutes into the interrogation, Lambert decided it was time to stop prowling around and go in for the kill.

'Where were you this afternoon?'

Hickson's mouth opened in surprise. 'This afternoon? I don't see what that's got to do with anything.'

'Don't you? Well, why not let me decide what is and isn't relevant in this investigation. I repeat: where were you this afternoon, between, say, two and six?'

'I was just pottering around.'

Ellis, sitting next to Lambert, simulated incredulity. 'Pottering around?'

'No law against it, is there?'

Blanche decided it was time to intervene, brushing a hand through his wavy hair. 'Inspector, has a crime been committed this afternoon? If my client is not under suspicion for any misdemeanours that took place in Swansea today, why would you feel it necessary for him to answer your question?'

Lambert glared at the solicitor. 'Because, Mr Blanche, your client is involved with a criminal who was recently released from prison, whose body was found in a car boot on Saturday, and today is only Monday. I would have thought some indication of his movements since then will help establish his innocence.'

The solicitor bit his lip as he considered this, then turned to Hickson. 'If you could be specific, Steve, it might help.'

Hickson tilted his head up, trying to remember, but Lambert could see it was part of an act. So far, Hickson gave the impression he was unconcerned, almost as if he was playing a game with them. One he thought he could win.

'Let's see now. When I say I was pottering about, I walked through the centre of Swansea, walked round the shops. It's my daughter's birthday soon, and I just thought I'd have a look round. Get a few ideas.'

'And this took the whole afternoon, did it?'

'I bought a paper to read and had a few beers.'

'Which pub did you use?'

'The Bank Statement. It's a Wetherspoon's.'

'I don't suppose you met anyone you know in there? Anyone who can vouch for it?'

'I'm afraid not.'

'How very convenient.'

Lambert could see that Hickson's solicitor was about to intervene, raised his hands to stop him, then turned to Ellis.

'Sergeant Ellis, would you make a note to check CCTV footage of Swansea town centre this afternoon to see if we can corroborate Mr Hickson's story of his walkabout there?'

Blanche made a rasping sound in his throat. 'Inspector, whether or not you find my client on camera in Swansea has absolutely no bearing on your enquiries as far as I can make out.'

Lambert gave him a frosty smile. 'Maybe I'm doing it to discover how truthful he is. And I intend to have that CCTV footage gone through thoroughly. Approximately what time did you go to Wetherspoon's?'

'I wasn't keeping tabs on the time.'

'Approximately.'

Hickson shrugged. He now wore a dark blue sweater over a light blue shirt and, as if to reassure or remind himself, pulled back the end of his sleeve to consult his precious Rolex. 'It was probably some time between three and five. I was in there a good hour, if not longer.'

So far Lambert had only questioned Hickson about his friend's murder. Time, he thought, to introduce the family connection.

'Mr Hickson, what happened when you found out that James Harlan had killed your niece in a drink-driving incident?'

If Hickson was shocked or surprised he didn't show it, but the strained silence was telling. And his eyes levelled into blandness, secure behind the lens of his glasses.

'I'm not with you.'

'It's a simple enough question, Mr Hickson. Your niece, Alice Mason, was run over by James Harlan. What happened when you learnt of this terrible tragedy?'

'I was devastated, of course. Anyone would be.'

'Yet you hadn't been close to the family for years.'

'Well, you know how it is. Starting a family of my own, and running the pub. It's a full-time job.' He grinned confidently. 'But I'm not sure whether being a parent is the full-time job or being a pub landlord.'

It crossed Lambert's mind that Hickson was not going to be easy to crack. The man was bright, cunning and unlikely to say the wrong thing, even under duress. The way he carefully considered his replies before answering showed how secure he felt about being questioned, almost to the point of enjoying being the centre of attention, knowing there was no proof and therefore there could be no adverse outcome as long as he kept his cool. And he was a cool customer, as Lambert was aware.

But everyone has a weakness, and Lambert needed to poke around until he found it. And then he would swoop.

'According to your sister, even before you became a father and ran a pub, you were not close to your family. Can you explain why that was?'

'So, you've met my sister. How did she strike you?'

'I'd like you to answer my question, please, Mr Hickson. You were not very close to your sister in the past, long before this terrible event. Why was that?'

'We never fell out or anything. We were just very different, that's all. Sheila was always a bit stuck up. Liked to pretend she came from a posh background. There's a bit of Hyacinth Bouquet about her, or perhaps you didn't notice.'

'I noticed she was still very distressed over the loss of her daughter.'

Lambert waited, giving his suspect an opportunity to add his own grievances to his niece's demise. But Hickson remained silent, his face inscrutable. A glance at the solicitor told Lambert, from the slight smirk on his face, he was pleased his client had done the right thing by remaining silent.

'After your niece died, your sister told us you became very close to her son. What did you and Mark talk about?'

'I just gave him a shoulder to cry on, seeing as we're family, and Alice's death seemed to bring us closer together.'

'I understand that, Mr Hickson. But can you remember what you actually talked about?'

Hickson stared impassively at Lambert and took his time in answering. 'This happened in February. I can't really remember what we said, to be honest.'

'We're into the start of the third week in March; it's not that long ago. Did you suggest to your nephew that you or he might take revenge on his sister's killer?'

'Of course not.'

'Why "of course not"? It would seem perfectly natural after seeing someone like Harlan – who had become a hated figure on all the news channels – to wish him dead. Did you talk to Mark Mason about how you would like to kill him?'

Not a muscle moved in Hickson's face. 'No, I didn't.'

'Even when you saw him leaving the court, talking and grinning on his mobile phone like he couldn't give a damn, you still didn't explode and suggest to your nephew that you would like to see Harlan dead?'

'No, I didn't.'

'Does that strike you as natural?'

'I'm not sure what you mean.'

'I mean most people, losing someone close to them, then seeing that monster showing no remorse, would at least make a threat, even if they had no intention of carrying it out. Why not you or your nephew?'

'No reason. We just didn't, that's all.'

'And you or your nephew made no threats against Harlan.'

'My client has already told you he didn't, Inspector,' Blanche interjected.

Lambert ignored him and stared at Hickson, who held his look, their eyes locked together like opponents about to slug each other.

\*\*\*

A silence fell on the Punch and Judy pub as the two uniformed constables entered. Even the sound of the cue ball on the pool table as it pocketed a ball gave out a soft clacking sound, suddenly less aggressive and controlled. There were only six customers present and they stared uninhibitedly at the constables. The two pool players postponed their game and stood with their legs splayed and their pool cues at their side like sentries on duty, glaring with open hostility, as if it was a Wild West showdown.

Behind the bar, the landlord, Roy Ellison, although he had never been in trouble with the police, had trained himself to distrust them almost as a matter of principle, and his gruff voice greeted them with a hostile, 'Can I help you?' He had already made up his mind they would get as little help as possible, whatever their inquiry.

The female constable, Jane Holland, removed the blown-up photograph from a folder as the male constable, Colin May, gave the landlord a restrained smile and an inquiring eyebrow as he asked, 'Would you mind looking at a photograph, sir, to see if you can identify him?'

'Oh, why's that then?'

Jane Holland placed the CCTV photograph on the bar and took over the questioning, as she often did, much to the annoyance of her partner.

'You've probably heard about the body in the boot of the car abandoned in Swansea city centre. This man probably abandoned the car and might even be the perpetrator of the murder. Do you recognize him?'

The landlord stared at the picture for a long time, recognizing it immediately. But the man who was murdered was an ex convict and a brutish enforcer for whoever paid him. If the man he was being asked to identify was a rapist or paedophile that would be a different matter, whereas the man in the boot probably deserved his end.

'Do you recognize him?' Constable May said.

The landlord nodded. 'I do. Yes.'

The constables exchanged an optimistic look and waited for the landlord to elaborate. He snorted and said:

'I recognize this bloke from the TV. I seen him on the television news.'

His bar cronies laughed loudly and he preened himself, while the colour rose in Constable May's neck.

'We have reason to believe he drank here regularly,' Constable Holland said, in her toughest voice.

'Oh, aye?'

'So you must have seen him, probably in the company of James Harlan, the man who got pissed in your pub and then drove home and killed that schoolgirl.'

'Hey! I only sell the booze,' the landlord protested, hands turned up in surrender. 'I'm not responsible for them that has too much of it. Apart from which, it was my son Daryl – who's only nineteen – looking after the bar that day. In any case, the police came round to get details the day after the accident.'

Holland tapped the photograph importantly. 'So, you must know this man.'

'I don't *know* him. I've seen him in here before, but I don't know his name,' he lied.

'And is he a friend of James Harlan?'

'I think so. I've seen them both together a couple of times, but I never got to know them.'

'Not even Harlan?' Constable May questioned.

The landlord stared at the young constable as if he was an idiot. 'Reason I know Harlan's name is because of all the TV coverage.'

Constable Holland gave an exasperated sigh. 'D'you mean to tell us you don't even know this man's first name?'

'No. They kept pretty much to themselves. And it's not like they was regulars. But if you wanna know this bloke's name, why not ask his mate? You must know where he lives.'

Holland didn't like to admit Harlan had done a disappearing act, and said, 'We'll ask him, but we're not sure he'll give us a truthful answer. Would you mind if we ask your customers?'

The landlord gestured over the bar. 'Be my guest.'

The pool players suddenly took a keen interest in resuming their game. The constables interrupted them, but their response to the photograph echoed the landlord's. The final customer they questioned was bald, and had a dent on his forehead, as if he'd been hit with a hammer. His response was the same as everyone else's.

As they questioned him, they missed the amused expressions exchanged between the landlord and the other customers, unaware they were questioning a man whose pub nickname was 'Dave the Liar'.

\*\*\*

Having suspended the interview with Hickson for half an hour, Lambert and Ellis met DC Jones in the canteen. As soon as the three of them had bought coffees, Lambert raised inquiring eyebrows at Jones.

'Any news on this Virgil character yet?'

Jones shook her head. 'E Division have had no luck. They've been back to the flat where he lived with that woman, but nothing more's been seen of him.'

'And what about Mark Mason? Have you tracked him down yet?'

'He's in Bordeaux.'

'What?'

'It's in France.'

'Yes, I know where Bordeaux is, Debbie. What's he doing there?'

'Work. I spoke to his fiancée. He flew out there yesterday evening.'

'When's he due back?' Ellis said.

'Late on Friday.'

Lambert slammed his cup into its saucer, spilling some of the coffee. 'Damn! We need to question young Mason as soon as possible. This is bloody inconvenient, to say the least.'

Ellis smiled thinly. 'Or bloody convenient for Mason. Away on business just as we're getting close to connecting him with Harlan's murder of Sonning.'

Deadpan, Lambert said, 'In self-defence, of course.'

Ellis chuckled. 'Don't you start.'

'Apart from the news of him flying to France,' Jones said, 'I spoke with his fiancée about how her boyfriend was coping with the loss of his sister. Not well, she said. She sounded very worried about him. The way he'd been acting lately, he seemed... like he was the guilty one. Those were her words. As if Mason blamed himself for his sister's death.'

Lambert winced as he sipped his coffee, put the cup down and said, 'Of course, he may have had another reason for acting guilty.'

'For taking revenge on Harlan, you mean?'

'Exactly. Or trying to'

Lambert spotted Kevin Wallace entering the canteen and could tell by the look on the young detective's face that he had the news they were expecting. He came striding over to their table and gave them a thumbs up.

'Confirmed. Mitchell identified Mark Mason as the man who bought his car.'

'So, it looks like he got Sonning to kill Harlan,' Ellis said. 'And it went horribly wrong.'

Lambert nodded towards DC Wallace. 'Kevin made the point that nobody takes revenge on behalf of someone else. Sonning would have wanted paying for the job. And it's far more likely that Mason, not Hickson, would have paid him.' He turned towards Jones, sitting next to him. 'Can you remember the name of Daniel Mason's financial services?'

'M and M Financial Advice. And I remember thinking at the time that the father knew something he wasn't letting on.'

'You noticed as well, did you, Debbie? And Daniel Mason said he was going to work tomorrow, so first thing in the morning, I'd like you pay him a visit at his office and see if you can get him to open up about whatever is on his mind.' Lambert glanced at his watch. 'Meanwhile, back to the grindstone. I've got a feeling we'll be very lucky to get anything out of Hickson. But we can hold him for twenty-four hours and I intend to do that, if only to inconvenience him. And I'm seeing the chief super early tomorrow. I'll see if he wants to extend it to thirty-six.'

*** 

Constables May and Holland, feeling discouraged by their visit to the pub, approached the small general store with apprehension, knowing their best bet for information had been the pub, and their inability to put a name to the suspect was a failure of epic proportions. They were both dedicated officers and were not looking forward to a return to Swansea Central with a big fat nothing to report.

The shop was cramped and overstocked with groceries, the shelves heavily laden with tins and packets, and they moved along an aisle crammed with stationery, a few cheap toys and greetings cards. Behind the counter a turbaned Sikh man, with a grey beard, and alert brown eyes, greeted them with a smile.

'Good evening,' he said. 'How can I help you?'

Constable Holland placed the photograph on the counter. 'We're looking for anyone who might have seen this man.'

The shopkeeper squinted and stared closely at the photograph. 'The face seems very… memorable. Yes, I think he's been in here to buy cigarettes a few times.'

Holland removed the photograph of Harlan and placed it next to the other one.

'We think this man might be a friend of his,' Constable May said.

The shopkeeper looked up after studying Harlan's photograph. 'Is this the man who killed that schoolgirl?'

'That's him,' said Holland.

'Terrible tragedy. The man so drunk and taking an innocent life like that.'

'Has he ever been in your store?' May asked.

The shopkeeper nodded and stared at them both, with a small smile now, knowing he possessed the information they wanted. 'Yes, they've both been in here together. Several times. To buy cigarettes.'

The constables exchanged a brief, sharp look, before staring expectantly at the shopkeeper. Holland found it hard to contain the excitement rising in her voice.

'And did you get the impression they were friends?'

'Oh, yes. I'm sure they were close friends. They look like each other. They look like brothers. But maybe not.'

Holland tapped Harlan's photograph. 'We know this man's name, obviously since he's been arrested and charged. But we're looking for this other man – his friend. And we're trying to find out his name and where he lives.'

'I don't know where he lives, but I think I can remember his name.'

Constable May almost barked with excitement. 'His name! You know his name?'

The shopkeeper beamed, enjoying the attention and drama. 'Not his last name. But I'm sure the other man, the drunken one, called him Jason. Yes, I'm sure of it. I think he called him Jason.'

'And you're certain it was Jason,' Holland said.

The shopkeeper said, 'Yes, as sure as eggs are eggs,' and grinned hugely, proud of his idiomatic English.

# Twenty-one

First thing Tuesday morning Lambert drove to HQ at Bridgend and attended a one-to-one with DCS Marden. The chief superintendent seemed preoccupied, as if he was only half listening to what Lambert had to say. Lambert wondered what the hell he was doing in the man's office, when he could have been getting on with the investigation, instead of going over stuff he had already emailed to Marden.

In a voice that lacked interest, Marden said, 'Are there any details absent from your report? Details you may have overlooked.'

'We have James Harlan's mobile number.'

'And?'

'We can't locate it. There's no signal. Presumably he knows enough to keep it switched off most of the time. But we also found out Harlan works – or worked, since he is now banned from driving – for Frank Masina. And since Harlan's now done a disappearing act, for all we know, Masina could be protecting him.'

Marden sniffed and tugged his hawk-like nose. 'That's doubtful. I think you're jumping to conclusions. According to your report, Sergeant Ellis went to Harlan's home yesterday and the man wasn't there. Nothing unusual in that. He might have a girlfriend he's staying with. He may not want to stay at home because of his notoriety.'

'But the connection to Masina is still a lead, and it's one we ought to follow up.'

Marden made a chopping motion with his hand. 'Leave it, Harry. I promise you, Masina's in our sights.'

'OK. But what about Harlan's house?'

'What about it?'

'The killing of Robert Sonning took place indoors somewhere. There were cheap carpet fibres found on his body. This could have happened at Harlan's house, which is why he may have done a runner. According to Tony Ellis, the place has an abandoned feel about it.'

Marden flaunted a smug smile. 'Perhaps when Sergeant Ellis got no reply his overactive imagination took over. So, what are you saying? You want to get a warrant to search Harlan's place?'

'I think it would be a good idea. At least then we'd have concrete evidence that Harlan killed Sonning.'

'Probably in self-defence,' Marden said.

Lambert stopped himself from laughing. 'Can I organize a warrant and a forensic search of his premises?'

'Yes, go ahead. And just what do you intend doing with this Hickson, who is clearly involved in the killing?'

'Sergeant Ellis is grilling him as we speak. We've got him for another ten hours. Unless we can keep him for another twelve – with your authority, of course.'

'That depends. If you get nothing out of him between now and this evening, coupled with the fact that you've got no concrete evidence linking him to the murder, his solicitor will want us to come up with a very good reason to hold him for thirty-six hours. What are you doing about this man who was seen on CCTV?'

'We're making every effort to find him. We know his first name is Jason, and he has a spider and web tattoo at the base of his thumb, and a local shopkeeper identified him as a friend of Harlan's when they both visited his shop together.'

'So, he shouldn't prove too difficult to find.'

'I feel confident we can nail him before the end of the day.'

Marden's mouth turned downwards sceptically. 'I hope so. I really hope so. A simple case of revenge is becoming a major headache. But your team is working well, I hope? All singing in the same choir?'

*And from the same hymn sheet.* Lambert quickly wiped a hand over his mouth to cover his smile. 'I've no complaints with my team. Although...' he hesitated, not wanting to be unfairly critical of one of the members.

Marden pounced. 'Yes?'

'Oh, nothing really. I just find Mick Beech a bit hard to communicate with.'

'But he ticks all the boxes? Does a good job?'

'I would say faultless.'

Marden shrugged and showed Lambert his palms, challenging him to explain the problem.

Lambert screwed up his face. 'It's tricky, sir. Hard one to explain. I suppose getting on in a team's not just about the work.'

'Don't give me that, Harry. You're talking about after work boozing and banter. We've all been there and we've all done it. At the end of the day, it's not what counts in a major investigation.'

'No, I know that. But for the last major investigation we had Roger Hazel. A good job *and* a good bloke. When this one came up on Saturday, I asked Sergeant Ellis to put in a request for Roger.'

'He wasn't available. He's on annual leave.'

Marden looked at his watch and Lambert took that as his cue to leave. As he stood up, he said, 'And how is the investigation going in conjunction with SOCA?'

Marden stared at him expressionlessly, then said dismissively, 'That'll be all for the moment, Harry.'

As he left the building, Lambert felt a contraction in his chest, and he wondered if it might be the beginning of something worse, the precursor of a heart attack. Or maybe, he thought as he strode towards his car, his hands balled into fists, it was how Marden affected him. But a comical thought suddenly tickled him, and he relaxed and almost laughed aloud as he told himself that no matter how reasonable Marden behaved, he would never sing in the man's choir.

*****

As soon as Lambert swept into the incident room, he could see by the expression on Debbie Jones's face, frowning with concern but with a slightly triumphant smile, that she had important information to impart. She tapped her notebook with a pen, then dropped it on to a desk, knowing its contents off by heart.

'What happened with Mason's father?' Lambert said. 'Did you manage to speak to him?'

'It wasn't easy. But I got there in the end. I'll cut to the chase, shall I?'

Lambert nodded.

'Over the years he'd taken his father's advice regarding his finances and savings. But his father was deeply worried because he knows his son's bank manager very well – in fact, it was the father who advised banking at that bank – and the manager called him to tell him his son had withdrawn eight thousand in cash, less than a fortnight ago.'

'Hmm. That looks as if this was money he used to pay Sonning to kill Harlan.'

## Chapter Twenty-one

'Life comes very cheap,' Jones said, twisting the pen in her hand.

'I've known some paid murders that were done far cheaper, Debbie.'

Jones giggled nervously. 'Why am I not surprised? Oh, and I also found time to contact Verve Initiatives.'

'Who?' Lambert said, then clicked his fingers. 'Oh, yes, his employers.'

'They know nothing about sending him to Bordeaux. They have no clients there and it's unlikely they will have. Mark Mason phoned the MD of Verve on Sunday evening, said he had to tie up some loose ends to do with family matters, and as it was reasonably quiet at work, would they mind if he took a week's annual leave starting on Monday. I then phoned his girlfriend, Julia Redfern, who told me he left late on Sunday evening to drive to Heathrow to catch a flight to Bordeaux, intending to leave his car for five nights in the long stay car park. But she's now beside herself with worry.'

Lambert stared at Jones, accusation in his expression. 'You didn't tell her about him lying about his flight, did you, and giving his MD a different story?'

'Of course not. She was already worried about where he went. And she was puzzled.'

'Oh? Why's that?'

'Because she found his passport. He didn't take it with him.'

'Ah! So what the bloody hell is he up to?'

'Maybe he only gave Sonning a down payment, and when he received news of his death, knowing Harlan probably killed him, he's found someone else to finish the job.'

'Harlan's missing, and for all we know he could already be dead. And Mark Mason wouldn't have known of the failed murder until Sunday, at least. So how would he find another hit man in less than twenty-four hours?' Lambert laughed and shook his head. 'Look in Yellow Pages? No, it doesn't make sense.'

'There's always the wicked uncle. And we know how he likes to take the law into his own hands.'

Pulling a face of uncertainty, Lambert said, 'He'd have had to act fairly quickly, even supposing he knew where to find Harlan. And we've had him in custody since last night.'

Suddenly, he became animated and tapped his pocket, checking he had his mobile, a gesture Jones recognized as a call to action.

'Come on, Debbie,' he said. 'Let's get to Swansea Central and have another go at Hickson, seeing as we've got fresh information about his nephew.'

\*\*\*

They met with Ellis and Wallace who had spent the last ninety minutes interrogating Hickson, who was now on a refreshment break. Ellis admitted defeat, had got nowhere with his suspect, and the solicitor was now obstructing them because they were going over old ground and asking the same questions. They needed some fresh evidence, which Lambert thought they had with the information DC Jones had obtained concerning Mark Mason.

Lambert instructed Ellis and Wallace to continue the search for the man named Jason, who could lead them to Harlan, and offered the hypotheses that he might have a previous record, even for a minor crime, and suggested the tattoo might not show up as distinguishing marks on his prison identification details because it could be a D-I-Y tattoo done while serving time. He also told them to organize a warrant to break into and search the empty home of James Harlan, telling them they shouldn't have much difficulty getting a magistrate's approval as DCS Marden had already given his blessing.

He and DC Jones planned to continue the interrogation of Hickson.

*** 

After announcing a change of personnel for the benefit of the tape, Lambert resumed the cross-examination.

'What happened to the eight thousand your nephew paid to your friend Sonning to kill James Harlan?'

Hickson tilted his head sideways with a puzzled frown. 'I have no idea what you're talking about.'

'We now know where Mark Mason is at this very moment,' Lambert bluffed. 'You might as well tell us everything you know – unless you'd like us to add perverting the course of justice to the charge of aiding and abetting an attempted murder.'

Deadpan, with not a flicker in his eyes, Hickson replied, 'I think I know where Mark is as well as you. He returned to work after Alice's funeral. He's in Bristol.'

'You know that's not true. He may have gone back to work immediately after the funeral, but he's not there now. And I think you know where he is.'

'If he's not in Bristol, I've no idea where he is. Have you tried his parents?'

'They have no idea where he is. But I think you do. And I'd like you to tell us where he is.'

'I thought you said you know where he is.'

'Don't play games with us, Mr Hickson. Where is Mark Mason?'

'I've just told you. As far as I know, he's in Bristol.'

'He was up until Sunday. Did you phone him on Sunday?'

Hickson took his time replying, considering his options. 'I may have given him a quick ring.'

'What about?'

'I was concerned about him. Just ringing to see how he was.'

Lambert could tell Hickson was smart enough to admit to the phone call as there would be a record of it with his mobile telecoms provider.

'Did you discuss Sonning's murder with him?'

Another long pause while Hickson weighed up the question.

'Mr Hickson,' Lambert snapped, 'can you please answer my questions without long delays?'

Lambert wasn't certain, but he thought he could detect the trace of a smile on Hickson as he replied.

'I didn't talk to Mark about Robbie's death, no.'

'When we gave you the news on Sunday at Burry Port, you seemed pretty shattered by it. And then as we were leaving we saw you phoning someone on your mobile. Would this have been your nephew?'

Hickson tilted his head up as he considered the question. Lambert, his temper rising, rounded on the solicitor. 'Can you please instruct your client to answer in a reasonable time span, Mr Blanche? Otherwise we might think he's obstructing the investigation.'

'Inspector,' Blanche replied in a clipped tone, 'my client has answered all your questions and you seem to be going around in circles. Apart from which, if you ask anyone what they were doing a few days ago at a certain time, they would have to think about it. My client is being very reasonable and answering your questions with care and consideration.'

'Yes, with long silences while he considers his options.' Seeing Blanche about to speak, Lambert waved a hand dismissively at him before turning his attention back to Hickson. 'Why did Mark Mason buy the second-hand car that was found in Swansea with your dead friend in the boot?'

Frowning, Hickson replied, 'I know nothing about Mark buying a car.'

'We have proof, Mr Hickson. The man who sold him the car identified him from his photograph.'

'Then you'll have to ask Mark that. I know nothing about it.'

'But you were the one who phoned up about the car from the ad in the paper.'

'I've never phoned up about a car. Other than the one I bought in mid-February. A blue Renault Megane.'

'So, you don't remember ringing this chap in Llanelli about the Rover?'

'I didn't ring anyone about a car. Other than my Renault a while back.'

The way Hickson looked at him, Lambert could tell he was momentarily confused about being told the location of the Rover was in Llanelli instead of Port Talbot and knew damn well where it was purchased. Even though it could have been Sonning who phoned about the car, Lambert knew Hickson was lying. But knowing it was one thing; proving it was another.

*** 

Just before midday, Wallace returned to the incident room at Cockett police station armed with a warrant to enter and search Harlan's house. DS Beech was at his desk, busy devouring a doorstop sandwich.

'I got the warrant, no problem,' Wallace said. 'How did Tony get on with the search for this Jason's ID?'

Without bothering to turn around, Beech raised a thumb in the air.

'He got a result?' Wallace said. 'Who is it?'

Beech jerked the same thumb back at one of the desks. 'It'll tell you there.'

Irritated with Beech's taciturn manner, Wallace said, 'Where's Tony?'

'Gone to the loo. Don't get comfortable. You and he will be dashing round to the man's gaff any minute now.'

'Christ! And I'm starving. I was hoping for some lunch.' Wallace walked over to one of the desks and had a look at the photograph lying face up. The face that stared into camera was the usual prison mugshot, a hard-man pose, but the eyes signified nothing but a worried distraction.

As he was studying the mugshot, Ellis burst into the room. 'I hope you're not starving hungry, Kevin.'

'Well, as a matter of—' Wallace began, but Ellis interrupted him.

'Only this is the best lead so far. We've got the bloke's address, so I think paying him a visit will be a priority. As of right now.'

'Who is he?'

'His name's Jason Crabbe. He lives only fifteen minutes from here. He was sentenced to a year in Cardiff prison in 2009 and was released after ten months. It was a first offence for burglary, stealing from garden sheds and selling tools and various items at boot sales.'

'Not exactly gangster of the month, then. What about searching Harlan's place?'

'I think that can wait. We need to get after this bloke, who might lead us to his mate Harlan.'

'Unless he's done a runner, as well.'

Ellis grabbed his coat from where it was draped on the back of a chair. 'Soon find out, won't we? See you later, Mick.'

\*\*\*

Having given Hickson his statutory break for lunch and feeling frustrated by the way the interrogation was failing, Lambert left the police station and went to the Cross Keys Inn for a pint of lager and a cottage pie. Offered the choice of chips and peas or salad with the pie, he unconsciously tapped his guilty waistline as he chose the former.

While he sat and waited for his food, he received a text from Tony Ellis, telling him the man known only as Jason had been fully-named and traced, and they were on their way to his address to question and possibly apprehend him.

After receiving the text, Lambert's pessimism dissipated and he began to relax, and even felt a tremor of excitement at the challenge that lay ahead in solving the body in the boot killing, which was starting to seem straightforward, even though the gathering of evidence was elusive.

Feeling refreshed after his lunch and pint, he walked towards the exit. His jaw dropped open with surprise as he almost bumped into Roger Hazel arriving at the pub.

'Roger! I thought you were on holiday.'

The young detective sergeant smiled wryly and said, 'An hour-long holiday. It's called a lunch break, in between gathering evidence for Geoff Ambrose.'

'But Marden told me you were on annual leave.'

Hazel shook his head vigorously. 'I wish I was entitled to more leave, but it's all been eaten up.' His eyes shifted to the bar. 'And talking of grub…'

Lambert patted his stomach again, this time consciously. 'I've just had a modest portion of cottage pie and one pint, and I'll pay the price. Whereas you'll devour a Desperate Dan cow pie and several pints of Guinness and won't put on an ounce.'

Hazel laughed. 'As you keep reminding me, Harry, there'll be a day of reckoning. But until that time comes, I'll give you oldies a run for your money.'

'Yeah, thanks a bundle. In spite of your insults, it's a shame you're not office manager on my current investigation. Tony Ellis asked for you, but we got DS Beech for our sins.'

'Beech was on Ambrose's team, who are heavily involved with SOCA. I think Marden did a swap, and I've taken Beech's place.'

'But the reason he gave for your unavailability was annual leave. Why would he say that?'

'No idea. But you know what he's like.'

'Only too well. He likes us to think outside the box.'

Hazel chuckled and added, 'I'm glad you flagged that up, seeing as we're all singing from the same hymn sheet.'

Grinning, Lambert said, 'I won't keep you from your mountain of food, Roger. *Bon appetite!*'

As Lambert walked away from the Cross Keys, frowning deeply, he wondered why Marden had lied to him about Roger Hazel. And then, as he neared the police station, preparing to tackle Hickson one last time, he pushed thoughts of Marden's manipulative behaviour to the back of his mind.

\*\*\*

Jason Crabbe lived in what had been a glorious mansion in 1873, but in the1950s it had been converted into a warren of flats, which had not been well maintained, and the flaking plaster and paint on the exterior walls of the building had been in a state of disrepair since the 1980s, when the building had been purchased by a property developer who had hoped to get planning permission to demolish the building and build a modern block of at least sixteen purpose built flats. Planning permission had been turned down, and the landlord had no intention of spending money improving the property for the benefit of his low-rent tenants.

Crabbe's flat was a rundown bedsitter halfway up a flight of stairs leading to the first floor. It was euphemistically referred to as the studio flat by his landlord, who never asked his tenants for references because all he cared about was his rent being paid on time.

When his doorbell rang, Crabbe guessed it was the police, and had wondered how long it would take them to catch up with him. He leapt out of his chair and switched the television off, even though anyone standing on the porch outside would be unlikely to hear it, and he prayed that his unwelcome visitors hadn't heard the faintest sounds of Formula 1 racing followed by a sudden silence.

His bell rang again, this time long and piercing. He decided to ignore it, and not feel tempted to creep to the window and peer through the grubby net curtains, just in case one of the coppers decided to walk to the back of the building and look up at his window. He felt vulnerable, but as his adrenaline kicked in, he also felt the excitement of the challenge. Outsmarting them. Fucking useless coppers. Without all their technical back-up, CCTV, computers and all that forensic shit you get on TV, they were a bunch of muppets. And he was one step ahead of them. He guessed they probably knew what sort of car he drove and was glad he'd taken the precaution of parking his Volvo in the next street, rather than in the car park at the back of his block of flats. And if he didn't answer the door, and providing they had no search warrant, he could wait until they got bored and went away.

He heard another bell ringing in the flat below him and counted himself lucky that he barely knew the other tenants, although he occasionally caught glimpses of them in passing. Most of them were out at work all day, and he knew at least two of them did shift work, guessing that one of the women on the ground floor was a nurse, coming and going at unusual hours. It was fortunate that he was probably the only tenant in the building at this moment, and they wouldn't be able to gain access to the building.

He heard the faint ringing of a bell as they tried another flat, and hoped it wasn't someone's flat who worked an early shift and was at home for the evening. He waited, tense and frightened now, wondering if they might break his door down if they gained access to the building. As he heard the insistent ringing of the bell, he cursed Jimmy for getting him into this shit. He'd saved his mate's life, that was for sure, after he'd recognized that bastard Sonning. But now he was involved in murder. Serious stuff with serious consequences. And his picture in all the papers and on TV, although he was relieved the crime had been overshadowed by the events in Japan.

Eventually, the ringing stopped, followed by a short silence, then he heard a car start up, and guessed they'd got tired of their search. But they'd be back, maybe next time with a search warrant, and by then one of the other tenants would probably be home and they would gain access to the building. He decided to give it another fifteen minutes, just to be on the safe side, then pack a few things and get out. Go somewhere. But where? He couldn't go to his parents or his sister's place because it was just a question of time before the cops knew everything there was to know about him. And after that row he'd had with Tricia there was no way he could call on her and beg for mercy. Not since he'd beaten her up. Bad move that. If only he'd known then…

Now he needed somewhere to hide. But where? Those two words kept ringing in his ears.

He suddenly felt desperately lonely. There was no one he could turn to for help. Maybe he could just get in the Volvo and drive. And then he remembered he needed to get to the motorway services to see if he could buy a pair of driving gloves to cover the tattoo. At least that would give him a reason to get out of this shit-hole. And once he'd got the gloves he'd feel more secure and he'd be able to find some place to hide out. But where? Over and over again those words kept repeating themselves. But where?

# Twenty-two

Just after four, Lambert and Jones dashed back to the incident room at Cockett police station where they met up with the rest of his team.

'I've organized our small band of forceful entry men like you requested,' DS Beech said. 'They'll be at the location at half-four.'

'Good,' Lambert said. 'What about forensics?'

'They'll be there at the same time.'

Lambert took a couple of paces towards the whiteboard, stopped and paced back again. The rest of the team could see he was wound up, tense and excited, like a horse at the starting line.

'What happened about Jason Crabbe?' he asked Ellis.

'There was no reply from his flat. Either he refused to answer or he's scarpered. The block had its own car park and there was no sign of his Volvo.'

'Shit!' Lambert said. 'Everyone seems to be doing a disappearing act. I suppose we're going to need another warrant to get into Crabbe's place.'

Ellis looked at Wallace and they shared a triumphant glint. 'No need for a warrant, Harry. We got the landlord's number, and he'll get there at five and let us in. He's got keys to Crabbe's bedsit.'

'Studio flat.' Wallace said with a grin.

'And he's happy to give you access?' Lambert said.

'Once we'd explained the serious nature of why we wanted Crabbe, he bent over backwards to help us.'

Wallace's grin widened. 'And it might have something to do with Crabbe being two months behind on the rent.'

'So, what's happened with Hickson?' Ellis asked.

'I had to let him go. We were just going round in circles. The man is guilty of aiding and abetting an attempted murder – I've no doubt about it. But we just haven't any evidence, certainly nothing with which to hold him.'

'Suppose he does a runner?' boomed Mick Beech. 'Everyone else seems to be disappearing. Why not him?'

Lambert, irritated by Beech's observation, snapped, 'I wouldn't have let him go if I hadn't felt confident we can pick him up whenever we like. He's got a pub to run. And I get the impression he puts family first.'

'Which is why he's helped his nephew to avenge the sister's death,' Jones said.

Lambert patted his mobile pocket and glanced at the clock 'OK. Let's get over to Harlan's house and see what we can find.'

***

As soon as Hickson arrived back at his pub, he rushed inside to reassure his wife that everything was going to be fine, at the same time dreading the explanation he would have to concoct about his involvement with the murder of Sonning and was surprised to find Phil still serving behind the bar.

'You still here, Phil? What's happened to Pat?'

'When you phoned to say you were on your way, she took Kelly to a children's party. And then she had an appointment at the doctor's.'

'What's wrong with her?'

'She didn't say. She looks all right though.'

'Did she take the car?'

Phil shook his head as he came from behind the bar and grabbed his coat from a row of coat pegs. One of the regular customers nodded at Hickson who acknowledged it with a brief wave.

'The party's round the corner.' Phil said. 'Walking distance.'

Hickson walked over to the barman and placed a hand on the coat, lowering his voice. 'Listen, Phil, do me a favour. I'll pay you another twenty quid if you stay till either Pat gets back or I do. I'll only be an hour, top whack.'

Phil, his ruddy-complexioned face contorted into a grimace of conflict as he wrestled with the lure of easy money against his disabled wife's needs, levelled his voice to match his employer. 'As long as it's only an hour. Only I have to see to Gwyneth.'

Hickson held his hands up. 'One hour – maybe less. I promise.'

'All right, Steve. Won't do no harm, just this once.'

The barman returned behind the bar as Steve glanced nervously over his shoulder, worried in case his wife suddenly returned before he could leave. He strode hurriedly to the bar and tapped the counter urgently.

'Let me have the car keys, would you, Phil?'

The barman got the keys from where they hung on a hook by the telephone and handed them over.

Hickson spoke rapidly. 'Listen, Phil, if Pat gets back soon, please tell her everything is OK. Nothing to worry about. I've just got to see someone urgently. I'll be back in an hour or less.'

\*\*\*

'Christ! What a dump.' Wallace said as they arrived back at the crumbling Victorian house. 'It hasn't improved since we were here an hour ago. I can't wait to see the inside.' There was a red Range Rover parked right outside the main entrance, blocking the narrow lane to the car park at the back. 'Think that's our landlord? At least he's here and on time.'

They waited while the driver of the Range Rover moved it, and they followed it around the back and parked next to it.

'Mr Giselli?' Ellis enquired as he got out, his ID at the ready. 'I'm Sergeant Ellis. We spoke on the phone.'

The man nodded and offered Ellis his hand. As Ellis shook it, the landlord looked towards Wallace, waiting for an introduction.

'And this is Detective Constable Wallace.' Ellis said.

Ellis wasn't sure what he expected the landlord to look like – probably a corpulent man, smooth and flashy and dripping bling. Instead the landlord was probably no more than mid to late thirties, lean and fit, and wore an expensive-looking track suit and trainers.

'You want to search Crabbe's flat, yes?'

'That's why we're here,' Ellis said. 'We could have got a warrant, but this has saved us some time. We appreciate your cooperation, sir.'

The landlord nodded thoughtfully and jangled a large bunch of keys he carried in his left hand. 'Right, shall we go in and have a look?'

He opened the front door, leading to an enormous hall dominated by a stunning feature: a conspicuously ornate staircase with carved banisters, which may once have been grand but was now coated in white paint that was scuffed and had faded to a dirty beige. A faint boiled fish and onion smell lingered in the air and a blast of the six o'clock TV news theme came from one of the downstairs flats. As they ascended the staircase the landlord turned and spoke to Ellis, who was following closely behind.

'So, what's Crabbe done?'

'You mean you haven't seen the news?'

'I've been away, doing a bit of climbing in Snowdonia.' The landlord tried several keys in the lock, muttering, 'Bloody thing's here, I know it is. Ah! Here he we are.' He unlocked the door, which was on a small landing halfway up the stairs, and pushed it open.

There was a narrow hall, with an open door on the left, which Ellis and Wallace could see was the bathroom. They carried on into a large room, which was open plan: a kitchen, bedroom and living room combined. It was depressingly drab and functional, and had a musty smell combined with a slight scent of cheap after-shave. Under limp, unwashed, net curtains covering the window, stood a small writing desk. There was no computer or telephone on it, and it seemed to be mainly home to takeaway pizza leaflets and other bits of junk mail and a pad of paper.

The detectives paused for a moment, surveying their surroundings.

'Sorry,' the landlord said. 'You didn't tell me what Crabbe's supposed to have done.'

Ellis stared at him for a moment before speaking, amazed at how many people seem to have no idea what's going on in the world, and are oblivious to anything but what concerns them directly.

'Well, Mr Giselli, on Saturday a car was discovered in the centre of Swansea with a body in the boot. The man had been shot. Murdered.'

The landlord's eyes lit up. This was exciting stuff and he couldn't wait to tell his wife when he got home. 'And you think Crabbe did it?'

'He certainly got rid of the car. He was seen on CCTV. It was on all the news.'

'I think I might have glimpsed it in the bar of the hotel in Llanberis where I was staying.'

'And you didn't think to come forward when they gave details about the tattoo on his thumb.'

The landlord smiled sheepishly. 'I didn't even know Crabbe had a tattoo. I know you're going to find this hard to believe, but I've never seen him.' He chuckled. 'Well, I have now you've mentioned the CCTV footage on the news. But the truth is, I'd never set eyes on him before then.'

Ellis's eyebrows shot up. 'You mean, when he became a tenant here you never met him?'

'That's right. Occasionally people hear there's a flat available and they ring me up. We do it over the phone. I give them my bank details and get the keys to them via a bloke who does occasional maintenance for me.' He shrugged apologetically. 'It's pretty much a floating population. People come and go. And I've got a load of other properties to attend to. Mainly in Cardiff.'

Wallace, who had only been half-listening, and had been searching through a chest of drawers, opened a built-in wardrobe door and exclaimed.

'Gone!' He turned to Ellis and said, 'There's hardly any clothes left in the chest of drawers and the wardrobe's practically empty. And there's not a suitcase anywhere to be seen. I think he's scarpered.'

'Looks that way,' Ellis said, then he went to the desk and looked down on the white pad, which had a local phone number scrawled across it. He turned back to speak to the landlord.

'There's no phone in the flat.'

'There's certainly an outside line. It's up to the tenants if they want a phone put in. But most of them use their mobiles now, unless they need a computer and broadband.'

Ellis showed Wallace the phone number on the pad. 'This looks like he might have phoned someone from his mobile. And it wasn't a number he knew, otherwise it would have been in his mobile address book.'

'He might have rung directory on his mobile to get that number,' Wallace said.

Before he'd finished speaking, Ellis took out his mobile and dialled the number hurriedly. Wallace watched him intently, as did the landlord, who thought the story for his wife was getting better by the minute.

Ellis sighed as the ringing tone went on for what seemed like minutes. Eventually it was answered by a weary female voice, who said good evening first in Welsh and then in English.

'Hello. Who am I calling?' Ellis asked.

'This is Pont Abraham Services.'

'The motorway services?'

'That's right.'

Ellis coughed lightly before continuing. 'I'm Detective Sergeant Ellis, and I promise you this isn't a wind up. You can check with Swansea Central police station if you like. But this is urgent and important. Can you tell me if you've had many phone calls in the last half hour or so?'

There was a pause, and he imagined her trying to digest this sudden cloak-and-dagger information. After a small squeak, a stifled exclamation of excitement, she said, 'We had three phone calls, two was from members of staff, and one was from some bloke who got right uppity when I couldn't tell him if the shop sold driving gloves or not. I said...'

Ellis interrupted her. 'How long ago was this?'

'Ooh, about ten or fifteen minutes ago.'

'Right, thanks for that information,' Ellis almost shouted in his excitement. 'You've been a great help.' He didn't wait for her response. He hung up and said to Wallace, 'Crabbe left here less than fifteen minutes ago, and he's heading for Pont Abraham Services. If you can put your foot down, Kevin, we might get him.'

***

Donny had parked the van one hundred yards up the road from the harbour car park, where they were out of sight of the prying eyes of CCTV cameras. Kyle lit another cigarette, his third in only twenty minutes, and blew the smoke out noisily in a display of impatience. 'If you ask me, this is a waste of time. Why don't we find a boozer, sink a few sherbets and come back later?'

Virgil stared at the boats, moored neatly in rows, like oversize toys or replicas. But then his circumstances seemed unreal and had a dreamlike quality, as if he was suddenly living inside a film and this was happening to someone else.

'If we come back later,' he said slowly, spelling it out, 'we might miss him.'

Annoyed at being spoken to by his father as if he were a small child, Kyle glanced towards Donny for support. But his partner was staring out of the van's windscreen with a secret smile on his face, lost in his own mysterious world, drumming his fingers on the steering wheel. Kyle, who was squashed uncomfortably between his father and Donny, wriggled in his seat and coughed loudly before sucking on his cigarette, which brought his partner out of his trance.

'Why don't you keep calm? You're starting to annoy me.'

Sandwiched between the two men, Kyle was unable to suppress feelings of impotence. He felt a pinprick sting of tears behind the eyes because he was shit-scared. But he was powerless to act, to change the course of his destiny, a direction which he suspected he would later regret.

'Won't be long now,' his father said, as if this was merely a day trip to visit the marina, and everything was ordinary and conventional, and they were planning nothing more than an extension to a short vacation. 'His wife said he comes here nearly every day.'

Donny leant forward and looked across Kyle at his stupid father. 'Nearly,' he growled. 'Suppose we've picked one of the days he ain't coming.'

Virgil had remembered the conversation between the landlord and his wife from last Christmas, while he was busy planning to burgle their pub. Her laughing and joking, saying something about her husband loving *Esmeralda* more than he loved her, which turned out to be a boat which was moored here at Burry Port. He hadn't known at the time how valuable that information would be, but it had been filed away and might still prove to be useful, if only he could keep Donny happy and convinced that the man would turn up.

Virgil glanced at his watch. 'He'll be here. Any minute now.'

Donny's lip curled into a sneer and he gave a short, sharp laugh of derision. 'Oh, fucking psychic, are you? Tuned in to some spiritual airwave. You didn't tell me you were telepathic. You left that bit out. If you knew he'd be here around four-thirty, why have we been sat here since three? Eh?'

Virgil shrugged annoyingly. 'Look, let's give it till five o'clock. What have you got to lose? I'm paying you ten grand from those rocks after I sell 'em. And all you've got to do for it is drive this van and help me out.'

'Yeah, and I've had to pay money up front for the hire of this vehicle, so I expect my share whether this geezer turns up or not.'

'You'll get your money. You don't have to worry on that score.'

Cold menace in Donny's voice as he stated flatly, 'I'm not worried, Virgil. Whatever happens I'm going to get my money.'

'I don't see why we had to hire it,' Virgil grumbled. 'We should have just nicked an old one.'

'You still don't get it, do you? If we're driving a stolen vehicle and we're stopped—' Frustrated by Virgil's stupidity, Donny thumped the steering wheel hard. 'This vehicle's been hired in another man's name. It's all above board. If we're stopped I can show documents. No problem. And I'll tell you something else, you imbecilic, half-witted, rat-faced arsehole. As soon as it's done, I'm returning the vehicle to the rightful owners.'

'What the hell for?'

'Because it's hired, you fucking moron. If it's returned to the hire company, it goes unnoticed. Nobody will suspect a thing. Jesus Christ, Kyle, I can't believe how mind-numbingly imperceptive your old man is. It's like wading in a swamp with a lump of faecal matter for company.'

Kyle sniggered nervously and glanced towards his father. But his father wasn't at all fazed by the insults and accepted them as if it was routine banter between two old buddies.

'I s'pose you learnt all of them fancy words in chokey.'

'Which is more than you did. I spent my time constructively.'

'You had a longer stretch than me.'

'Yeah, yours was for some petty crime. This what you're trying to prove now? Like you're someone to be reckoned with?'

Virgil shifted uncomfortably and changed the subject. 'So, what you gonna do with the ten grand, Kyle.'

'Well, I hadn't really thought about…' Kyle began, but his partner jumped in.

'I'll tell you what *we* are going to do with it. We are going to convert that ten K into a small fortune.'

## CHAPTER TWENTY-TWO

'Oh yeah? How you gonna manage that then?'

'We are going to open what looks like a legit business, on some small unit on an industrial estate. Buy stock. Build up credit. Get companies trusting us as we always pay the invoices in under twenty-eight days. Then once we have their trust, we go for the big kill. Big orders. Big disappearing act. Sell all the gear and go to Northern Cyprus for a few years, until things die down a bit. Not that I intend to do any of this in my own identity. But Northern Cyprus is just a safety valve in case they get on to us.'

'You've got it all worked out then,' Virgil said, with a mixture of admiration and jealousy. 'But why Cyprus?'

'Not just *Cyprus*. Northern Cyprus. There's no extradition treaty.'

'Oh, I didn't know...' Virgil started to say, then stopped as his attention was drawn to a blue Renault that flashed past them and turned into a parking space. He watched as the brake lights dimmed and the door opened. Steve Hickson climbed out clutching a Sainsbury's carrier bag.

'It's him! I told you he'd be here. Let's go. Let's get the bastard.'

The three of them had come prepared, wearing sweaters with hoods, which they raised to mask their faces from the cameras. Leaving the van doors open, they dashed across the road to the Renault as Hickson turned slightly on hearing their running footsteps. The last thing he noticed was three hooded men bearing down on him, before a fist smashed into his face.

\*\*\*

Lambert stood in the middle of James Harlan's small, neat living room. The man obviously went for minimalist and it looked as if the room was only ever used to watch television and DVDs. There was a collection of films on top of a built-in cupboard in an alcove, mainly war and adventure films, and there was a two-seater sofa in white leather, contrasting sharply with a bright blue carpet, and a matching easy chair. But the only item that interested Lambert was the telephone answering machine in front of the DVDs on the cupboard. The light was flashing on it, so Lambert pressed the play button.

'You have four new messages,' said the robotic female voice. 'Message one.' And then Lambert heard a click before a gruff male voice spoke through the crackles of the digital recorder. 'Jimmy? It's Dad here. I'm just ringing to see if you're all right, and if there's anything I can do. I know it's not a good time for you, and I know how you must be feeling. But please come round if you want to and don't give a shit about what our neighbours think. Bollocks to them. Anyway, I hope you're OK, son. Anything we can do, just ask. See you soon, hopefully. Bye for now.' Click. Then the female voice announced the second call. Harlan's father again. 'Meant to say, Jimmy, why not call round at night if you like. That way you don't have to worry about the neighbours. Just a thought. Bye, son.' When the third call started playing its message, Lambert's attention became razor-sharp. It was a young man's voice, very matter-of-fact, and for a moment Lambert imagined it was all a performance, because the content of the message contrasted so sharply with the way it was spoken.

'You might have got away with it this time, you bastard, but now I'm going to do the job myself. If you think you're going to get away with four or five years for manslaughter, you're mistaken. This isn't going to get as far as court, because you'll be dead by then. Oh yes, you fat bastard, I'm going to kill you. Why should the government waste public money on scum like you? So I'll be doing everyone a favour by killing you myself. OK, so this will be an act of revenge – pure and simple. But it's the only way I can get any closure on this. So, when you least expect it, I'll kill you without warning. You can take this as your warning.'

A pause followed by a click as the caller hung up. And then the female voice announced the fourth and final message, but the caller didn't speak and cut the call after a few seconds. Hurriedly, Lambert dialled 1–4–7–1, took a notebook and pen out of his pocket and took down the number. It was a Swansea number and he dialled it on his mobile. It was answered after only two rings.

'Hello?'

'Who am I speaking to?' Lambert said.

'Do I know you?' demanded the croaky, male voice.

Lambert was in no mood to play games, and said, 'Would this happen to be Mr Harlan, senior, by any chance?'

'Who wants him?'

'I'm Detective Inspector Lambert, Swansea CID. I'd like to know the whereabouts of your son James.'

'I wish I knew. I've been trying to get hold of him myself.'

'Well, his case comes up next week, and if he skips bail, he'll be in serious trouble.'

The voice became sharp and rasping. 'I've just told you, I haven't got a clue where Jimmy is.'

Lambert believed him. 'OK, Mr Harlan,' he said. 'If your son contacts you, get in touch with me at Swansea Central police station immediately. Ask for Inspector Lambert.'

'I'll think about it.'

'I'd do more than think about it, if I were you.'

Lambert cut the call. He then unplugged the answering machine from its socket, wound the flex around it, and carried it out to the hall.

Hughie, looking at the floorboards beneath the rolled-up carpet in the hall near the front door, looked up and shook his head. Others on the SOCO team shuffled about, waiting for further orders now that their job was almost done. Lambert sighed deeply.

'Big fat nothing for your trouble, Hughie?'

Hughie pushed his bottom lip out like a sulky child. 'Carpet's nothing like the fibres we found on Robert Sonning's body. That was real cheap shit, whereas this one's good quality. And there's no stains on or under the carpets anywhere in the house. If Sonning was shot by James Harlan, I can tell you in complete confidence, it didn't happen here. There's no evidence of anything untoward in this house. What about your searches, Harry? Find anything interesting?'

Lambert held up the answering machine. 'There's an interesting message on this machine. And I think there's someone who'll be able to identify the voice, so I think I'll appropriate this. Apart from which, it has now become vital evidence. But it's the only bit of evidence I've come across. No address book or anything with his contacts or the people he knows.'

'Young bloke like him will go for the latest gizmo, which will be grafted on to his hand. They don't use diaries and address books, Harry. Days of the quill pen are over. You want me to take a last look round before we tidy up?'

Lambert rubbed his forehead, trying to rub away his frustration. 'Not much point. The house is neat and smart. The furniture's expensive and quite tasteful, not what you'd expect. But everything's impersonal. Usually when you look round someone's home you see something of their life. But not this one. It's as if the place is a temporary residence.'

Hughie pulled his sleeve up and checked the time. 'It's nearly six. I'll just pop upstairs and have a word with Chris, then I'm going to call it a day.'

As the forensics officer went upstairs, Lambert called out, 'Sorry you've had a wasted journey, Hughie.'

DC Jones came out of the kitchen.

'Anything of interest?' Lambert asked.

'The man did very little cooking. Bin's full of Chinese takeaway and KFC cartons.'

'And nothing in the bin that'll give us a clue to his whereabouts? You know, the discarded book of matches with the name of a nightclub and a phone number scribbled inside.'

Jones laughed. 'If only life were that simple.'

'Yes, if only. Except for Hickson, most of our suspects seem to have vanished. And Harlan's due in court next week, so if he's planning on jumping bail they'll throw the book at him. He must know that.'

'You think someone's protecting him?'

Lambert stared at the wall and Jones could see there was something on his mind, something he was keeping to himself. After a pause, he looked her in the eye and said, 'I think that's a strong possibility. And I've got a hunch who might be sheltering him. The trouble is the chief super wants me to leave this person alone.'

'What on earth for?'

'Drugs, Debbie. They've had this man in their sights for some time now, and they're close to busting him.'

'But surely a murder enquiry—'

Shaking his head, Lambert cut in, 'It's out of our hands, Debbie. We've got SOCA pulling our strings on this.'

Lambert's mobile rang and he took the call hurriedly. 'Tony! What's happening?'

Jones watched her boss as he listened carefully, his eyes lighting up with anticipation, and she knew there had been a sudden development in the case. He looked at his watch.

'You might just make it, Tony. Go for it. And tell boy-racer to go like the clappers. Let me know what happens.'

Lambert ended the call. 'Keep everything crossed, Debbie. Tony and Kevin are hurtling towards Pont Abraham services. Looks like that's where Jason Crabbe is headed, to buy himself a pair of gloves.'

'And presumably Kevin's driving,' Jones said.

Lambert winced, knowing how Tony Ellis hated reckless driving, ever since his parents had been killed in a car crash when he was still quite young. And once Kevin was let loose behind the wheel...

Still, it had to be done.

\*\*\*

They drove around the car park slowly, several times. Having missed the dirty green Volvo the first-time round, they eventually found it parked a long way from the main entrance to the services.

'That's the one.' Wallace said, peering at the number plate. 'Bingo! He's still here.'

'Park in the space next to it and we'll head for the shops and cafes,' Ellis said. 'Just in case he abandons the car and is met by someone.'

'Doubt that very much' Wallace said as he got out of the car and looked into the back of the Volvo. 'His suitcase is still there. Wherever he's headed, he'll need a change of underwear and a toothbrush.'

'But just to be on the safe side, Kevin, we'll head for the main entrance and wait for him outside. And from there we can keep an eye on the Volvo.'

As they neared the main entrance they spotted Jason Crabbe coming out, carrying a Costa coffee bag, and heading straight towards them. They put on a spurt and were perhaps less than three or four metres away from him when he suddenly realized, by the determined way they were striding pointedly in his direction, who they were. Of course, attempting to evade capture was impossible and foolhardy, seeing as he was well and truly caught in a trap. But perhaps it was the instinct of a cornered animal that made Crabbe react. He gave a guttural roar, hurled the Costa bag at the detectives, and took off towards the main entrance.

The bag caught Wallace on the side of the head and he swore loudly. Ellis lunged forward after Crabbe, who hurtled through the main doors, knocking an overweight man aside, who also swore loudly, but instinctively stood to one side to make way for Ellis. Wallace recovered and dashed after them, into the crowded entrance hall. Crabbe lurched through the crowd, knocking people aside. Ellis zigzagged after him, trying to avoid colliding with the service customers, and Wallace followed closely behind. Crabbe barged his way into the Costa coffee shop. Crash! Someone's tray went flying and there was a clang of cutlery hitting the floor and crockery smashing. Angry shouts and people screaming as fear and anger began to grip the services, and cries of confusion and panic as diners and shoppers thought they were in the clutches of something far more dangerous than one man's futile attempt to escape the police.

Crabbe barged his way across the coffee shop, out the other side and into the shop opposite. He sent a woman flying, and her angry husband tried to grab hold of him, but he punched the man's wrist, who cried out in pain. And then Crabbe ran straight into a display of Easter eggs and chocolates which he sent flying. Ellis was close behind him now and lunged, sending him smashing into the cold drinks display, where his head smacked cans of Coke which clattered and dropped to the floor. Several cracked open and jet streams of fizzy drink shot out in 360 degree arcs as the cans spun like Catherine wheels and sticky cola doused startled shoppers who shrieked and yelled with alarm and indignation.

Crabbe fell to the sticky wet floor with Ellis astride him, and Wallace followed up with the handcuffs and squeezed them onto Crabbe's wrists.

They raised him to a standing position and Wallace took out his warrant card as the uniformed security man arrived on the scene.

'Police!' Wallace said. 'It's all in hand. We'll be OK from now on.'

The security man scratched his chin and looked around the shop. 'Yeah, but what about all this mess?'

Wallace chuckled. 'His fault. Not ours.'

Ellis, unnerved by the sea of faces staring at them like an audience watching a drama, said, 'We'll get him out of here. Safely locked up before the crowd decide to string him up for all the trouble he's caused.'

One either side, they dragged Crabbe away, and the people stood back to make way for them, most of them curious and excited, rubber-necking the scene like at most disasters. By now Crabbe was resigned to his capture and walked briskly across the car park, keeping pace with his captors. Ellis bundled him into the back seat of the car and sat next to him. Wallace got behind the wheel and turned the ignition.

Crabbe's head had sunk on to his chest and Ellis stared at him with anger and contempt.

'There was nowhere to bloody go,' he said. 'You're stuck in the services, and you couldn't get to your car. So why didn't you just come quietly? All that aggro. It was unnecessary.'

Crabbe sniffed and said. 'Instinct, weren't it. You was chasing and I was the hunted. I had to give it a go, didn't I?'

Wallace turned around and grinned at Ellis. 'You can't argue with that,' he said.

# Twenty-three

Steve Hickson groaned through the gaffer tape covering his mouth as he came out of his semi-conscious state. His head felt as if it had been split open by the hefty blow he'd received. And before bundling him into the van, half conscious, they had given him a brief but frenzied kicking.

He'd been taken completely by surprise and hadn't stood a chance. The journey, wherever they were taking him, seemed to take forever, and every time the van went over a bump, he felt searing pain in his ribs as his body shifted.

He was short-sighted and his glasses were gone, probably smashed to bits. He blinked several times, trying to focus on what was inside the back of the van, but as night was descending fast, he couldn't see anything, other than the vague shapes of the heads of his three captors in the front seat, outlined by the glow from the setting sun.

His arms were numbed with pain. There was no slack on the rope that bound his hands tightly, cutting off the circulation. As the van turned a corner, his body rolled along the empty interior, and his head encountered metal. A sharp pain cut into his head like a razor and he screamed through the gaffer tape, frightening himself by the intensity of the noise.

Then he heard a chuckle from the front seat. 'Nearly there. Not long to go now.'

The voice was relaxed. Matter of fact. But there was still a chilling menace in the tone, like the calm prior to a gory bomb blast. Steve shivered uncontrollably with burning and freezing fever. His brain was scrambled with remnants of memory as he tried to focus on what had happened at the marina. There were three of them, and he recognized one of them as the scumbag who had burgled his pub that time. But not the other two who had jumped him. Who were they and where were they taking him?

And then an extreme fear gripped his throat, an icy metal hand that choked the life out of him as he thought about revenge. It was an eye-for-an-eye time, and hot tears stung his eyes as he thought about the horror of what might happen to him. How much pain could he stand? And it wasn't as if they wanted anything from him other than his suffering. It was all down to revenge. He had brought this on himself. He had gone all out for revenge and now it was his turn. Payback time. A stupid vicious circle. And what crossed his mind was the phrase *what goes around*. Why had he sought revenge so intensely, both for the scumbag burglar and his niece? Why couldn't he leave well alone? And now the thoughts of the terrible retribution that would be taken was too mind-numbingly horrific to contemplate.

He wanted to say how sorry he was. Be given another chance. He thought about Pat and Kelly, and a sentimental memory of his daughter's baby smell when she was tiny comforted him briefly. There was no smell like it in the world. Pure and unsullied by adult indulgences. And how he longed for a reconciliation with life affirming goodness now it was too late.

Needles of pain shot through his nervous system as the van's wheels hit a pothole. He tried not to scream and clamped his mouth tight, but he could taste blood in his mouth from where he'd been hit. And he could tell by the way the van bounced over stony ground that they were taking him somewhere remote. They were going to torture him, and his brain screamed at the anticipation of the slow pain that lay in store for him.

If only he could wind back the clock. Please, dear God! A second chance.

\*\*\*

As Pat Hickson neared the pub, with her daughter Kelly holding her hand and swinging her plastic party bag with the other, for a moment the landlady felt elated and optimistic – excited even – but then she thought about her husband and her mood clouded over. Once he'd been released he had telephoned to say he was on his way home, and told her there was nothing to worry about, but she still agonized over why he'd been arrested in the first place. No, not arrested, she told herself, just helping the police with their enquiries. But he was still heavily involved in something dreadful, and she wished he'd never had anything to do with that unpleasant Sonning creature, who had been found murdered in the middle of Swansea. But then Steve had been released, so she guessed he was only involved in the murder since Sonning happened to be a friend of his. And with this thought in mind, she entered the pub in a lighter mood, although she dreaded facing the regular customers, whose insatiable craving for gossip echoed her own love of scurrilous events, and she almost felt she deserved being on the receiving end of the steaming gossip.

Trade was good for a Tuesday evening; much better than usual, so maybe word had got around. And this was confirmed by the way they all stared at her as she entered, nodded their greetings but remained silent. But she could tell by their curious, enquiring looks that they were dying to know. Give us the low-down, their expressions urged.

*Chance would be a fine thing.* She gave them all a cursory wave and nods, and looked enquiringly at Phil.

'Where's Steve? He phoned me to say he was on his way back.'

Phil, his eyes darting to the side, checking for nosey customers, leant across the bar and lowered his voice. 'He came back. He said everything was OK, but he had to go out again.'

'What!'

'Just for an hour he said.'

'How long ago was this?'

Phil looked at the pub clock. 'About half an hour ago. If you want to get Kelly ready for bed, I'm happy to stay another thirty minutes, but after that I've got to get back and—'

'Yeah, thanks, Phil,' Pat interrupted him. 'If Steve said he'll be back in an hour...' She shrugged. 'But if he's not, I'll come back down to relieve you. It's much appreciated.'

As she raised the counter flap and went behind the bar with her daughter, Phil smiled at Kelly.

'And how was the party, sweetheart? Was it fun?'

Kelly held up her party bag. 'Look what I got.'

'Cor!' Phil exclaimed. 'Lucky old you.'

As Pat was about to usher Kelly through the door leading upstairs, she stopped to ask the barman, 'Did Steve say where he was going?'

'No. He just said he had to see someone.'

Pat frowned deeply, wondering what was so important that her husband had to dash off so suddenly after having been released from police custody. As she took Kelly upstairs, the frown deepened into a scowl, and her forehead looked as if there were deep scars etched on it. The little girl, sensing all was not well, looked up at her mother and asked her what was wrong. The landlady relaxed her forehead and told her there was nothing to worry about. She took her into the kitchen, sat her at the kitchen table, and sat opposite, while she deliberated on the recent events, and wondered whether to share her news with her daughter. She was undecided for a moment, because she had planned to tell her husband when they were all together as a family. But now she felt angered by Steve's absence, and that, coupled with the realization he was involved in something dirty, decided her.

'Kelly,' she said. 'Mum's got something to tell you.'

But Kelly wasn't listening and was involved with searching the contents of her party bag. 'Oh, cool!' she whooped. 'I've got a Kinder Egg. I wonder what's inside it?'

'Kelly,' her mother said again, 'I've got something to tell you. Some good news.'

But Kelly was still searching the contents of the bag and tugged out a yo-yo, followed by a small plastic dinosaur, which she studied with a frown of concentration as she tried to remember the name of which one it was.

Pat raised her voice, not so much in anger but to convey the urgency of her need to communicate with her daughter. 'Leave that for a minute, Kelly. Please. I want to tell you something. It's important. Come here and give me a cuddle. You can go back to the party bag afterwards.'

'Oh, but, Mum…'

'Please, Kelly! Just for once, do as you're told and come here. Mum's got something important to say.'

Pouting, Kelly reluctantly abandoned the party bag's contents and shuffled over to her mother. Her mother turned her chair away from the table, held out her arms, and sat her daughter on her lap.

'Guess what,' she began.

Kelly stared at her with a serious and attentive expression and shook her head.

'Your Mum's going to have a baby. You're going to have a little baby sister or brother. After all this time – all these years – and now we're going to be a bigger family. What would you like Kelly? A brother or a sister?'

A long silence followed, while Kelly stared at her mother's smiling face. 'I suppose,' she began slowly, 'a brother might be fun.'

Teasingly, her mother said, 'But what if it's another little girl. You won't be jealous, will you?'

'Not as long as she plays with me.'

Pat laughed and squeezed her daughter tightly. 'She'll be too young at first. All she'll do is sleep all day. But you'll be able to look after her.'

'Does Dad know?'

'Not yet. But I can't wait to tell him.'

Perhaps that'll knock some sense into him, she thought.

***

The van rattled and banged over stony ground as the light faded. Electricity pylons disfigured the lonely moors like the skeletons of weird machines, and high on a distant hill a light twinkled in a farmhouse. Kyle shivered, partly from finding himself as an urbanite forced into a ghostly rural setting which was alien to him, but mostly in anticipation of what was about to happen.

Donny carried on driving along the track until they came to a gate, and then drove off the track and on to a grass verge near to one of the pylons. 'This'll do,' he said.

Virgil, a grin on his face, turned to look back at the trussed form of his captive. 'Right, this is the end of the line. This is where you get off.' He chuckled. 'You only got a single ticket for this trip.'

He reached under the seat for Donny's sawn-off shotgun and a torch.

Kyle, who couldn't stop one of his legs moving up and down rapidly, whispered to his father, 'Dad! You sure you want to go through with this?'

'It'll be pitch dark in a minute, Kyle. Let's get on with it.'

Donny put the headlights on full beam and, behind the pylon's grey metal, a dry-stone wall lit up, behind which was a hillock and some trees, shielding them from the distant farmhouse.

'What are you doing?' Kyle hissed to his partner, his leg bouncing even more rapidly. 'The battery'll go flat and we'll be stuck here.'

'Relax, my friend. It's just so we can see what we're up to. I'll switch to parking lights afterwards.'

'But what if someone up at that farm sees the light and decides to investigate?'

Donny put a hand on the bouncing leg to calm him. 'All they'll see from behind that hill is a slight glow. They'll think it's a trick of the light. The crepuscular light.'

'Fuck's sake! You really swallowed a fucking dictionary when you was inside,' Virgil said. 'We gonna do this or not?'

'Yeah,' Donny replied. 'Let's get the show on the road.'

The three of them climbed out of the van, inhaling the sweet smell of damp grass. Virgil coughed and spluttered as if the air was toxic. They slid the van's doors open on the side. Virgil shone his torch inside, and the beam picked out Hickson's terrified eyes, blinking in the glare. He made a muffled appeal for mercy through his gag and Donny couldn't resist doing a ventriloquist impression. 'Gottle of geer! Gottle of geer!'

Laughing, Virgil grabbed a handful of his captive's hair and pulled him towards the van's door. Hickson screamed with pain and his body protested as shards of glass shot through his nervous system. Donny and Virgil grabbed him under the arms and dragged him out of van and he fell to his knees.

'Get the spades,' Virgil instructed his son.

There was a clang of metal as Kyle leant into the van and picked up two spades and Hickson, realizing what they intended to do with him, shook uncontrollably as his muffled screams grew loud and frantic. They tried to force him to stand and walk towards the pylon, but his legs were like jelly and his bladder gave way to a warm trickle running between his legs, which soon turned to a freezing wetness. He sobbed and thought of his wife and daughter. He wanted them to remove the gag, so that he could negotiate, offer them money. Anything to stop this dreadful insanity.

They reached the pylon and he fell to his knees again. The muffled screams echoed in the dip in the valley and Donny worried in case a farm dog heard him and started barking furiously.

'Hurry up!' he told Virgil. 'Get it over with and shut him up.'

But Virgil wanted to prolong Hickson's agony. 'You think I should give you another chance after what you done to me? Then shut up for a minute and listen.'

As if a radio had been switched off, and thinking he might still escape this terrible end, Hickson stopped screaming. His mind was alert now to whatever his captor had to say, now that he might have a chance to survive. Maybe they were just trying to scare the shit out of him.

'You might think I'm over-reacting. But these stripes you give me, I've got 'em for life, see. So, in a way, it's a life sentence. I'm stuck with these scars till the end of my days. Which is why I am sentencing you to death. A life for a life. Understand?'

Hickson's eyes bulged with horror and he had no breath left to scream. As Kyle arrived alongside his father, carrying two spades, Virgil aimed the shotgun at the back of Hickson's head and pulled the trigger. In an instant, the landlord's head became a mess of blood and bone, spattering fragments like a hideous piece of decaying fruit, and the shotgun blast thundered across the valley.

Kyle stared with fascination at the bloody remains of Hickson's head, and then moved aside and vomited. Donny patted Virgil on the shoulder.

'Welcome to the club,' he said.

# Twenty-four

After DC Jones had given the date, time and details of those present in the interview room for the sake of the tape recording, Lambert leaned back and stared at Jason Crabbe, taking his time and letting the long pause unsettle him. Crabbe was a slimmer version of Harlan, thinner-faced, with a long nose, sharp along the ridge like a knife, with a head shaved close, but there were tufts of fluffy hairs growing on the back of his neck indicating the need for a trim.

The duty solicitor, grey and unassuming, sat next to him. His name was also unassuming – Derek Smith, but there was just one bit of sartorial daring attempting to colour his greyness. A pink silk handkerchief was tucked into the breast pocket of his cheap grey suit, barely discernible, but clearly worn as an adornment to send messages that here was a more interesting individual struggling to reveal himself.

Lambert made a show of glancing through a folder to study Crabbe's file, although he already knew most of its contents. 'Well, well, well,' he mused. 'Stealing from garden sheds and flogging gear at boot sales. Pathetic, isn't it? So how come you went from petty theft to murder in one giant leap?'

Lambert saw Crabbe's Adam's-apple bobbing as he swallowed nervously. He knew the man was probably thirsty from fear, his throat parched and his mouth dry.

But Lambert intended to keep him from any refreshments as long as possible, because he could see his suspect was desperately vulnerable and wore his fear like a badge.

'I never killed no one.'

Lambert raised his eyebrows in mock surprise. 'No? We have you on CCTV getting rid of the car on Thursday night, the one with Robert Sonning's body in the boot.'

'Yeah, OK, I drove the car with his body in it, but I didn't have a hand in killing him.'

'Then who did?'

'I don't know.'

'Oh, come on, Mr Crabbe! Are you trying to tell us you got rid of the body for an unidentified person? Why would you do that?'

DC Jones, deliberately playing good cop, leant forward and gave him the trace of a smile. 'I expect,' she began softly, 'you're trying to protect a friend. That's perfectly understandable, and it's something we can all relate to. But do you really want to go to prison for life to protect someone whose friendship is – well, to put it bluntly – I think he's using you.'

Lambert slammed the cardboard folder on to the desk. 'Come on! Let's stop beating about the bush. Why did James Harlan kill Robert Sonning?'

Crabbe shook his head rapidly and his eyes retreated in fear. 'I don't know.'

'But we all know that your mate Harlan did the killing and then got you to get rid of the body in the car. Where did this happen? Where did the murder take place?'

'It wasn't murder. It was self-defence.'

Lambert exchanged a brief look with Jones before continuing. 'So why did Sonning attempt to kill Harlan?'

'We think he was paid by someone?'

'Who?'

'The brother of the girl Jimmy accidentally killed – when he was pissed.'

'So how did he know Sonning was a paid killer out to get him? Was he given advance warning?'

Crabbe's mouth clamped tight, showing a reluctance to elaborate, and Lambert could see the wheels turning in his mind as he considered his options.

'Mr Crabbe, we know Harlan killed Sonning and you got rid of the body, so now all we need is the details. I'll ask you again: how did Harlan know Sonning planned to murder him?'

There was a tense rasp in Crabbe's throat when he spoke. 'He didn't know. Sonning would have taken him by surprise if it hadn't been for me.'

'Go on.'

'I recognized Sonning from Cardiff prison. And I knew what he did for a living. Course, I had no idea he was planning to kill Jimmy. I thought he'd gone round to rough him up. Break his arms. That sort of thing.'

'Why would you have thought that?'

'Well, when I was coming away from Jimmy's I sat down on a wall to send a text to an ex-girlfriend. That's when I spotted Sonning getting out of his Rover.'

'The one you used to get rid of his body?' DC Jones asked.

Crabbe nodded and continued his story. 'Sonning started acting suspiciously. Pretending to look at the cars, but he was behaving all shifty, like. Kept looking around him. Seeing if the coast was clear, just in case there was a customer in the office.'

Lambert raised a hand. 'Just a minute. Where did this take place?'

'All Star Cars. It's a used car dealership.'

'What was Harlan doing there?'

'He worked there. Since the drink-driving charge he had to give up the long-distance lorry driving, so he worked flogging cars.'

'This is for Frank Masina?'

'I think so.'

'What happened after you spotted Sonning behaving suspiciously?'

'I phoned Jimmy to warn him.'

'And after you phoned him what did you do?'

'I hung around for a bit, in case Jimmy needed help. Then I heard loud noises coming from the office, the sound of a fight. Because Sonning hadn't seen me, I thought I could take him by surprise, get him from behind. So, I crept up the steps into the office. The door had been left wide open. That's when I saw Jimmy struggling with Sonning. He was on top of him. Sonning had a gun but Jimmy managed to turn it on him. And then it went off. Jesus Christ! I wasn't expecting anything like that to happen. You've got to believe me.'

With the forensic evidence they'd got so far, Lambert was sure that was how it had happened. And he knew Crabbe, now that he had begun to unload his story, felt relieved and wanted to get it off his chest. Lambert had seen it happen so often; once the interrogators pushed the suspect's right button, then the confession tumbled out like the jackpot on a fruit machine.

'OK. So then what happened?'

Crabbe's eyes became distant as he remembered. 'Jimmy saw me standing in the door. He climbed off Sonning's body and told me to shut the door. After that we panicked for a bit, wondering what to do. We waited until it was getting dark, moved some of the vehicles on the lot to make room for the Rover, then backed it up to the office steps and opened the boot. Once it was dark we heaved Sonning's body down the steps and stuck it in the boot.'

'And did Harlan ask you to get rid of the car or did you offer to do it?'

'He begged me. He was shaking and he was shit-scared. I mean – Jesus Christ! – he hadn't meant to kill anyone. It was self-defence. If he hadn't defended himself, Sonning would've killed him.'

A corner of Lambert's mouth tugged itself into an expression of disdain as he said, 'It might have been better for everyone if he'd succeeded.'

'Inspector, I don't think those sorts of comments are helpful and have nothing to do with your questioning of my client,' the solicitor said.

It was the first time he had spoken, and the detectives realized he was just going through the motions and making his presence felt to justify his attendance. Lambert acknowledged the man with a small acquiescent nod before turning towards DC Jones, giving her an opportunity to ask the next question.

'Mr Crabbe,' she said, 'you mentioned you thought Sonning could have been paid to kill your friend by Alice Mason's brother. How did you know that?'

'Well, I didn't. Not when I saw Sonning on the car forecourt behaving suspiciously. Like I said, I knew what he did for a living, and why he'd been in prison. I thought he was there to put the frighteners on Jimmy and beat him up. I didn't know what for at that stage.'

'When *did* you work out it could have been the girl's brother?'

'After Jimmy calmed down a bit, he went through Sonning's pockets and found his mobile phone. There was quite a few texts on it from a mate of his, and one of them said the bloke's cousin would offer eight K for the job. So, Jimmy guessed it was something to do with Sonning being paid to kill him by this bloke's cousin and he was determined to find out who was out to get him.'

'And how did he go about doing that?' Lambert said.

Crabbe broke eye contact with the detectives and stared at the table as he mumbled, 'He found the bloke's name in Sonning's address book.'

'The one on his mobile?'

Crabbe nodded. 'That was when he decided to ring his number.'

'When was this?'

'The next day. On Friday.'

'Why did he leave it until the following day?'

'He needed to clear up the All Star Cars office. There was blood on the carpet, and he needed to buy some bleach and spend some time clearing it up.'

Lambert stifled a smile. It was laughable the way Harlan thought he could just wipe away traces of the killing. Forensics would find the residues and enough evidence for the prosecution.

'What was this bloke's name?' Lambert said. 'The name Harlan found in the address book.'

'His name was Steve. I've no idea what his surname was.'

'So why did Harlan ring him?'

'I don't know. Maybe he just wanted to find out who was trying to kill him and why.'

'But the attempted murder of your friend had failed. And there was nothing to be gained by going to all the trouble of getting this information, was there?'

Crabbe looked as if he'd painted himself into a corner and he suddenly became unresponsive. He shrugged and stared at the door, as though he was hoping someone would enter the room to break up the interrogation. Lambert leant forward, ducking his head, and made a point of trying to catch Crabbe's eye.

'When he rang this Steve bloke, what happened?'

'I don't know.'

'Oh, come on, Mr Crabbe! He must have told you.'

'After I'd got rid of the car, I told Jimmy I wanted nothing more to do with it.'

'And did he accept that?

Crabbe looked down at the table and nodded.

'I'm sorry, Mr Crabbe – is that a yes?'

'Yes. I had one more meeting with Jimmy – we met in a pub. That's when he told me he'd found out that Sonning's mate was the landlord of a pub called the Earl of Richmond.'

'How did he manage that?'

'He called his mobile number and heard a lot of background noise and guessed it was in a pub. And then he asked him if it was Steve at the Black Swan, and the bloke only went and told him it was Steve in the Earl of Richmond. After that call, Jimmy did a bit more delving and pretty soon he had the full SP.'

'And did he tell you what he planned to do with this information?'

'I ain't gorra clue.'

'And this meeting you had in the pub with Jimmy. When was this?'

There was a slight pause as Crabbe carefully considered his reply, and Lambert saw the way his eyes darted sideways.

'It was on the Saturday. We were watching the rugby in Wetherspoon's.'

'And was that when Jimmy told you he'd found out this Steve was the pub landlord at the Earl of Richmond?'

'That's right.'

'So how did he or you know he was the landlord of the pub? When he phoned this Steve's mobile and heard the pub background chatter, your mate wouldn't have had any inkling he wasn't just a customer in a pub, seeing as it was a mobile he was ringing?'

A shield seemed to drop over Crabbe's eyes and he tugged nervously at a hangnail on his tattooed thumb. 'I don't know. We was involved in the rugby, and I don't s'pose I was really listening to everything Jimmy said.'

'Jimmy got you to get rid of the car. Was there anything else he wanted you to do?'

'Like what?'

'I don't know. You tell me.'

'No, that was it.'

'Are you sure, Mr Crabbe?'

'Yeah, of course I am. I told Jimmy I wanted nothing more to do with it.'

Lambert raised his eyebrows, exaggerating mock surprise. 'Oh, so he *was* planning something else he wanted you to do.'

Crabbe became flustered and looked towards the solicitor for guidance. But Smith avoided eye contact with his client and rubbed hard at the palm of a hand with the thumb of his other hand.

*Wiping away responsibility*, thought Lambert, suppressing a wry smile. Like Lady Macbeth wiping away imaginary blood.

'Mr Crabbe,' he said, 'did James Harlan tell you if he was planning to do something else when he met you at the pub?'

'No, of course not.'

'Then why would he go to all the trouble of finding out who this Steve bloke was?'

'Maybe he was just curious. I don't know. You'll have to ask Jimmy himself.'

Lambert snorted. 'Except he's done a disappearing act. Where did he go?'

Crabbe pushed his lower lip up and shrugged.

'I asked you a question, Mr Crabbe. Where has your friend James Harlan gone?'

Suddenly the solicitor came to life and intervened. 'Perhaps the first time my client thought it was a rhetorical question, Inspector.'

Lambert glared at him. 'I assure you it wasn't.' He focused back on Crabbe. 'Where has James Harlan gone?'

'I haven't a clue. I tried to ring him but couldn't get hold of him.'

'Was this on his mobile or at home on his landline?'

Crabbe paused, wondering how convincing his lie would be. 'At home on his landline.'

'Now that is interesting. We searched his premises and there were only four calls on his answer machine, and yours wasn't one of them. So why are you lying about it? I'll ask you again: when did you last speak to Harlan?'

'I told you. It was on Saturday, during the rugby. I tried to ring him on Monday...'

He saw Lambert was about to interrupt and added hurriedly. 'Sorry, I made a mistake about the landline... got confused... it was on his mobile. Yes, now I remember. I tried calling him on his mobile but I got a single tone. You know, like a discontinued one.'

'And you've no idea where he went?'

Crabbe placed a hand on his heart and looked Lambert in the eye. 'I swear on my mother's life, I haven't a clue where Jimmy is.'

Lambert stared back at Crabbe, wondering if he was capable of a decent performance. His deception so far had been abysmal. Lambert knew he had told the truth about the killing, but when it came to the story about Harlan seeking further help, his lying skills had plummeted like a burning fighter plane.

Lambert was about to go back and question him about doing Harlan further favours after he'd got rid of the body, when the door to the interview room opened, and a uniformed constable came in and handed him a piece of paper. After Lambert read the paper, he rose and suspended the interview.

Crabbe looked up at him expectantly and Lambert smiled. 'Don't worry, Mr Crabbe. At least now you can have a bite to eat, seeing as how you've wasted your grub by chucking it at my arresting officer. As you're under arrest for accessory to a murder, you'll be remanded in custody until your trial. And we'll know where to find you when we need to ask you further questions.'

# Twenty-five

As Tony Ellis and Kevin Wallace marched up the front path of the Mason's house, it was already quite dark, the temperature had dropped considerably, and in their light suits they both felt the cold, especially as they were so tired now, and in the car Wallace's stomach had complained loudly about lack of food.

'Never mind,' Ellis consoled his colleague. 'This is the last task before home time.'

'But not one I'm looking forward to.' Wallace held up Harlan's telephone answering machine as he thought about Mason's parents' reaction to the death threat. 'And it seems pretty obvious the threatening phone call came from Mark Mason.'

'Yes, but we both know,' Ellis said as he pressed the doorbell and took out his warrant card, 'we have to have confirmation. It's no use guessing, Kevin.'

'I know. I know.' Irritated at Tony Ellis pointing out the obvious, Wallace wished he hadn't complained.

As soon as Sheila Mason opened the door, the stoic expression she adopted for visitors fell apart and her vulnerability showed in her quivering lips and shallow intake of breath.

Ellis introduced them both and asked if they might come in and have a brief word. Shaking now, wondering what terrible news they had to impart, and saying nothing, she stood aside by way of invitation and directed them to the living room. Her husband, strain showing in his cadaverous face, rose from an easy chair as they entered. The flesh seemed to be shrinking away bit-by-bit from his high cheekbones.

'What seems to be the trouble now?' he croaked. 'Is this about Mark? I hope everything is all right?'

'We'd like you to help us with our enquiries,' Ellis said.

## CHAPTER TWENTY-FIVE

Sheila Mason gestured to the sofa. 'Would you like to take a seat?'

Ellis could see in the strained politeness that going through the ritual of routine courtesies was proving difficult for her. It looked as if she might go to pieces if he didn't get to the point very soon.

'We've got a telephone conversation – a message on an answering machine – that we'd like you to listen to and see if you can identify the voice.'

Sheila Mason put a hand to her mouth. 'Oh, God! It's not Alice, is it? I don't think I could bear...'

'No,' Ellis replied quickly, 'it's a male voice.' He indicated the telephone in Wallace's hand. 'If we could just plug it in somewhere.'

'There's not a phone point in here,' Daniel Mason pointed out.

'That won't be necessary. Just a normal socket will do. We don't need to use the phone, just play the message.'

Mason pointed to a spare socket close to the sofa. Wallace bent down, plugged in the telephone, and clicked through the first two messages until he came to the third. He clicked play and remained in a stooped position while it played, carefully watching the Masons' reaction, as did Ellis.

As they all listened to the cool hostility in the voice, the parents showed no signs of recognition. But when the telephone message reached the final statement about killing Harlan without warning and when he least expected it, Mason crumpled into his easy chair and buried his head in his hands. His wife stood by the fireplace, gripping the mantelpiece tightly for support.

'Well?' Ellis said. 'Was the voice familiar to you?'

Sheila Mason nodded tearfully. 'It sounded like Mark. But I don't understand. Whose phone did he leave that message on?'

'James Harlan. The man who killed his sister.'

'You mean, he... Mark wouldn't do anything like that... I know he wouldn't. Perhaps he got carried away when he made that threat. People say things without meaning...'

Unable to finish speaking, her eyes flooded with tears. Ellis nodded to Wallace who unplugged the phone from the socket. He turned to look at Sheila Mason, who took a dainty handkerchief from her sleeve and wiped her nose and eyes.

'I'm sorry we had to play you the recording,' Ellis said. 'Only none of us have ever heard your son speaking and we couldn't be sure it was him. If it's any consolation, we don't think he's carried out his threat.'

Sheila Mason composed herself, nodded and asked, 'Have you any idea when the phone call was made?'

'He called Sunday evening, around five o'clock.'

Sheila Mason went and stood close to her husband's chair and squeezed his shoulder. 'Thank God, Daniel. He must have been at Heathrow airport when he made that call. He was probably brooding in the departure lounge and it got the better of him. I expect his work will keep him busy in France and take his mind off this senseless revenge.'

As Wallace stood up and wound the flex around the answer phone, he caught Ellis's eye and wondered if he was going to say anything. He could see the sergeant frowning thoughtfully, tossing up between keeping quiet about their son's deception and disappearance and telling them what happened in case they might be able to shed some light on where he might be.

'Mrs Mason,' Ellis began slowly, 'how did you know your son was going to France?'

'He telephoned us on Sunday afternoon. Why?'

As if he'd just remembered something he'd been meaning to ask earlier, Ellis said, 'Oh, I meant to ask you: what sort of car does your son drive?'

'He has a Saab. A silver one. It's a company car. But you didn't answer my question about Mark telephoning us on Sunday afternoon.'

'I'm sorry, Mrs Mason, we had a word with your son's fiancée and it doesn't look as if he's gone to France.'

'You spoke to Julia? But why would she...'

'You need a passport to fly to France. And his fiancée discovered he hadn't taken it.'

Mrs Mason clutched the cross she wore, her hands opening and closing around it. 'Well, perhaps there's some sort of explanation. Perhaps he just forgot it, and when he got to the airport...'

'We also spoke to his boss at his workplace. Apparently, your son telephoned him on Sunday afternoon and asked him for a week's leave of absence. He had no intention of flying to France for work or otherwise.'

A sudden moan from Mason, and DS Ellis thought he might be about to have a heart attack.

'Are you all right, sir?'

He looked up at Ellis, angered by the question, and a thin stream of spittle appeared on his bottom lip as he spoke. 'Of course I'm not all right. Stupid question really. My son tells lies, goes missing and threatens to kill someone, and you ask a stupid bloody question like that.'

An uncomfortable silence followed his outburst, which his wife broke with a feeble admonishment a moment later.

'Daniel!'

'I-I'm sorry,' he stammered. 'I didn't mean to… it's just the worry. That phone call Mark made – it's upsetting.'

'I know he wouldn't do anything bad,' his wife said. 'That's not the way he's been brought up.' She let her pleading look travel back and forth between the two detectives, begging for reassurance and a comforting word of agreement. 'Mark has always been considerate and kind. I'm sure you'll find out he's just depressed and is still finding it hard to face up to the world. His sister's death has affected him terribly. It has all of us. But all we want now is for that man to be sentenced so we can get some peace, even though it'll never bring Alice back.'

Ellis cleared his throat softly before he spoke. 'Have you any idea where your son might be at this moment? Any close friends he might be staying with?'

'Mark had a group of close-knit friends in Swansea, but you know what it's like when people commit to a relationship and go their separate ways. His best friend, Owen Jefferies, moved to Aberdeen. They keep in touch, but Owen's married now, and Mark will soon be married himself. I doubt Mark would have gone to Owen's in Aberdeen.'

'And is there any likelihood he might have sought out his uncle, Steven Hickson?'

Scars of worry were etched into her forehead as she thought about this possibility, and then she shook them away. 'I doubt it. I can't see Mark going to Steven's pub. He's only ever been there once and I don't think he considered it – well – the sort of place he wanted to frequent regularly.'

Ellis, knowing they'd had Hickson in custody from late evening yesterday, until late afternoon today, also thought this was unlikely, and nodded thoughtfully. 'And you don't think there's anyone else he might be staying with?'

'Well, I suppose he could have gone to stay with any of his old friends, but it's doubtful. I'm not just saying this, but we're a very close family. We always have been. If Mark came back to Swansea, why wouldn't he have come home?'

'I can't answer that, I'm afraid.'

'I can't understand why Julia didn't say anything about the trip to France. I told her about the visit from your Inspector Lambert, but she said nothing about Mark's disappearance and not taking his passport.'

'Perhaps she didn't want to upset you.'

'This is very worrying. I can't think where Mark might have gone. Julia must be beside herself with worry, especially as he's lied to her. That's not like Mark. They had a good relationship. And he had everything planned for their future together and had saved enough for a deposit…'

'Not any more he doesn't,' Mason cried. 'Not anymore.'

Mrs Mason's head swivelled towards the tortured voice of her husband and there was a sudden coldness in her tone. 'What are you saying, Daniel?'

He waved a hand in the detective's direction. 'Ask them. They sent a policewoman round to see me at work to ask about his finances. Mark withdrew £8,000 of his savings.'

'What? Why would he do that? It doesn't make sense.'

'How the hell would I know?'

'Why on earth didn't you tell me?'

'Because this only happened yesterday.'

'But you didn't think to tell me when you came home.'

'I didn't want to worry you. I was confused. I couldn't think why Mark needed so much money in cash.'

'Cash!'

Mason sank deeper into his chair, as if he wanted to vanish into the fabric. 'Oh, God! I just wish I knew what was going on. Why on earth would Mark take out the money he was saving for their marriage, their deposit, to spend on what? It doesn't make any sense.' His final sentence faded out and his face became a mask of despair.

His wife turned to Ellis. 'Have you any idea why Mark would withdraw so much cash?'

The moment he'd been dreading. Ellis had considered the possibility they might confront him with the question, but up until now he had put it safely to the back of his mind. Now it was crunch time.

'We think he may have used the money to pay someone to kill James Harlan.'

Sheila Mason's face turned to stone, and at first she seemed unable to comprehend what Ellis had told her; but suddenly, from deep inside her came a painful sound, growing in intensity, until she moaned loudly like a wounded animal, and clutched her mouth and stomach before running from the room to be sick in the downstairs toilet.

***

Julia Redfern sat and waited in one of the interview rooms, her beige handbag open on the table, while she rummaged its contents, searching for nothing in particular. She tugged out a lipstick and examined it closely, but in her head a voice reminded her that her fiancé was missing, and she returned the lipstick to the depths of the bag and fiddled with a hairbrush instead; but as another voice protested that Mark was missing because he chose to go missing, she let go of the hairbrush, and pulled out a small golfer's diary, flicking the pages randomly, while yet another voice – this time ominous and threatening – told her again what she dreaded hearing: that Mark had lied to her. As she let go of the diary, her frustration building, she snapped the handbag shut and looked round at the ghastly, characterless room, depressing in its blandness, and she wondered why she had come here.

She had spoken to Mark's mother who told her of the visit from the police, and also told her about the phone call from the local vicar about the police visit to his church. At first, she felt uneasy, which soon gave way to a distressing and deep foreboding as her brain attempted to cope with her suspicions that Mark was involved in something terrible. Just how terrible she didn't know, but her imagination ran away with itself and she pictured all kinds of dreadful scenarios, each one worse than the last, and she kept telling herself that she was being foolish; but nagging away at the back of her mind was Mark's relationship with his sister, a relationship which was fast reaching sinister proportions.

The door opened and Lambert entered, followed by DC Jones.

'Miss Redfern?' he said. 'I'm Detective Inspector Lambert and this is Detective Constable Jones. You asked to see me.'

They both sat at the table opposite her and Lambert gave her a tentative smile, designed to put her at ease. He could see, by the tension in her shoulders, and the way her lips were clamped tightly together, how worried she was. But even her anxiety and lack of sleep had done nothing to spoil her beauty. She had jet black, shoulder-length hair, a natural tanned complexion that suggested she spent a great deal of time outdoors, and an almost perfectly sculpted face with high cheekbones, tapering attractively into a delicate rounded chin and a slender neck. She was dressed in black jeans, a blue crewneck sweatshirt and an ancient waxed weatherproof coat, as though she had dressed hurriedly without giving much thought to what she would wear.

Lambert, who had taken in at a glance her perfectly proportioned figure, looked into her dark brown eyes as he asked his first question. 'Why did you ask to see me?'

'Because Mark's mother told me you'd been to ask them about Mark.'

'And did she tell you why we called about him?'

'She said something about you collecting evidence about Alice's death for the Crown Prosecution Service. But I don't believe that.'

Genuinely surprised, Lambert said, 'Oh? And why is that?'

Julia Redfern, her jaw clenched tight, leant forward and said through gritted teeth, 'Please don't treat me like an idiot. Why on earth would a Detective Inspector collect minor details of drink-driving case when the man responsible is clearly guilty? And you also questioned the family vicar about Mark, because he telephoned Sheila Mason afterwards to ask her if everything was all right. What did you want to see Reverend Eastman about?'

Lambert hesitated. He suspected Mark Mason's fiancée was an intelligent woman, and he didn't know just how much the vicar had told Sheila Mason about her son seeking retribution for his sister's death. He weighed it up carefully and decided the vicar would have avoided any mention of Mason's thirst for vengeance, and probably telephoned to comfort the mother.

After a brief hiatus, during which Julia Redfern's eyes locked on to his with a piercing intensity, he decided to give her part of the truth, omitting to mention the recruitment of Sonning as a hitman. Even as the word 'hitman' flashed through his head, he realized how absurd it would sound to a young woman planning a wedding in a quiet suburb of Swansea.

'We think your fiancé wants to kill James Harlan.' For a moment, he wondered if she had comprehended what he had told her, because her face was expressionless; but she nodded slowly, almost as if it was confirmation of information she already knew or suspected. 'But, if it'll put your mind at ease, we don't think he's managed to track down James Harlan yet, who seems to have disappeared.'

'How do you know that? If they've both disappeared, it could be too late. Mark might already have…' She broke off, her hands clutched tightly on the tabletop.

'I'll be brutally honest with you,' Lambert said. 'Your boyfriend left a message on Harlan's answering machine threatening to kill him, and we think Harlan disappeared shortly afterwards. He was probably scared, which is why he ran off.'

'But a man like this Harlan – I saw him on television when he came out of court – he looks a typical thug. Why would a man like that be scared of Mark?'

Lambert could have told her about Sonning but felt it would worry her unnecessarily to know that the man in the boot of the car was a criminal her fiancé had hired to kill Harlan.

'Man like Harlan's a coward, and his tough guy image is an act; deep down he's a coward. He's not going to hang around to see if your fiancé means business. But that's why we need to apprehend one of them as soon as possible, to prevent any further tragedies.'

Julia Redfern narrowed her eyes as she regarded him shrewdly. 'Which other tragedies are you talking about?'

Lambert was prepared for this question. 'The drink-driving death of his sister.'

DC Jones decided to intervene and addressed Julia Redfern in a soft tone. 'Why do you think Mark Mason has taken this so badly and wants to take his revenge on this Harlan.'

Redfern flashed the DC a look which suggested she was asking something which was painfully obvious, and then shook her head as if it didn't merit a reply.

'You might want someone dead,' Jones persisted. 'That's only natural. But to actually go ahead with plans to kill someone rather than letting the law do its job seems a bit extreme.'

'The law,' Julia Redfern said with lip-curling contempt. 'He'll probably be paroled in three years or less, so where's the justice in that?'

'All the same, there have been many instances of people losing loved ones by perpetrators, and yet not many take this draconian measure. And by all accounts, Mark Mason wasn't like that, having been brought up as a churchgoer. So why the drastic change?'

Julia Redfern's eyes suddenly glistened with bitter tears and she spoke with suppressed anger. 'Why do you think? There was always something lurking in the back of my mind concerning Mark's relationship with his sister. It seemed extreme and went beyond… I mean, it was always Alice this and Alice that. And when she was killed, he went to pieces. So much so, that I suspected his feelings for her were unnatural.'

There followed a deathly and uncomfortable silence, and each of them became aware of muffled voices coming from the corridor outside, voices they hadn't noticed up until now. Lambert, his expression deadpan, stared at Mason's fiancée and waited for her to continue.

She smoothed a hand over her handbag, wiping away an imaginary blemish before making eye contact, first with DC Jones and then Lambert. Her voice was husky when she eventually spoke. 'I'm not saying anything ever went on between them. I think it was a suppressed desire. They probably didn't even know it themselves.'

'But it would explain your fiancé's lust for revenge.' Lambert looked at his watch and sighed. 'If you've no idea where he might be, I suggest we get on and continue our investigations.' Lambert moved his chair back and stood up. 'I'll contact you and let you know of any progress we make. Where can I contact you?'

'I'll probably stay with Mark's parents'

'A good idea,' Lambert said, going to the door and holding it open for her, making it clear the meeting had ended. 'I'll contact you there as soon as I have some news.'

\*\*\*

'I'm glad that's over with,' Ellis said as they sped away from the Masons' house. 'If their son really does intend killing Harlan, his parents will be collateral damage.'

Wallace swerved to avoid a pothole.

'Careful!' Ellis warned, his stomach lurching.

'Bloody council!' Wallace complained. 'Where d'you reckon this Harlan creep's gone? He can't drive, for a start. If he's done a runner any great distance, he'll have to use public transport.'

'I wouldn't bet on it. A ban from driving's not going to deter a shit like him.'

'Yeah, but after the accident, I think he sold his BMW for scrap. He's got no wheels.'

Ellis's mobile rang and the display indicated it was Lambert. He clicked the green button and Wallace heard him saying, 'Hi, Harry. Yes, they identified the voice as their son's. What?' A pause, and then Ellis said, 'All Star Cars. I don't know it. Have you got a postcode and I'll feed it into the satnav?' Out of the corner of his eye, Wallace saw the sergeant scrambling for pen and paper to write down the postcode. Wallace gripped the steering wheel tightly, and inwardly cursed their luck. He could tell by the way Ellis was being given instructions that they were far from finished for the night, and he also saw his dreams of an ice-cold lager vanishing faster than their current suspects.

'OK, Harry, leave it to me,' Ellis said. 'I'll organize forensics and we'll see you there.' He cut the call and turned to speak to Wallace. 'Jason Crabbe's confessed. Sonning's murder took place in the office of a second-hand car dealership. And Harry thinks that's where Harlan might get another set of wheels from.'

'So now we head for All Star Cars,' Wallace sighed. 'I happen to know where it is. I pass it on my way home.'

'Right. Well, we need to get there right away. On the other hand.' Ellis pointed with his pen to a public house at the corner of a street, which indicated there was a car park at the back. 'Park at the back of that boozer, Kevin. We may as well organize forensics with a pint in our hands.'

'Sensible move,' Wallace said with a grin.

\*\*\*

As soon as Lambert and Jones arrived back at the incident room at Cockett police station, Lambert saw Mick Beech's head swivel round while he was speaking on the telephone, and heard him say, 'Here he is now. I'll just transfer you to the other line.'

Beech pointed to Lambert's desk and transferred the call, which immediately began flashing on Lambert's telephone.

'Who is it?' Lambert asked.

'Mrs Hickson, the pub landlady.' Beech smirked. 'She wants to know what we've done with her husband.'

Jones watched her boss as he sat on the edge of the desk and picked up the telephone, frowning deeply as he listened to what Pat Hickson had to say, his face a study in concentration. She saw him tap out an impatient rhythm on the desk with a knuckle, and then he almost barked into the phone:

'We let your husband go at half-four this afternoon, Mrs Hickson, and it's now eight-thirty. If he said he was going to see someone, then I expect that's what he's done. It's too early to class him as missing. And to be perfectly honest, your husband is more than economical with the truth. If he doesn't turn up by, say, eleven tonight, then I suggest you might give us another ring and we'll see what we can do first thing tomorrow morning.' As he listened to his caller's protests, Lambert rolled his eyes. 'Well, I expect his mobile is switched off. Look, I'm sorry, Mrs Hickson, but I have something urgent to attend to. And I really can't do anything until your husband has been gone for some time and we're sure he's missing. If we hear anything, don't worry, you'll be the first to know. Bye for now.'

Lambert slammed the phone down, stared at Debbie Jones, then banged his forehead with a hand. 'Christ! I should have known all along where Mark Mason is.'

She threw him a quizzical look while she waited for him to elaborate. Instead, he leapt up and said, 'Don't take your coat off, Debbie. We're going to see if we can apprehend the reluctant bridegroom. Debbie will phone you with our actions on the way there, Mick. But we need to move on this. Oh and, Mick: ring the Harbour Master's office at Burry Port and tell them we'd like to access the marina. Tell them it's urgent.'

# Twenty-six

The light was fading rapidly as they sped towards Llanelli, and by the time they reached Burry Port it was dark. Lambert barely reduced his speed as he drove along the deserted street leading to the small town and they hit a speed bump. They both shot up in the air as car protested noisily and Jones's stomach lurched.

'Ouch!'

'Sorry,' Lambert said with a laugh. 'Didn't see it in this light.'

'Or at this speed,' she said.

They crossed the small roundabout, turned into the road leading to the harbour, and Lambert's headlights picked out the lifeboat house, which loomed towards them as he hurtled towards the car park. There were seven or eight cars parked neatly in a row, with several gaps between some of them. Lambert turned at speed into a space close to a Mitsubishi four-by-four, braked sharply close to the wall at the edge of the harbour, and Jones's stomach heaved again. She blew out her breath noisily, and with relief as Lambert killed the engine.

'I think I spotted Hickson's Renault just the other side of the four-by-four,' Lambert said. 'We'll see if one of the other cars is a Saab. You got the registration number?'

As she opened the car door, Jones held up her notebook and said, 'Got it here. But wouldn't it be quicker to see if there's a light in the boat's cabin? If that's where Mason's hiding out, and his uncle is with him, they won't be sitting in the dark.'

'True. But as we've got to walk across the car park, we may as well check to see if Mason's Saab is here. Then we'll know for sure they're on the boat. And if they refuse to open the door – or would you call it a hatch? – we'll break it in.'

'Unwarranted intrusion?'

'Hardly, Debbie. We've got enough evidence now to arrest Mason, along with his uncle, for conspiring to murder Harlan. Let's go.'

As he slipped out of the car, Lambert looked out over the marina, which seemed unnaturally still, apart from the watery sounds of the sea gently lapping the sides of the boats. Less than a quarter of a mile away, the town seemed quiet and abandoned, no traffic sounds, just a faint aggravated yapping of a small dog. The night had a frosty clearness about it, with a salty tang in the air; but the clean, tranquil atmosphere was leant a touch of eeriness from the ghostly masts of some of the taller yachts casting long shadows along the harbour walls, and the sodium street lamps which glowed with little warmth in their light.

Debbie Jones shivered and turned the collar of her coat up as she and Lambert walked away from the car, Lambert half-turning and clicking the automatic locking device, which sounded intrusive in the unruffled mood of the night.

'Well, it's definitely Hickson's Renault,' Jones said, pointing out the dark shadow of a vehicle the other side of the four-by-four. She screwed her eyes up as she read the number plate. 'Yes, definitely Hickson's.'

As they neared the car, Lambert's foot met something which scrunched beneath his sole. He looked down and saw a strip of something black, and a slight glint reflected by a piece of glass. He bent down and stared closely at the object. A pair of glasses, mangled and broken beyond repair.

'What have you found, Harry?'

He carefully took hold of a corner of the glasses, straightened up and held them out. Jones squinted in the darkness as she stared at them. 'Looks like a pair of glasses.'

'Black frames,' Lambert said. 'And who do we know wears glasses with black frames?'

'What the hell's been happening here?'

A scrunch of footsteps on tarmac, and a voice, subdued and hesitant, said, 'Inspector Lambert, is it?'

Jones started with a shallow intake of breath. 'You made me jump,' she said.

It was the young, bearded man who had let them on to the marina the previous Sunday when they had first spoken to Steven Hickson.

'Sorry about that,' he said. 'I got your phone call and I came down here right away. They said it was important.'

'Thank you,' Lambert said. 'You're Tom, is that right? Thanks for coming out tonight. We need to get to the *Esmeralda*.' He turned to Jones and offered her the broken glasses. 'Careful, Debbie, just hold them by the end like I did. Here are my car keys. You'll find some brown paper bags in the glove compartment, go back and stick these glasses in one of them. I don't think we'll bother to look for Mason's Saab.'

'There's a Saab parked right at the end there,' Tom said. 'This is all very—'

'Exciting?' Lambert offered. 'The excitement might be just about to kick off.'

As Jones turned away, holding the glasses delicately, she said, 'I'll put these in the car. But please take your time getting down onto the marina. I don't want to miss the fun.'

Lambert chuckled, although there was a nervous tremor in it. 'OK. We'll walk slowly. You can catch me up.'

'There's a brick next to the gate,' Tom called after her. 'I'll leave the gate propped open with it.'

Lambert watched as she hurried back to his car, which was parked about 150 yards away, and then turned and followed Tom towards the gate and walkway. He peered into the blackness until his eyes focused on the last boat moored along the far pontoon, and he could have sworn there was a faint glow coming from the cabin's porthole. He glanced back towards his car and saw Debbie's silhouette outlined against the vehicle as the lights flicked on when she unlocked the door.

Tom Bradley unlocked the gate and Lambert led the way down onto the pontoon. As soon as he stood there looking at the long stretch leading to the end where it branched off to the left leading to Hickson's boat, he took a deep breath and prepared himself for a possible confrontation with Mark Mason. Aware that Tom had every intention of accompanying him to the *Esmeralda,* Lambert took a moment to think about the consequences. He was reluctant to involve the young man, mainly because he had no idea what lay ahead. Anything could happen. Mason's hunger for revenge seemed grossly inflated, as if the man had gone completely berserk, unleashing a violent streak that had been suppressed by his spiritual upbringing, and he might react unpredictably. And there was a distinct possibility he could be armed. How else did he intend to kill a thug like Harlan?

Lambert took Tom's arm and spoke quietly. 'I don't think you'd better accompany me any further.'

Although it was dark, and he couldn't observe the expression on the young man's face, he recognized the monotone of disappointment when he spoke.

'I don't mind coming along if you need some support.'

'I think it's better if you don't, Tom.'

## CHAPTER TWENTY-SIX

'Why? What's going on?' There was a nervous quiver in his voice now.

'Just taking precautions. Probably nothing to worry about. But it's better if you stay here and wait for DC Jones.'

He saw the young man nod and heard him swallow.

'Thanks,' Lambert said, and set off stealthily along the pontoon. He was about halfway along to the end where it branched off to the left when suddenly the air thundered and was split in two, like a parting of the Red Sea. In a fractured second he thought his eardrums would burst as a massive crack tore the air to shreds, and the area shook as the pressure burst outwards from the blast like a mighty wave, and he was thrown backwards on to the pontoon, one of his elbows banging and scraping painfully on the planks as an arm was sucked into the cold sea water, and he had to clutch the side of the pontoon to stop himself being sucked into a gap between the pontoon and a small craft. With a great effort, he pulled himself sideways and instinctively rolled on to his stomach to shield himself from any debris from the bomb blast and put his hands over his head to protect himself.

As she was shutting the glove compartment of the Mercedes, the enormous blast caused DC Jones to jump and she banged her head on the roof of the car. From the corner of her eye she saw the flash of the explosion and, rubbing her head, turned in time to see the deadly blast creating a dark pall with a bright flare at its core. The air crackled and fizzed, and she heard metal tearing and wood splintering. It took her a moment to register what had happened and recover from the shock of the blast, and then she ran as fast as she could towards the walkway leading down on to the pontoon, to see if Lambert had suffered any injuries. As she ran on to the pontoon, she saw Bradley huddled in a protective heap, and heard him exclaim, 'Jesus Christ!'

'Harry!' she yelled as she stumbled along the pontoon. 'Are you OK?'

He groaned. 'I think I'll survive, Debbie. Call the emergency services; we need the fire brigade here quickly to put out the blaze.'

She helped Lambert to his feet and then took out her mobile and dialled 999. As she made the call Lambert looked towards the *Esmeralda* as it burned, the fire throwing ripples of light across the water, the acrid smoke and smell of burning oil drifting across the marina towards Lambert, making his eyes water.

He heard voices, shouting, people running from the opposite side of the harbour along the edge of the marina now, coming towards the disaster. Lambert took out his warrant card, ran back to the walkway and shouted to Tom, 'Help me stop them coming into this area. We've got to keep them out. This part of the marina's now a crime scene, and the less people that contaminate it, the better.'

As soon as Lambert reached the car park, accompanied by Tom, he raced towards the crowd who had spilled out of the yacht club and were approaching the car park not far from the burning vessel. Lambert waved his warrant card in front of him.

'Police!' he yelled as he ran towards them. 'Keep away from here. In case there's another bomb about to go off.'

He saw a young woman tugging her boyfriend's arm, pulling him backwards. 'Terry!' she shouted. 'It's a bomb. Come away. Let's go back to the yacht club. We can see everything from there.'

\*\*\*

Little more than an hour later the marina resembled a scene from a science-fiction film as fireman fought the blazing *Esmeralda*, and police cars, lights flashing in the dark, bordered the edge of the marina like a squad of alien machines. The entire area had been taped off, and a large forensics team had arrived, with arc lamps set up to give them light in which to carry out their search, and the SOCO officers shuffled about in their white coveralls, heads and shoulders hunched, torch beams rising and falling as they searched the ground all around and along the marina, and their forms resembled strange creatures from another planet as they meticulously sifted through discarded pieces of litter or an imprint on the ground for clues. The crackling sound of fire, the steady hiss of water from the firemen's hoses as they doused the burning boat, and the stench of charred wood and burning paint gave the scene a strange feeling of familiarity, as if time had slowed down or been suspended and was being experienced again and again.

Lambert, who had found Hickson's smashed glasses, fetched them from his car and gave them to the forensics officer in charge, explaining that he thought they probably belonged to Steven Hickson. And when they searched the area near the lifeboat house, they found a Sainsbury's carrier bag which looked as if it had blown across the car park and lodged itself between the building and a water pipe. Nearby they found what looked like the scattered contents of the bag: a chicken sandwich, two cans of Budweiser, a packet of Kettle crisps and a plastic container of assorted melon and grapes. Inside the carrier bag was a supermarket receipt, showing the items had been paid for in cash and had been purchased at 5.36 p.m. that day.

Lambert and Jones surveyed everything going on around them and watched the SOCO team going about the investigation like an army of white ants moving in slow motion, and for a moment they both seemed momentarily lost. Lambert, feeling tired and drained, rubbed forcefully at his eyes with a thumb and forefinger, and then blinked several times, his eyes watering from the smoke which drifted over from the boat.

'What do you make of the glasses we found?' DC Jones said.

Lambert pursed his lips and shook his head. 'Looks like someone got to him.'

'You don't think he was on the boat then?'

'I think Mark Mason was, and I think his uncle was taking food for him. But he was waylaid by someone before he got there. Before the blast, I could swear there was a light on in the cabin. Yes, I think it was probably Mark Mason who was on the boat.'

'If that's the case, Mr and Mrs Mason will have lost their son soon after losing a daughter,' Jones said, shivering at the thought of informing the parents.

'That's what happens when you take the law into your own hands,' Lambert said with a shrug, more despairing than offhand. 'Revenge is ongoing. Where does it end?'

'You think it might have been James Harlan? Getting to Hickson and his nephew before they got to him?'

'Well, I think Harlan is scared. But for someone like him to do something like this...'

Lambert waved a hand in the direction of the boat. 'It would require someone who knows something about explosives.'

'Like an army demolition expert? An ex-SAS man, maybe?'

Lambert nodded. 'Exactly. To pull a stunt like this requires a certain amount of expertise.'

'It certainly looks like the work of someone like Frank Masina.'

Lambert threw her an enquiring expression, wondering how she knew about Masina. She returned his look with a knowing smile and tapped the side of her nose.

'I'm a detective. Remember?'

He returned the smile. 'And a good one, Debbie.'

'The question is,' she said, 'why on earth would Masina do something like this? What possible motive would he have for killing Mason? He probably doesn't know him. Or his uncle.'

'I've no idea. But Harlan's an employee of his, and the spooks from MI7 have him in their sights.'

Jones gave her boss a grim smile. 'Well, let's hope the Serious Organized Crime Agency,' she said with emphasis, demonstrating an unwillingness to give them a nickname, 'can get their claws into him soon.'

The young man from the Harbour Master's office came over, his expression a mixture of concern and exhilaration. 'You wanted a word, Inspector.'

'Yes. It's about the harbour CCTV.'

'No problem with that. It covers the entire marina from different angles. We have to guarantee security for the boats.'

'Of course. But what about the car park?'

Tom Bradley shook his head. 'We don't have the car park covered.' He saw Lambert pull his lips tight into a disgruntled and disappointed expression, and added, 'But the lifeboat house have CCTV now which covers the car park. Ever since they had lead nicked off their roof.'

Lambert's face relaxed into a smile. 'Ah, that's more like it. We'll need to look at that.'

Bradley coughed lightly as a preamble to what he was about to ask. 'Have you any idea why anyone would want to blow up Steve's boat, Inspector?'

'None at all. But it might have been an accident.'

'Accident?'

'Yes, you know. Some sort of Calor gas explosion or something.'

'Seems a bit of a coincidence, though. You arriving here urgently and then the explosion. You must have known something was up. And what about Steve?' Bradley looked over towards the smouldering wreck. 'Was he on board?'

Lambert stared into the young man's eyes and told him honestly, 'We don't know. But we don't think so.' He patted Bradley's arm. 'But thanks for your help, Tom. Sorry we had to involve you. But as soon as there's any news – about Steven Hickson – we'll let you know.'

Bradley nodded thoughtfully and said, 'I'll get in touch with the lifeboat people for you, about the CCTV.'

As soon as Bradley had walked off, Lambert looked over towards the road leading to the marina, where he could just about make out the deputy chief constable talking to the chief super, his round owlish face and hooked nose mirroring Marden's avian features.

'Come on, Debbie,' Lambert said. 'Time we had a word with our senior officers.' He flashed her a cheeky grin. 'See if we can wangle an early night for a change. There's not much more we can do here except leave it to the techies.'

As they neared Marden and DCC Chessman, Lambert noted the worried lines on the chief super's face, and knew he was probably agonizing over their stretched resources, especially as there was already a forensic team busy searching and unearthing evidence of the killing at the office of All Star Cars.

'Ah, Inspector Lambert,' Marden greeted him formally. 'You seem to have a way of finding trouble wherever you go.'

Ignoring Marden's comment, Lambert stared into the deputy chief constable's round, jowly face and mumbled a 'good evening, sir.' Chessman was dressed in a navy blue suit, light blue shirt and yellow silk tie, and Lambert guessed that the bomb blast had disturbed a social event.

'So how come,' Chessman said without preamble, 'you dashed over here just as a bomb went off?'

Lambert shook his head. 'I didn't know a bomb was about to explode. And if I'd arrived a minute later, I wouldn't be standing here talking to you, sir.'

'Anyone on that boat, you think?'

Lambert said, 'I can't be sure, but I think it's probably a man called Mark Mason, who was out to seek revenge for his sister's death.'

'Yes, Clive's updated me on that. Perhaps you could bring me up to date on the immediate situation.'

Lambert had no reason to conceal anything from the DCC and quickly told him everything he knew, and his reason for coming to the marina to search for Mark Mason and his uncle. When he finished, he looked pointedly at Marden and said, 'It looks like the finger points heavily in Frank Masina's direction.'

Marden coughed into his hand and shook his head. 'Let's not go there, Inspector. I can't see what possible motive Masina would have for doing this.'

Chessman stared at Lambert, his eyes glinting and catching the light from the squad cars. 'Does Masina know this young man?'

'I doubt it.'

'So, we have absolutely no reason to suppose he was responsible for the bombing?'

'Not so far. No.'

'And you've found this young man's car.'

Lambert jerked a thumb to the car park in front of the Harbour Master's office. 'A Saab. Parked just along there.'

'And how near are you to apprehending this James Harlan, who is definitely wanted for the Robert Sonning killing?' Marden said.

'I'm hoping Sergeant Ellis gets a lead from the second-hand car premises he's searching. I've asked him to see if he can find an inventory of their cars, on the assumption that Harlan may have taken one of the vehicles to distance himself from Swansea. And first thing tomorrow morning I intend talking to everyone who knows Harlan: friends, relatives, girlfriends, acquaintances.' Lambert fixed a steady gaze on Marden and added, 'Except for his employer. I'll leave him to Geoff Ambrose and SOCA.'

Marden nodded thoughtfully, tapped Lambert on the arm with a show of familiarity, and said, 'You're looking jaded, Harry. There's not much more you can do here, except leave it to the SOCO team, and I should think it'll be some time before they come up with any answers. You and your team have been swamped with this investigation almost non-stop since Saturday. So why don't you hit the hay and make a fresh start first thing tomorrow? And that goes for the rest of your team.'

Lambert suspected Marden's display of understanding was for Chessman's benefit who nodded approvingly.

'Right,' Lambert said. 'I can't say I wouldn't welcome a good night's sleep for a change.'

He was about to walk away, when Marden halted him with an over-familiar touch of his arm.

'And a word of advice with regards to the search for Harlan – what you said about a thorough but routine investigation of everyone who knows him. Might I also suggest you start thinking outside the box.'

Lambert could feel DC Jones looking at him and deliberately avoided eye contact with her. Instead, he gave Marden an exaggerated look of agreement and said, 'An excellent suggestion, sir.'

# Twenty-seven

First thing Wednesday morning, Lambert organized his team to question everyone who knew Harlan, however slender the connection, starting with Harlan's parents. He also got Ellis to question Jason Crabbe again about any friends Harlan might have known from the past: old school friends, girls he'd been out with, and even people who were not necessarily that close to him; anyone, in fact, with whom he associated. And Lambert did his best to avoid succumbing to the frustration he felt in pursuing pointless information, because he suspected that the only man who could shed light on Harlan and his disappearance was his employer, Frank Masina, and Marden had made it perfectly clear that questioning this villain was strictly out of bounds.

Just after lunch, Lambert was summoned to the chief super's office at Bridgend headquarters and for once he was glad of an excuse to get away from the drudgery of the incident room and the chore of organizing the routine questioning, which seemed to be getting nowhere. Besides, he wanted to know if there was any news from forensics about the bomb blast, and if they had identified anyone caught in the blast. As soon as he was seated in front of Marden's desk he asked about updates from forensics about the explosion.

'There is news,' Marden said, 'and I'll get to that in a little while, because I want to have a word with you about something of grave importance.'

Lambert wanted to say something about a bomb blast that may have killed someone in a cosy marina last night scored pretty highly as crucial in an investigation. Instead, he said, 'Is this meeting something to do with Frank Masina?'

Marden drummed his fingers on the desk, stared at them thoughtfully, and then gave Lambert a piercing look and cleared his throat. Lambert guessed he was about to make a lengthy speech.

'We suspect that the amount of Class A drugs Masina has swamped South Wales with runs into an excess of fifty million pounds worth. And we also suspect James Harlan worked as one of his drug runners, along with lots of other dirty and illegal activities. He was very close to Masina, and the gangster regarded him as a friend and confidante. Which is why we need to concentrate our efforts on finding Harlan, who we think is more vulnerable and would probably trade his boss for a lighter sentence. If we can get Harlan as a witness for the prosecution, we could be home and dried. Of course, I'm quite aware the bomb explosion last night could have been Masina's work, but if we get him for the massive number of drugs he's peddled over the last twelve years – maybe longer – he'll get a hefty sentence, and he won't see the light of day until he hobbles out on a Zimmer frame. So really, Harry, it's down to you and your team to find Harlan.'

Feeling pressure building in his chest, Lambert let his breath out slowly. 'We're working flat out trying to find the man. And we think we have the vehicle description and registration of the car he might be driving. He probably helped himself to it from the second-hand car dealer where he worked since the drink-driving accident. We've already circulated the entire force with the details. But then, of course, he could be hiding at the one place which you tell me is out of bounds.'

Marden stared at Lambert with raised eyebrows, and an expression on his face implying that he would be unbending on this issue, and Lambert was wasting his breath even considering it as an option.

'We don't think Harlan's at Masina's place.'

'We?' Lambert questioned.

'DCI Ambrose and Superintendent Bewes from SOCA. They've had Masina's place under surveillance since the weekend. Which was another reason we didn't want you to go anywhere near the man like you did last Friday. And SOCA have even put an electronic tail on his four-by-four. So, unless Harlan's staying at another of the man's properties, it doesn't look as if Masina's sheltering him.'

Marden pulled open a desk drawer, took out a sheaf of papers, rifled through them, and handed a sheet to Lambert. 'That's a list of some properties Masina owns – mostly holiday cottages. And as it's not yet Easter, he's probably got quite a few empty. So, you could try some of those. Harlan might be hiding out in one of them.

Lambert took the paper and glanced down at the list of about twenty properties scattered over quite a wide area to the west of Swansea, some as far away as Tenby and Newquay. He frowned, almost scowled at the list, wondering why Marden had kept this list from him until now.

As if he could guess what Lambert was thinking, Marden said, 'You know what SOCA are like, Harry – they tend to treat everything with the utmost secrecy as if they trust no one. They only gave me this list late yesterday, not long before the pyrotechnics at Burry Port.'

'Talking of which,' Lambert said, 'you said you were going to tell me if there's any news from forensics yet.'

Marden sighed deeply. 'A body – if you can call it that – was found in what was left of the boat.'

'Just the one person?'

'It looks that way so far, but it might be too soon to tell. But there was one item indicating who the victim was.' Marden paused dramatically before continuing. 'There was a key with a Saab key ring still attached to it.'

Lambert nodded. 'Just as I thought. It looks like it *was* Mark Mason on the boat.'

'Forensics are still working on getting a DNA match, and there was a reasonable part of the victim's head and jaw left intact, so any dental records should give us confirmation. They may have the evidence later this afternoon. But it is starting to look that way. And you've interviewed Mason's parents over his sister's death. How did they seem?'

'They were devastated, and both looked as if they were on the edge. And now, if they find out their son's dead—'

'Those poor people,' Marden said, rubbing the lower part of his face with the flat of his hand. 'I doubt they'll ever recover from this.'

'They'll never be the same, that's for sure. And Steven Hickson's still missing. His wife is beside herself. Keeps ringing to find out what's happened, so I had to tell her about the boat. If she happened to see or hear the news she'd have found out, and she'll think her husband was aboard when the bomb went off, although no one's been named as a victim yet.'

'But if she knows he's been missing for nearly twenty-four hours,' Marden stressed, 'and his boat's gone up in flames, she's bound to think the worst. What do you think happened to Hickson? Has he been killed separately by the bomber, d'you think?'

'I don't know what to think, sir. Obviously Hickson and Mason were in it together, planning to kill Harlan, so maybe Harlan – or someone like Masina – had him killed. But if Hickson was on his way to the boat with groceries for his nephew, why wouldn't the bomber have waited until they were both aboard the boat and the bomb would have taken care of both of them? And it looks as if Hickson was just dropping off Mason's food but wasn't planning on staying.'

Marden tapped the desk with his fingers to emphasise a point. 'All of this rests with finding Harlan, you know.'

'I know, sir.' Lambert stood up to leave, then frowned, knowing he had to tread cautiously with what he was about to say. 'This is just a thought, sir, but what if we can't find Harlan?' Hurriedly, before Marden could object, he added, 'I mean, what if he's already dead? We're doing all we can to find him; working flat out on it, but—'

Marden raised a hand to stop him. 'I know you are, Harry. Let's give it another twenty-four hours. If by that time you haven't managed to track down Harlan, then we'll regroup and consider our options.'

# Twenty-eight

Rubbing the sleep from his eyes and feeling unwashed despite throwing himself under a hot shower bang on seven-thirty, Lambert would have given anything to go back to bed for another couple of hours. Too much booze the previous night, that was the problem. A couple of pints of beer and probably the equivalent of a bottle and a half of the pub's house red. Would he never learn?

He stared with loathing at the untouched instant coffee on the desk in front of him, as if it represented every hardened criminal he wanted to collar. He knew he had decisions to make, his team demanded nothing less, but his brain was fuzzy and useless. The telephone in front of him rang. As he reached for it, although he was not a superstitious man, Harry Lambert for once experienced a strange sensation of premonition. Or perhaps it was desperation and he was clutching at straws, hoping this would be the break he was waiting for.

He reached out and picked the phone up slowly. There was no reason to suppose the call was anything other than a customary enquiry, one of the hundreds of tedious and repetitive areas of routine they had to deal with on every case, but as soon as he gave his name, and then heard a throat-clearing sound before the person spoke, with background sounds of traffic, he knew this was the phone call he had anticipated, perhaps a micro-second before the phone even rang.

Maybe he had dreamt it. Or maybe he was getting superstitious in his old age. He couldn't explain it, but he just knew who this was going to be before he even spoke.

'I think you might have been looking for me,' the voice said in a monotone, bored and despondent.

'Where are you, Mr Harlan?' Lambert said as he scribbled furiously on a scrap of paper, waving it so that it rustled to catch someone's attention. On it he had written in bold letters the word TRACE.

It caught Kevin Wallace's attention, and Lambert raised three fingers to indicate he was on line three as Wallace dashed out of the office to use another phone to get the call traced. Lambert glanced at his watch to check out how long he could stretch the phone call. It was one minute past ten.

'Never mind where I am,' Harlan said, his voice breathless and urgent now, and Lambert knew he would say what he had to say and hang up before they could trace the call. 'Just listen, will you? I saw you on television asking for witnesses to come forward, which is why I asked to speak to you and not Ambrose.'

'Has this something to do with Frank Masina and drugs?' Lambert said quickly. 'So why didn't you want to speak to DCI Ambrose?'

'I have my reasons. Now listen carefully: I felt bad about killing that girl and was willing to do time for it. But then her brother hired someone to kill me, and I swear I killed the bloke in self defence. Then her brother said he was coming after me himself.'

'So, you had Masina blow up the boat on which he was hiding.'

'I swear… I had nothing to do with that.' A slight choke in Harlan's throat, as if he was stifling a sob. After the briefest of pauses, he managed to control himself and continued. 'Frank was just supposed to put the frighteners on him; rough him up. Christ, I never thought he would go that far.'

Lambert glanced at his watch again. Only twenty-five seconds had gone by. He had to keep Harlan talking.

'Why would Masina go to all the trouble of helping you out of a tight spot by killing Mark Mason?'

'Because I threatened to turn Queen's Evidence if he didn't. But, Christ, I never thought he'd… the man's a lunatic. Now listen: I don't have much time. I'm willing to turn QE now, in return for all the evidence you need to get Frank. I can give you enough to put him away for life. Now don't interrupt, cos I know you're tracing this call. I know you'll have to go to a higher authority with this. I'll call you same time tomorrow and you can let me know about turning Queen's Evidence. I'll give you my location and I want you to come along. Not Ambrose.'

The line went dead. Lambert looked at his watch. The conversation had taken about one minute and ten seconds in total. It seemed highly unlikely they could trace the call, and he doubted Harlan was stupid enough to call from a mobile whose radio frequency could easily be traced.

As soon as he replaced the phone, tensely holding his breath, he realized

Jones and Beech seemed to be holding their breath as well, waiting for him to report details of the call.

'That was James Harlan,' he said. 'He wants to turn QE, and hand Frank Masina to us on a platter, along with his drugs empire.'

Wallace returned to the incident room shaking his head. 'The conversation was too short. By the time they'd found the—'

Lambert raised a hand. 'It doesn't matter, Kevin. Harlan's ringing us at the same time tomorrow. He wants to turn Queen's Evidence.'

DC Jones came over to Lambert's desk, her brows furrowed questioningly. 'Hasn't he been involved in too much killing to do that? I mean, a lighter sentence maybe, but—'

Shaking his head, Lambert cut in. 'As Mick keeps reminding us, the killing of Robert Sonning was in self-defence.'

Mick Beech glanced over from his workstation, his mouth hanging open, uncertain whether Lambert was being sarcastic or complimentary. Lambert barely noticed him.

'But there's also the drink-driving incident,' Jones continued. 'He can't walk away from that one. The public won't stand for it.'

Lambert shrugged. 'Well, you must know what dealing with SOCA is like. Not to mention Customs and Excise. They might agree to anything to land the bigger fish. Although it's doubtful he'll get off scot-free and with complete anonymity; especially in view of the fact he's just admitted the bomb blast was his fault. He says he blackmailed Masina into committing the act – says he threatened to turn QE unless Masina got Mark Mason off his back. But he claims he thought Masina would just rough him up.'

Wallace laughed. 'Yeah, and I might win the Euro lottery on Friday.'

Lambert rose and grabbed his coat from the back of his chair. 'I'm going to shoot over to Bridgend and have a word with the chief super about James Harlan turning Queen's Evidence. Would you contact him, Mick, and let him know I'm on my way? And tell him I need a confidential meeting in private.'

'Will do,' Beech replied, picking up the phone.

'Where's Tony?' Lambert asked Jones.

'Sorting out forensic evidence from the All Star Cars office. And there's plenty of it. They didn't do a very thorough job of clearing the mess up. But now it looks as if we might be getting a full confession out of Harlan.'

'We still need everything we can get for the CPS to throw at Harlan's defence barrister when it gets to court,' Lambert replied. And then he gave her a lopsided smile as he started for the door. 'That's if it ever gets to court.'

\*\*\*

As he sped along the M4 motorway, Lambert wondered about DCI Ambrose and why Harlan was reluctant to deal with him. He knew SOCA and Geoff Ambrose had got very close to breaking Masina's gangster grip on South Wales, but something had always gone wrong at the last minute. And had it not been for Harlan getting drunk and killing the schoolgirl, they still might not have got anywhere nearer to nailing Masina. It was only because of Mason and his uncle's attempts to avenge his sister's death that they were on the verge of ending Masina's criminal organization. Revenge. That's what had done it. A craving for vengeance, a compulsion that was almost a basic instinct, and had been an evil driving force for thousands of years. It was, as Lambert well knew, one of the best reasons to have a good criminal justice system.

But as he passed the Port Talbot turn off, he was again reminded of his father, who had returned to live there when he had split up with Lambert's mother. And revolting thoughts of his father's depravity continued to haunt him. Why else would his sister have fled to Australia, never to be seen again? The older sister who became a stranger to him, a person he had never known beyond his childhood. And now that she was dead, along with his parents, he would never learn the truth. However painful that truth was, it was at least something tangible. It was not knowing that had somehow become a jeering, macabre joke. He often lay awake at night and imagined his father was still alive. Followed by confrontation and accusation, grabbing his father round the throat and throttling out his confession. How often he had battered his father's leering face. But it was all in his imagination. The foul truth would forever elude him. Which, on reflection, was just as well, because had he known or even suspected his father had driven his sister thousands of miles away from home because of sexual abuse all those years ago, then Lambert knew his reprisal would have been unimaginably brutal. He had always believed in law and order and the justice system, but when it came down to personal issues, he realized how different his standards could become. And it was these dark thoughts which helped him to understand the feelings of Hickson and Mason.

But Frank Masina was a different matter. He was in it for the money and power. And it was he, more than anyone, Lambert wanted imprisoned, where he would spend the rest of his life in everlasting tedium. That would be the state's revenge. Maybe it all boiled down to the same thing in the end. Revenge. Because trying to rehabilitate men like Masina seemed pointless.

\*\*\*

When he entered Marden's office, the chief super raised his head from a document he was reading and stared at Lambert as if he was the office cleaner. It was a look which never fazed Lambert, who had become immune to his boss's hostility, and almost regarded it as a challenge, something to be opposed with subtle insolence.

'Why the sudden meeting with no warning?' Marden snapped.

'Makes a change when the boot is on the other foot,' Lambert countered.

Then again, maybe not so subtle.

Marden looked as if he was about to choke on a lump of bile, so Lambert hurriedly dropped into a chair and spoke quickly.

'This has to be a private meeting in confidence, because I'm about to discover the whereabouts of James Harlan, whose location will be revealed to me in return for turning QE and giving you all the evidence you need to bring Frank Masina to justice.'

Marden's lined and scowling face suddenly smoothed into a more relaxed appearance as he absorbed Lambert's news. 'When did this happen?' he said.

'About half-an-hour ago. He rang me in person, said he wanted to deal with me and not Geoff Ambrose.'

Deep lines formed on Marden's brow again. 'Why you and not Geoff?'

'He said he'd seen me on television.'

'I wouldn't have thought that was a good enough reason…'

Lambert interrupted with an apologetic shrug. 'Well, sir, maybe he knows something we don't about someone Masina's got on the inside. A mole I believe it's called.'

Marden laughed humourlessly. 'Oh, come off it, Harry. I have complete trust in Geoff.'

'Yes. Same here,' Lambert agreed. 'But the fact remains: Harlan wants to deal with me. And he wants to know by tomorrow morning whether we can accept his offer.'

'And if we don't?'

'He didn't say. But – and I'm only guessing here – he'll probably refuse to cooperate and provide any incriminating evidence on Masina.'

Marden stared thoughtfully at his desk phone for a moment. 'I'll need to take this right to the top. And have a word with Superintendent Bewes.'

'Of course. That's only to be expected. And what about Geoff?'

'Well, he's been working closely with Superintendent Bewes, so it'll be difficult to keep him out of it.'

Lambert was about to object when Marden stopped him with a pointed finger. 'Why did Harlan single you out, that's what I want to know?'

Trying not to let his impatience show, Lambert spoke slowly and forcefully, 'He knows I'm the one working on the case, trying to bring him in for the killing of Sonning, and like I said, he has some ulterior motive for not wanting to deal with the team working on the drugs investigation. Clearly, he knows something we don't. In fact, he knows a great deal we don't, which is why he wants to turn QE and spill the beans about his boss.'

'This is going to be awkward trying to keep Ambrose out of it. I trust the man implicitly. And if I don't back my fellow officers...'

Marden stopped and sighed deeply, staring into the distance, nervously rubbing a thumb backwards and forwards across his fingers.

'If I could suggest, sir,' Lambert began, waiting for Marden to look him in the eye, 'when Harlan contacts me, if I and my team are first on the scene to interrogate him, we could bring Geoff and SOCA in a little later. Because by then, if he's scared of his confession getting leaked to Masina...'

Marden stopped the nervous twitching of his hand and smacked it on to the desk. 'This is ridiculous. He must know that once he turns QE it'll get back to Masina. Once we've got everything we need to convict Masina, he'll know exactly where the knowledge came from, which is why Harlan will demand protection as part of the package.'

'Which is why, if he deals with me, and my team get to him first, he'll know he's protected. Then Geoff and our spook from MI7 can enter the scene.'

A stern, schoolteacher look from Marden, which Lambert tried to dispel with a disarming naughty-boy smile and shrug. Marden ignored it.

'OK, Harry, I want you to keep me informed every step of the way between now and tomorrow when Harlan calls. And I will do likewise, and let you know we have clearance regarding an agreement for Harlan to turn QE. But I think SOCA will want to go in not long after you've arrived at his location.' Marden snatched a look at his watch. 'Now I think I'd better put these wheels in motion.'

Lambert rose and walked to the door, where he turned and couldn't resist saying, 'I suppose Mark Mason avenging his sister's death has given you the lucky break you needed to convict Masina. Funny old world.'

# Twenty-nine

Lambert felt a flutter of excitement as he stared at the phone, willing it to ring. Harlan had said he would ring at the same time as the previous morning and it was already ten minutes past the allotted time. Although, as Lambert guessed, he was probably ringing from a telephone box and there might be someone else using it. Lambert found it difficult to concentrate on anything else, so focused was he on the telephone.

And others in the incident room were also finding it difficult to concentrate. Ellis was fast forwarding, pausing and rewinding the Harbour Master's office CCTV of a dark figure scaling the harbour wall and creeping stealthily along the pontoon and ducking out of sight of the cameras by the area where the *Esmeralda* was located. But Ellis was unable to make any sort of identification or find any small clue as to who it might be. It was a black moonless night and it was difficult to see much of the figure, just a dark shadow, a black phantom, so there was absolutely no way they would ever be able to identify this person or use it as evidence. Wallace fared slightly better with the lifeboat house CCTV, as it provided clear images of Hickson arriving at the car park and being viciously attacked. The trouble was, the three men who attacked him were hard to identify because of their hoods; although there was one man, the one Wallace had christened 'the fat fuck', and his hood had fallen back in the skirmish, revealing his face in profile for a moment. It was probably enough to get a still picture blown up from it. And to the edge of the frame was the van, although only half of it was in the picture. Consequently, half the number plate, but at least there were the first two letters and one number of the registration, and Debbie Jones was about to get on to DVLA to see just how many vans could be identified by just two letters and a single number. Probably hundreds, if not thousands, Wallace suggested. But when they considered the five figure numbers of vehicles whose owners the police had to interview and eliminate before they eventually caught Robert Black for the serial killings of the young women he abducted and raped in Scotland, before dumping their bodies in the midlands, their task didn't seem half as daunting. But prior to making the registration search, Jones hovered close to Mick Beech, talking quietly to him about their recent activities and what they needed to achieve in the ongoing investigation, which included a frantic dash to wherever Harlan was located as soon as his call came through. And even if Harlan was found, and Masina was brought to justice, there was still the problem of what had happened to Hickson. Having thoroughly studied the CCTV of the attack on him, Jones thought the scrawny physique of one of the hooded figures might be the man they called Virgil.

Lambert knew they were all finding it difficult to concentrate. The expectancy in the incident room was a palpable tension linking them as they waited. Although Lambert felt the stirrings of disappointment, in case Harlan might not ring, he felt better able to cope than on the previous morning. He'd had an early night for a change, and was fast asleep by midnight, having drunk only two pints of beer and had a proper dinner, so he was feeling much better prepared than the day before.

'Come on ring, you bugger,' he muttered. 'Ring.'

'Maybe he's changed his mind,' Ellis said.

Still staring vacantly at the phone, Lambert shook his head. 'Doubt it, Tony. Turning QE's his only option.'

'I still can't believe they agreed, after all he's done.'

'With certain conditions. You any closer to identifying the bomber?'

'Not a hope in hell. A man in black on a moonless night?'

'Holy *Esmeralda*!' Wallace exclaimed. 'He's probably back in his bat cave by now.'

'Yes, and I happen to know where that is,' Lambert said. 'It's a pretentious southern mansion on the Gower peninsula.'

Jones, feeling restless, came and stood close to Lambert, to be near the phone when, and if, it rang. 'You think the bomber's Masina, don't you?'

'Well, I don't go along with Kevin's suggestion. It's not Batman – or the Joker or the Penguin. It's definitely Frank Masina.' Lambert waved a dismissive hand at Ellis's monitor. 'But the CCTV proves nothing, of course.'

Lambert, aware they were all talking for the sake of talking, killing time as they waited for the crucial ring, had a terrible sinking feeling. Perhaps something had gone wrong. He didn't think Harlan had changed his mind. But supposing someone got to him before he was able to make the call? And that someone seemed to be hell-bent on a destructive course, almost as if they wanted to get caught. He had seen it so many times in certain criminals. One minute they had everything under control and were living a lifestyle they could never hope to achieve by honest means. And then, suddenly, the rapid change as a crazy greed took over their lives, resulting in an almost inevitable death wish and an urge to self-destruct.

Lambert was startled out of his reverie as his desk phone rang, and the rest of the incident room stopped what they were doing and held their breath. Lambert took his time as he reached across the desk and picked up the phone.

'Lambert,' he said.

Harlan's voice seemed huskier than before, possibly because the fear was getting to him. 'No need to trace this call,' he said, 'because I hope we have an agreement for me to turn Queen's Evidence, which means you'll soon know where I am.'

Lambert bit his bottom lip before telling Harlan the deal. 'With certain conditions.'

A pause, then Lambert could have sworn there was a sharp intake of breath from Harlan. This was followed by a noisy rumbling sound, possibly a heavy lorry passing wherever he was phoning from.

'What conditions we talking about?'

'You'll have to stand trial for the drink-driving, and you'll probably go down for it.'

'No way, man. No way. I can't do that.' Harlan started to gabble. 'If I go inside they'll get to me, man. They'll get to me.'

'Listen to me, Jimmy. The public would never stand for it if you got off the drink-driving charge, and then the girl's parents would probably pursue it. If you turn QE and give us all the evidence we need to convict Masina, we'll give you all the protection you need. After the smoke clears, you'll get a new ID and a cushy open prison somewhere in the south of England. And let's face it, after what you've been involved in, it's the best you can hope for.'

There was another long pause and Lambert could tell Harlan's brain was racing as he considered his options. A sudden whoosh, as another vehicle went by in the background. Eventually, Harlan cleared his throat nervously.

'OK,' he said. 'What choice do I have?'

'So where are you, Jimmy?'

'I'm a few miles northwest of Llanelli on a B road just past a village called Dolwen.'

As Lambert wrote it down on a scrap of paper, he said, 'Is that where you're phoning from now?'

'Yeah. Why?'

'We could be with you in less than half an hour. I suggest you wait there for us.'

'No way, man. I'm not going to hang around on the road. I'm not taking any chances.'

Lambert realized the man was scared out of his wits.

'OK, Jimmy, so tell me where we can find you.'

'Go through the village and a hundred yards up the road on the right, past the phone box, is a small track. Go along the track and you'll find a gate leading to a field with a large oak tree. I'm camped in a tent just behind the oak. If you open the gate and turn into the field, you'll see my car – a red Toyota – parked to the left of the gate. And, Lambert.'

'Yes?'

'Make sure you get here before any of your drugs people.'

'Like I said, Jimmy: less than thirty minutes.'

Lambert cut the call and stood up, waving the sheet of paper. He walked hurriedly over to Mick Beech. 'Right, Mick, I've got his location. Copy down the details.' Mick Beech started scribbling furiously. 'What I'd like you to do is inform Chief Superintendent Marden the whereabouts of Harlan. But I'd like you to do that ten minutes after we depart. It's vital we get to Harlan before anyone else. Is that understood?'

Beech's extra chins wobbled as he nodded. 'Don't worry. They've got to come from Bridgend, so you'll have a head start.'

'I'd still like that ten minutes, just to be on the safe side.' Lambert turned and spoke to the rest of his team. 'We'll go in a pool car. Kevin, you can drive.'

Lambert noticed Wallace's eyes light up at the prospect of a hair-raising drive. It was the second time in a week that Tony Ellis was being subjected to Wallace's hell driving, but Lambert knew they had to get there fast, and he couldn't waste time considering his sergeant's fear of high speed.

*\*\**

As they raced along the B road towards their destination, Lambert felt the surge of the car as Wallace kept his foot hard-pressed to the accelerator. He wondered how Ellis was coping with the neck-breaking speed. As they were about to leave the police station, Lambert had offered to sit in the front passenger seat but Ellis had commandeered it as if he was trying to prove something – possibly how he had put the past behind him and conquered his terrible memories.

And now, almost as if he guessed what Lambert was thinking, he turned around to look at Lambert and Jones in the back seat and smiled. 'It's OK. I think I'm getting used to our boy racer's driving now.'

But just as he said it, his stomach lurched as they took a corner at speed, and an enormous Shogun almost sideswiped them. Kevin swerved to avoid the Shogun, and the car rumbled along the edge of the road and glass verge as he gripped the steering wheel tightly to keep the car from losing control. Leaves and branches swept noisily along the left side of the car until Kevin managed steer it away from the hedgerow and back on course.

'You were saying, Tony?' Wallace said with a nervous laugh.

'Just concentrate, Kevin,' Lambert warned. 'You'll have to slow down as we go through this village. We don't want to kill anyone.'

Wallace killed his speed as they passed through the village. Just beyond the phone box, Wallace drove slowly until they found the dirt track. He turned off the road and the car rumbled and bumped along the potholes and muddy ruts. They couldn't see into any fields because there were large hedgerows on either side, but they hadn't gone far when they found the opening between the high hedges, leading into a field. A large iron gate had been left wide open and Wallace pulled into the field, the car bouncing over the rough ground. He turned the car round as soon as they were in the field, so that it was almost facing the exit, ready for their departure.

As they all got out of the car, they spotted the Toyota, parked surreptitiously behind the hedge, away from the gate, so that it couldn't be seen from the narrow track.

In the centre of the meadow was the enormous oak tree, the leaves now thick and full grown, although it was still only mid March. They strode towards the tree, Lambert leading the way, the grass rustling beneath their tramping feet. As they got close to the tree, they could see in a dip in the field a light green tent, just about big enough for one person. Lambert guessed that after the threatening phone call from Mark Mason on the Sunday, Harlan perhaps contacted whoever owned this piece of land to see if he could hole up here. Maybe he had an old friend who was willing to support him, who could always deny knowing Harlan was camping on his land if asked.

As Lambert turned sideways to ease down the steep slope into the hollow where the tent was pitched, Jones came sliding after him and had to lean her hand on his shoulder to stop herself slipping.

'Sorry,' she mumbled.

But he hardly noticed or heard her. His eyes were fastened on to the dark stains smeared across a large area of canvas, and he feared the worst.

'Jimmy!' he called out, hardly daring to raise the tent flap at the entrance. Silence. He knew it was futile. Jones came up beside him and he became aware of her quick intake of breath.

'Oh, God!' she said.

Ellis and Wallace stared at the tent, their faces taut, bracing themselves for the shock, the terrible disclosure they were now prepared for. In unison, they both looked towards Lambert, waiting for him to make the first move. He composed himself, took a deep breath of the sweet air of the pasture before pulling back the flap.

'Jesus!' Wallace said, almost shielding his eyes from the blinding horror of the bloodshed.

The tent was soaked with Harlan's blood, the groundsheet swimming with pools of gore beneath what was left of his body, which had been pounded by multiple shots. Whoever had shot him had probably kept firing long after he was dead, leaving behind an unrecognizable carcass, just a hideous mess of blood, flesh, protruding bones, brain, cartilage, and what was once a human being.

Lambert was the first to look away. 'I don't think anything can be done for this man,' He laughed grimly at his ridiculous choice of words. And then a wave of anger enveloped him. 'How come...' he started to say but was interrupted by his mobile ringing. He fumbled in his coat pocket and answered it hurriedly. It was Marden.

'Where are you, Harry?'

'We're at the location and—'

He was about to give Marden the bad news but was interrupted by his boss's panicky voice, higher-pitched than normal. 'That electronic tail we have on Masina's vehicle. He's in your area. You need to protect the witness at all costs. But be careful of Masina—'

It was Lambert's turn to interrupt. 'It's too late.'

'What d'you mean?'

'I mean Harlan's dead.'

'You sure of that?'

'Course I'm bloody sure,' Lambert shouted. 'He's got more bullet holes in him than...' He tried to think of an analogy but gave up. He saw Wallace's mind ticking over and shook his head warningly. He yelled into his mobile, 'We need SOCO out here right away. Meanwhile, I think we need to get over to Masina's. And an Armed Response Unit might be a good idea. The bastard's gone crazy. Christ! I've just realized. We almost collided with his vehicle on the way here. How could he possibly hope to get away with this?'

'Impossible. He must have flipped.'

'And he'll be extremely dangerous. Nothing left to lose now. Whereabouts are you?'

'We're on the M4, just before the Llanelli turn-off. I think now we'll cut across to the Gower and see if we can talk Masina into giving himself up.'

Lambert laughed grimly. 'Yeah, and Swansea might win the UEFA championship.'

'Harry,' Marden said, his tone almost wheedling, 'Forget Masina. Don't go there.'

'What?'

'I'm concerned for the safety of you and your team.'

'I know you are, sir, but... hang on, I'm losing you. Bad signal.'

He clicked off his phone and began to scramble up the slope towards the oak tree. 'Come on,' he shouted. 'That was Masina's four-by-four Kevin nearly smashed into on the way here. And we won't be far behind him.'

As they followed Lambert hurriedly across the field to the car, Wallace grinned as he said to Ellis, 'Let's see if we can head him off at the pass.'

# Thirty

When they screeched to a halt in front of the drive leading to Frank Masina's house, they saw the gate was shut, and probably locked, so approaching the house was not an option.

'Now what?' Wallace said.

Without replying, Lambert got out of the car and stood in front of the gate, looking up at the house. He imagined the house was a fortress now, and Masina would be protecting his territory like a Texan at the Alamo. And the chief super had warned him not to go anywhere near the crazed killer. Not that Lambert had any intention of endangering his own life or anyone else in his team. And the fact that his quarry was now a cornered animal, mentally wounded and extremely dangerous, meant there was only one thing he could try now, and that was to see if his negotiating skills were any good.

As Ellis, Jones and Wallace joined him at the gate, he could feel their tension as they stared at the house, eyes wide with foreboding. Debbie Jones stood next to him, and he became aware of her clearing her throat, but delicately, as if she was afraid to disturb the pressure that was building up like a saucepan about to boil over.

After they had all stood immobile for a moment, staring at the house as if it was an entity that could burst into life at any minute, Jones moved a little closer to Lambert and turned to look up at him questioningly. He gave her a small, self-effacing smile as he fumbled for his notebook and mobile phone.

'Not that it'll do any good,' he said, 'but I've got his landline number and I'm going to try and talk some sense into him.'

'About all you can do,' Ellis said.

Although she felt hot, and was perspiring profusely, Jones shivered as she observed, 'After seeing Harlan's corpse – the amount of times he was shot – I think this man's on his final mission.'

'Yes, one shot would have killed Harlan,' Wallace said. 'Two maybe. But shooing him that many times means the guy's gone haywire. Angry and savage.'

As he dialled the number, Lambert could feel how edgy they all were, hot fear hanging in the air like heavy pressure before a mighty thunderclap. He held the mobile close to his ear, pressing hard, his hand taut and his knuckles white with tension. The line rang. Once. Twice. Three times. He ignored the stares of his team as they waited, their lives on hold for this extreme moment of conflict, looking and listening for any indication that Lambert's call had been answered. He counted to nine rings and was about to abandon it when the ringing stopped and he heard a click.

And then Masina's voice growled, 'Who is it?'

'Detective Inspector Lambert, Frank. We met last week, and listen, I should warn you—'

Before he could finish, Masina screamed down the phone, 'And you listen to me, you arseholes, there's only one way out of this mess. I need you to get me a helicopter.'

Now Lambert knew he was mad. An image flashed into his brain of an old James Cagney movie he remembered seeing years ago, with the crazed gangster calling for his mother as he blew himself up.

'I can't do that, Frank. I haven't the authority. And in a matter of minutes an Armed Response Unit will be crawling all over your property.'

'Yeah? And I'll be ready for the bastards.'

'There's no point in carrying on with this, Frank.'

'I've still got one fucking card up my sleeve,' Masina screamed. 'And if you don't believe it, just watch me.'

The line went dead. Lambert stuck it back in his pocket and shrugged in response to Ellis's inquiring expression. 'He's gone crazy, and he's capable of anything. Maybe we'd better clear these gates. It wouldn't surprise me if he runs out of the house firing from the hip like a demented soldier attacking a machine gun nest.'

But as he finished speaking, the front door of the house, which was only about twenty yards away, burst open. Masina had his wife's head in an arm lock, holding her so tight she was unable to speak or scream. And in his other hand he held an automatic pistol jammed against her head.

'You want me to kill the bitch? Is that what you want? I'm telling you to get me a helicopter. Or this bitch dies. I've never fucking liked her. In fact, I hate the fucking bitch.

'And if you don't believe me...'

'Oh, I believe you all right,' Lambert shouted, knowing he had to keep Masina talking for as long as possible. He guessed that the longer he kept the dialogue going between them, the better his wife's survival chances. It was risky, but what other choice did he have? 'But even if we get you a helicopter, Frank,' Lambert continued, 'where would you go?'

'Let me worry about that. Just do as I say, or the bitch is dead.'

The army of squad cars and vans hurtling towards Masina's house were travelling so fast that the wail of sirens burst upon them suddenly, shattering the silence of the neighbourhood like discordant screams. One squad car, lights flashing, flew past them and continued along the road, and Lambert guessed it was going to put a block on the road at the other end. Now the entire area would be cordoned off. Three other cars and two vans screeched to a halt and out of the back of the first car leapt Marden. Out of the car behind them came Superintendent Bewes of SOCA, accompanied by another suited man with a short-trimmed beard. Lambert and his team cleared the gates and went forward to meet them.

'I thought I told you to leave this to us, Inspector,' Marden barked.

'Sorry, I must have misheard,' Lambert shrugged. But, because of the urgency of the situation, Marden knew there was no time for recriminations and asked Lambert what the situation was. Lambert, distracted now by the armed police piling out of the vans, could see the deputy chief constable, in uniform this time, waving his arms about and giving instruction to some of his men, who dashed off along the perimeter of the wall probably checking to see if there was another entrance.

'Inspector!' Marden spoke sharply to get Lambert's attention, who gave him a brief explanation about Masina's threats and demands for a helicopter.

'Helicopter,' Bewes sneered as he arrived alongside Marden with the other man. 'The bloke must be mad.'

'That's a fair assessment of the situation,' Lambert said. 'He's watched too many Bruce Willis films and it's sent him loony.'

Bewes stared at Lambert as if he was an irritating insect, and then deliberately ignored him and spoke to Marden. 'What are the chances of getting this man alive?'

'It depends how serious this threat to kill his wife is. He might be bluffing.'

Lambert laughed but was deadly serious. 'I doubt that. I doubt it very much.'

Almost as if Lambert hadn't spoken, Bewes turned to his bearded colleague and said, 'We could do with this man being taken alive. Customs and Excise and Europol want the information and intelligence so the Dutch and German police can target the suppliers.'

The bearded man shrugged. When he spoke it was with a slightly effeminate lisp. 'At least we've got the main drug dealer in South Wales. That's something, I suppose.'

There was a yell from outside the house. 'Come on, you bastards! Or I'll kill the bitch in front of you.'

Marden strode to the gate and confronted Masina. 'Now listen, Frank...'

'No, you listen. I've given you my terms. A helicopter in exchange for this bitch's life.'

'We can't do that, Frank. And anyway, it's not practical. Where could you fly to? The Republic of Ireland, maybe? We could extradite you from there, and you know it.'

Masina was a terrified man clinging to a last desperate hope. His only way out was the crazy notion of escaping by helicopter. But now that Marden had dashed that one remaining lifeline, he became a man devoid of reason. The gangster's eyes bulged with fanatical rage, and with a flick of his wrist he turned the automatic from his wife's head and shot at Marden. In that brief moment the chief super had time to register the danger and leapt to one side as the bullet hit a bar of the metal gate, followed by the bang as the cartridge ricocheted off the gate and smacked into the road's surface. Fortunately for Marden, Masina's aim had not been accurate, possibly because of his wife trying to break free of his stranglehold. But for one instant Marden looked shaken, then recovered rapidly as he discarded the shock by physically shivering it out of his system, like a dog shaking off water.

'We'll be lucky if we take this man alive,' he told Bewes. He could see the SOCA officer was about to object and raised a hand to silence him before continuing frantically. 'About all we can hope for is one of our marksmen gets a clear shot at him, missing his wife. It's a risk we might have to take. Clearly there's very little hope of negotiation.'

'None,' Lambert said. 'I spoke to the man on the telephone prior to this confrontation and he's pressed the self-destruct button. He knows how long a sentence he'll get and I don't think he sees it as an option.'

Bewes sniffed loudly and his lip curled, and Lambert waited for the sarcastic comment.

'Thank you, Inspector, for stating the obvious.' Bewes turned and addressed Marden. 'I think it's best if we surround the house and wait. He's a man of action; an ex-soldier. He'll eventually get tired of a long and tedious stand-off.'

Lambert snorted, making certain Bewes saw his expression of pained disbelief. The SOCA superintendent was about to lay into him when Ellis, who had chanced a quick look from behind the wall next to the gate, suddenly shouted, 'He's gone inside and shut the door.'

By now all the armed police officers were lined up along the house's boundary, some leaning against the lichen covered brick, like an army of black ants using the cover of the brick wall, waiting to scurry across the lawn to attack Masina's fortress, scared of the shots that could be fired from any window in the house, and fearful of the extreme dangers of the shot that could prove fatal to any one of them. They knew, they had been forewarned by the DCC, that their target was himself a trained shot, an expert marksman. As they watched and waited, tensely waiting for the deputy chief constable to form a strategy, they saw him march forward to consult with Marden, and each man strained to hear the conversation, knowing how much it affected each one of them, and the risks involved.

'How much cover is there in the garden, Clive?' Chessman asked, his eyes glinting and keen with excitement.

'From what I could see through the gate, very little,' Marden said. 'A sloping lawn and flower beds, no trees. A few shrubs for cover but nothing substantial. And the driveway in front of the house is completely exposed.'

Chessman pursed his lips thoughtfully and shook his head. 'Which means I can't risk sending any of my men across the front. He could take a shot at any one of them. And he's a trained marksman himself. Ambulance is on its way; just in case.'

Bewes stepped between the two men. 'If I might suggest: we need to surround the house, so he has no way of escaping, and then we wait. Meanwhile, once he's calmed down, we try to negotiate again. It's the only thing we can do.'

And then they all heard a piercing scream from inside the house, and a shot was fired, echoing in the house like the boom of a distant flare. And then, perhaps less than a second later, another shot.

'Jesus!' Marden exclaimed. 'You don't suppose...'

He didn't need to finish the sentence. They all knew what he meant.

'As soon as we arrived,' Chessman said, 'I sent some of the men to recce the grounds around the house. Apparently, there's a lane at the end of this wall, and it leads to a gate, which is maybe a tradesman's entrance. In any case, it gives access to the garden at the side of the house. And one of my blokes thinks there's a garage and outhouse which would offer enough cover to get near the back of the house.'

'I know you can't take any risks,' Lambert said, 'but I have the distinct gut instinct that there are two fresh corpses in the house. We've seen cornered monsters before, and for some grotesque reason they decide to kill not only themselves but the people close to them.'

'I think you're right, Harry,' Marden agreed, then turned to address DCC Chessman. 'Why not give it five minutes, Peter, then get your men carefully up through the back door of the house? And I suspect, Harry's right about the two shots. It was also my immediate reaction.'

'Same here,' Chessman replied. 'I'll go and organize my men, and we'll go in five minutes.' He turned sharply and marched over to the armed officers to issue instructions.

There was a brief hiatus while they waited for Chessman to get his men ready for the onslaught. And that was when Lambert realized he'd missed something in all the excitement. Someone was missing. Someone who should have been present. Where was Geoff Ambrose? He had spent considerable time and effort trying to get enough evidence to convict Masina. And yet he was absent as the net tightened around his target. He should have been here, that was for sure. Perhaps Marden had deliberately kept these details from him. Lambert knew Marden trusted Ambrose, as Lambert did himself, but perhaps the chief super wasn't taking any chances. But now was not the time or place to mention Geoff's absence. It was something to be ironed out later.

Marden checked his watch and said, 'Three minutes to go.'

Wallace lit a cigarette and inhaled deeply, then examined the cigarette closely like a child staring at a chocolate bar between mouthfuls. Jones opened her handbag and looked inside, but for no apparent reason. Like Wallace's cigarette business, it was displacement activity. None of them wanted to admit to the horror of what they would discover on entering the house. They knew that men who take their own lives often destroy someone close to them. There were enough media reports of nasty, vicious crimes where estranged husbands, obsessed and fevered with hatred and thoughts of 'if I can't have you, nobody can', will wipe out an entire family. Except for Lambert, none of his team had experienced that hopeless, pointless, revengeful taking of innocent lives.

Linked by the same terrible thoughts, it was Ellis who verbalized their concerns.

'At least there's no children involved.'

'Has he never had a family?' Jones asked.

Lambert nodded. 'He's got a wife and two children. Divorced about six years ago. But pays the family a generous maintenance, apparently.'

'Huh! Not anymore.' Wallace said, discarding his cigarette and stamping on it.

Jones shivered. And then they saw DCC Chessman, about fifty yards along the wall, making a military-style forward gesture in the air, indicating the all-clear for the assault to begin.

Bewes and his bearded colleague were already striding towards the lane, and Marden and Lambert's team followed at the rear.

Before they reached the gate along the lane, there was a splintering crash as the battering ram smashed it open, followed by a yawning creak as it was wrenched from it's hinges. The armed officers, crouched and hunched, their weapons clutched tightly close to their bodies pushed their way through the narrow gap into the land behind the outhouse and garage, trampled over a kitchen garden, and flattened themselves against the wall of the garage, taking a moment to take stock before the next part of the assault.

As the men with the battering ram, followed closely by three armed officers for cover, dashed around the garage and headed for the back entrance to the house, the detectives ran across to the garage, pinning themselves to the wall, adrenaline pumping and breathing heavily, their minds surprisingly clear. As they waited by the garage, they heard the crash and tinkle of glass, followed by a wood-splitting crack and the tramping of heavy boots.

Feeling safer now that the armed officers had gained access to the premises, the detectives ran around the garage and towards the smashed door leading to a utility room and kitchen. They saw the armed officers darting along the hall, in and out of doors and alcoves, until one of them called out, 'In here!'

It was Masina's study that Lambert had visited almost a week ago. As the detectives piled into the room, first they saw Masina's corpse on the floor in front of his desk. A trail of blood ran across the antique top of the desk, and a glossy smear and a spray of red tarnished the bookshelf behind. Masina's head, what was left of it, lay in a pool of blood which had spread and soaked into the deep pile of the expensive carpet.

But at the sound of a faint sob, they all shifted their focus to the other side of the room where Masina's wife lay on the floor against a wall beneath an oval mirror, an uncomprehending, stunned look of shock on her face as she gazed into the distance through half-closed lids. Lambert elbowed his way through all the detectives and armed officers who had crowded into the room and knelt at her side. As he did so, he glimpsed the shattered mirror above her head.

'Vikki!' he said, quickly inspecting her body for any sign of a gunshot wound. But she appeared to be physically unharmed, and he guessed that Masina had changed his mind and shot at the mirror.

Her lids opened slightly as she looked into Lambert's eyes, pleading for understanding and sympathy.

'Frank loved me after all. He loved me. He couldn't do it. He said he would, but he didn't. So, he must have loved me, mustn't he?'

# Thirty-one

Masina's wife, shocked and traumatised, was carried out on a stretcher to the ambulance. For the first few minutes the scene was chaotic, and even though the crime scene was compromised by many tramping feet, they still needed to keep as much of it intact and as uncontaminated as possible for all the evidence that would be needed to clear up the case that had become a mess and a nightmare simply because of a man's drunken binge.

Amongst all the chaos and confusion, Lambert, after letting his eyes wander over Masina's study quickly, managed to slide out of the door unnoticed to go in search of the one item he needed to complete the investigation.

During his previous visit to Masina's house, he had noticed a narrow door near the main entrance, and he hurried along the hallway and pulled it open. Inside, a cloakroom with coats hanging on a rail. There was a genuine wax Barbour hanging at the end of the row, and he thought the coat was typical of a man like Masina, a flash gangster dressing with the image of a country squire. The coat felt reasonably warm, as if it had been worn recently, perhaps in a car with the heating on. And when he searched the pockets he knew he was right. He had the result he needed.

He quickly took Masina's mobile phone out and clicked on the log and received calls. Hurriedly, he took out his pen and notebook, wrote down the last three calls which Masina had received today, and returned the phone to its pocket, which would be discovered by the forensics team.

But Lambert felt he was ahead of the game now. It was time to finish it. But first, he needed to have a quick word with Chief Superintendent Marden. And he knew this time his boss would back him all the way.

# Thirty-two

As soon as Tony Ellis and Lambert arrived back at the incident room, Lambert sank thoughtfully into the chair by his desk. He asked Ellis to brief Mick Beech about everything that had happened, while he sat nervously chewing his lip, listening to Ellis's account of the affair, and watching Beech's reaction.

Eventually, when Ellis had almost ended his tale, Lambert took the notebook out of his pocket, reached across the desk and dialled the first number from Masina's mobile phone. He waited, holding his breath, while it made the connection. Click. And there was a ringtone on the other side of the incident room. Beech's mobile.

Confusion and doom spread across Beech's face, like low cloud sweeping over mountains. Beads of sweat broke out on his forehead as he scrambled to kill the noise.

'Too late, Mick. We've got you bang to rights.'

Beech switched his mobile off and began to stammer an excuse. 'I… I …I'm not sure I understand…'

Lambert looked at Ellis who had been briefed by him on the drive over from Masina's house. Ellis nodded and gave a faintly triumphant smile, although it was tinged with regret. None of them liked the copper who was dishonest and sold out to the criminals.

As he watched the beginnings of Beech's stammering excuse, anger began to well up in Lambert, so much so that he had to stop himself from leaping across the office and slamming a fist into the office manager's face. Instead, he directed his anger into a stare of utter contempt and channelled the intensity of his fury into words he almost found too difficult to articulate.

'You loathsome prick! We had no idea you were the bastard who worked for Frank Masina. And you were the one who warned him whenever Geoff Ambrose and SOCA got close to nailing him. The chief super couldn't prove it was you, so he got rid of you as office manager, and we got lumbered with you instead. The trouble was the chief super had no idea that the body in the boot was indirectly linked to Masina. That's where it all went wrong for you, otherwise you'd have got away with it. There was no way anyone could prove your connection with Masina.'

Apart from the beads of sweat breaking out on Beech's forehead, his face was a mask, shocked into a deathly stillness.

'And that makes you responsible for Harlan's death,' Lambert continued, struggling to control his temper. 'Not that I'm going to lose any sleep over that bastard. But once you found out he was turning QE, you knew you'd be implicated and he had to be silenced. You cowardly bastard. At least Masina had the guts to fall on his sword, whereas you...'

Lambert broke off as he felt the heat rising, and the desire to attack Beech became overwhelming. Ellis, seeing the ugly look of revulsion on his boss's face, found himself staring at Beech with such loathing that he wanted to beat him senseless, almost as if he and Lambert had become a crazed pair, feeding off each other as their anger escalated.

'How much did he pay you?' Ellis shouted. 'How much were all those lives worth to you? And I'm not talking about Masina or Harlan, but all the lives that have been fucked up through drugs because of you.'

Beech lumbered to his feet and held his hands out imploringly. 'It wasn't like that. I swear.'

'No? You mean you just did it cos you wanted to help our local drug dealer? Don't make me laugh.'

Beech's hands began to shake. 'No, I swear to you, it wasn't my fault. My wife and kids – he threatened them – told me if I didn't do like he said he'd kill them.'

'And you believed him?'

'I was scared.'

Lambert came striding over to Beech, who flinched, thinking he was going to hit him.

'You're lying, you bastard,' Lambert snapped. 'Maybe Masina did threaten you once you were in too deep. But to begin with he must have made it worth your while. And didn't you tell the chief super a while back that your wife had come into some money and you'd spent it buying a property in Spain?'

Tears formed in Beech's eyes. 'No, I swear to you...' His voice dissolved into a small croak.

'I think you know how this goes Michael Beech,' Lambert began. 'You do not have to say anything but it may harm your defence...' Lambert paused briefly as he watched Beech sinking into his chair... 'if you do not mention, when questioned, something which you later rely on in court.' Beech bent over, his head in his hands, stemming the flood of tears. 'Anything you do say may be given in evidence. I think you understand.'

Beech openly sobbed now, his back heaving as he tried to choke back tears. Lambert exchanged a look with Ellis, who regarded Beech's blubbering dispassionately.

'Do me a favour, Tony,' Lambert said.

'I know,' Ellis said, anticipating Lambert's request, 'you want me to go and have a word with the custody sergeant and get someone to prepare a cell for this bastard.'

'Be much appreciated, Tony.'

As Ellis left the incident room to make the arrangements, Lambert sat on the edge of the desk and stared at Beech with more hatred than was fitting for most criminals. At least the criminal classes were often born into a life of crime. But Lambert could never tolerate treachery such as Beech's. And when he thought about it, if it hadn't been for Beech, none of it would have happened. They would have had Masina behind bars months ago – along with James Harlan, who would not have been drunk on that fateful day when he killed an innocent schoolgirl.

He hoped Beech's sentence would be long and difficult.

# Epilogue: Four Days Later

It took forensics another three days to confirm to Lambert, almost beyond doubt, that the only person on board the *Esmeralda* at the time of the explosion was Mark Mason. But what had happened to his uncle, Steven Hickson, who was still on the missing list? Lambert was convinced the man they called Virgil had something to do with it, and strongly suspected an abduction in the van that had been parked at the Burry Port marina.

After laborious enquiries, he and his team traced the van to a Cardiff car hire company. It had been rented for twenty-four hours by a George Mackintosh, a respectable businessman, who discovered his driver's licence was missing from his wallet and was unable to offer an explanation or pinpoint the time of its disappearance.

They drew a blank.

Then, on the fourth day after the shooting at Frank Masina's home, Lambert – who had become bogged down by the myriad statements that needed taking – got a phone call on his mobile as he sat in the incident room, sighing over paperwork, and his eyes lit up as he listened intently.

Debbie Jones was suddenly alert as she watched him taking the call, and could tell by his demeanour, the way his shoulders jerked to attention, that there was a new development. He scribbled details on a writing pad, told the caller he and his team would be there right away, and ended the call.

'A man out walking his dog,' he said, shaking his head, with a wry smile tugging at his mouth, 'found a shallow grave with a corpse in it.'

He stood up, picked his mobile up from his desk and pocketed it. Ellis hurried over, unable to keep the excitement out of his voice.

'Anything to do with this case and our missing person, Harry?'

'That's the thing about murderers,' Lambert replied, 'they get bored with digging graves after committing their crimes. It seems this one was so shallow the wildlife had started tucking in and have eaten a fair bit of the corpse. But it does look as if it's our bloke.'

As Jones threw her jacket over her shoulders and slid her arms into the sleeves, she asked, 'How can you be so sure it's Steven Hickson?'

'Because a fox is unlikely to eat a Rolex watch – fake or real. Right, let's get to the crime scene and see what SOCO has found for us.'

'You think the killer might be this Virgil bloke?' Wallace said, grabbing a plastic bottle of Diet Coke to take on the journey.

Lambert stopped in the doorway and gave his team a reassuring grin. 'I would bet my life on it. And we'll get him and his accomplices, of that I have no doubt whatsoever.'

And Lambert had never felt so confident about the truth of his statement, knowing from experience how the most violent criminals risked getting caught by laying a paper trail to their convictions, as if their subconscious minds controlled their actions, despite any conscious lack of remorse.

'Come on,' he said. 'Let's find out if that watch is real or fake.'

Also from David Barry...

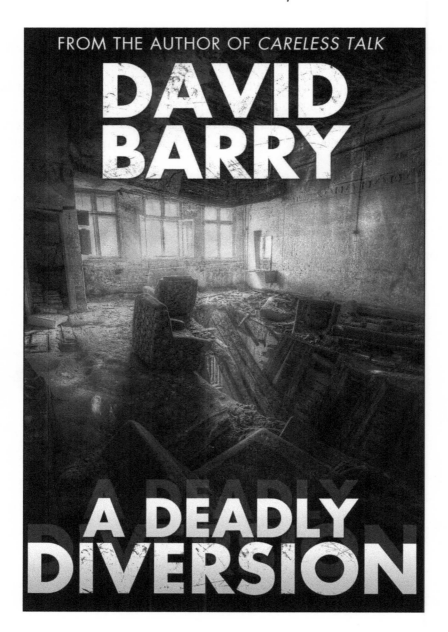

FROM THE AUTHOR OF *CARELESS TALK*

DAVID BARRY

A DEADLY DIVERSION